GLENN FISHER

Exile on Faith Street

The Destination

First published by Glenn J Fisher 2024

Copyright © 2024 by Glenn Fisher

All rights reserved. No part of this publication may be reproduced, stored or transmitted in any form or by any means, electronic, mechanical, photocopying, recording, scanning, or otherwise without written permission from the publisher. It is illegal to copy this book, post it to a website, or distribute it by any other means without permission.

This novel is entirely a work of fiction. The names, characters and incidents portrayed in it are the work of the author's imagination. Any resemblance to actual persons, living or dead, events or localities is entirely coincidental.

Glenn Fisher asserts the moral right to be identified as the author of this work.

Glenn Fisher has no responsibility for the persistence or accuracy of URLs for external or third-party Internet Websites referred to in this publication and does not guarantee that any content on such Websites is, or will remain, accurate or appropriate.

Designations used by companies to distinguish their products are often claimed as trademarks. All brand names and product names used in this book and on its cover are trade names, service marks, trademarks and registered trademarks of their respective owners. The publishers and the book are not associated with any product or vendor mentioned in this book. None of the companies referenced within the book have endorsed the book.

First edition

ISBN: 979-8-9852560-6-2

This book was professionally typeset on Reedsy.
Find out more at reedsy.com

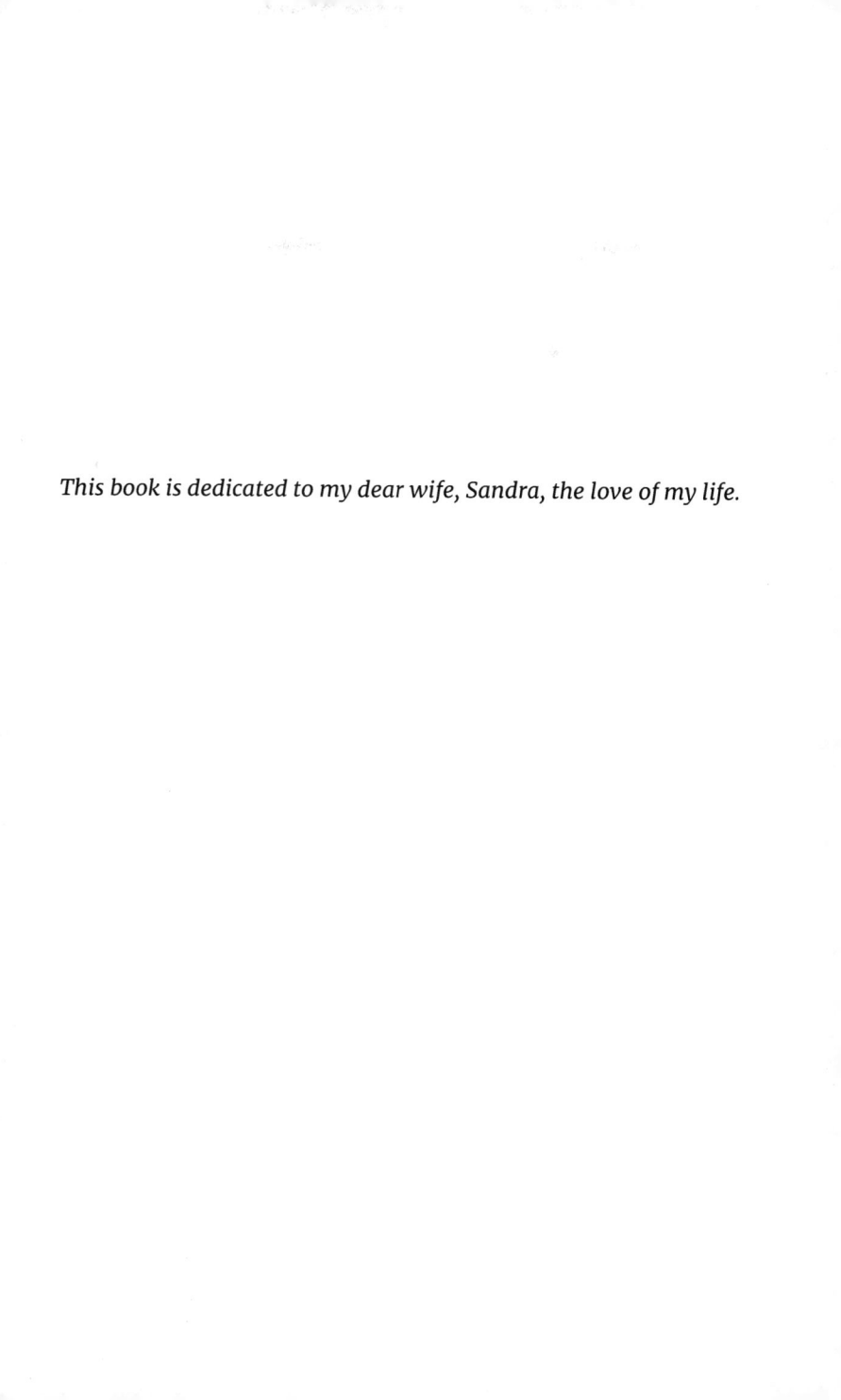

This book is dedicated to my dear wife, Sandra, the love of my life.

"Now faith is confidence in what we hope for and assurance about what we do not see."

Hebrews, 11:1

Contents

Foreword — iii
Acknowledgement — iv

I Prologue

Cheri — 3

II Memorial Day Weekend

The Shamrock — 19
Holiday — 29

III Paradise

Getaway — 47
Wildwood — 67
Not so Fast — 81

IV Paradise (Not Lost)

Fireworks — 105
Hilltop Vista — 117

V The Unraveling

Winter	125
The Chance	127
Dick's	143
Yukon Trail	168
The Party	177
Bad Juju	194
Coup de Grace	209
Fini	220
Christmas	233

VI Exile

Tuna Out	241
Chinatown	247
Better Things	249
The Noose	254
Homeland	256
Escape	261
Jeff	263
Asylum	267
Deep Freeze	270
Cannonball Express	273
The Dream	276
And then...	278

VII Epilogue

The Settlement	285

Foreword

I'm publishing this novel in two parts, "The Journey" and "The Destination" because one of the fictional characters - described in detail in "The Destination" - too closely resembles my wife (in her opinion). Per her expressed wishes (and the threat of divorce) I will postpone publishing "The Destination" until after I receive her permission or she passes away. While I'll continue to maintain that this entire novel is 'fiction' (come on now, who could possibly remember all that dialogue accurately?) I'll also honor her request. I can only hope she knows how magnificent a woman - truly worthy of being remembered throughout the ages - I lovingly modeled the character 'Cheri' after.

Acknowledgement

This novel would not have come to fruition without the great help of my sister, Carol, for which I am eternally grateful. As a long time editor and reporter for the Reading Eagle newspaper her suggestions are backed by a wealth of professional expertise. In my writing I rely on her for assistance of every sort, from guidance on 'grand design' to minute grammatical corrections. She remains a crucial partner in the creation and publication of all my work. Carol, "Thank you!"

I

Prologue

January 1980

Cheri

Her voice was studded with contempt, her delivery so venomous that one would have supposed the very intent capable of shredding him to naked, bleeding bone.

"Anthony, I swear to Christ I hate you! Get your miserable ass out from underneath that coat right now, you moron. You're getting blood all over my mother's chair - show some goddamn consideration."

This was pure malice - she was long past the point of simple anger. She wanted to drag him out into the open, ripped and wounded, where she could see him bleed. The fact that they were at her mother's house only made matters worse. How dare he cause a scene here? And if he hadn't already been paralyzed, broken and incapacitated before her onslaught, the added humiliation of having his emasculation occur in public would have been, in itself, reason enough to keep him under that coat until hell froze over.

Throughout all this, Anthony - a good looking Italian kid with a nice smile and curly black hair - didn't move an inch. He simply wasn't strong enough to face her scorn or sword hand any longer. He was clinging desperately to the wreckage of their affair, hoping to salvage something. He still loved her and needed her - he couldn't be away from her. His battered and brutalized brain was incapable of further reflection. He was safer underneath her coat, that much he knew.

Unfortunately, Cheri was without mercy or patience and she erupted once again.

"Get up you lousy prick!" she hissed scathingly. "Oh wait, how could I forget?" she added, in her most acid tones. "You can't get it up most of the time, can you? Besides it's much too small for me to call you a prick anyway, isn't it, Anthony?"

There was no response to these new thrusts except for a barely perceptible tightening of her coat down around his head as he pulled it closer for better security. She watched him carefully, like a cat toying with a trapped mouse, the nervous tapping of her fingernails the only indication that she wasn't yet satisfied with her handiwork and, in fact, remained dangerously angry. There was no further movement on his part.

"All right!" she lashed out, furious to the point of violence, cutting the air with a short, slashing motion of her right hand. "I've had enough of this! I'm going to call your wife and tell her to send the police over here to get you. Won't that be nice?"

She abruptly shifted gears, changing her tone to a disturbingly sweet manner that was in no way indicative of her actual mental state - sarcasm coming as naturally to her as breathing. She continued on in this patronizing, cooing fashion.

"Maybe we better send the poor little boy straight over to the psychiatric center where they'll let him hide underneath his coat. What's the matter little boy, do you want me to call your mommy?"

She knew she should stop, in the name of basic human

decency, but she couldn't. This was her nature - she was merciless and bloodthirsty in the clinch, respecting only strength. She went on, speaking in a dispassionate voice.

"You are pathetic, Anthony. I can't stand the sight of you... you need a shrink, not a girlfriend."

'Vicious' is the only word that adequately describes her delivery. It was deliberate and calculated to cause maximal pain and damage. And when she stopped yelling she was at her most devastating and remorseless, not wanting emotion to sway her as she measured her victim for the rending slashes.

The room was dark except for what light emanated from the television screen and kitchen. Cheri could see that her lover of late, slumped low in an easy chair, coat draped over his head, was not going to respond to anything she said. He was crying under there. She could hear an occasional whimper. She glared at him, frustration etched on her features. He made no sound nor gave any indication of stirring from his place of refuge.

Cheri glanced up to see if her mother was still witnessing the castration - she had been 'shushing' her daughter from the relative security of the kitchen, appalled at the spectacle of this pitiful man cowering and quailing beneath a jacket. Cheri's mother didn't have much sympathy for men either, however, and if the truth be known, she was curiously proud of her daughter's primal ferocity - this sucker's balls had certainly been professionally snipped off! (It's the same way with black widow spiders - he wants to fuck? Fine. Let him...she liked to fuck too! But he better be good and he better be nimble. Otherwise he'd merely be tasty.) Her mother had slipped away though, apparently unable to watch any further humiliation of what had basically been a pampered, philandering husband in over his head with a woman who'd broken tougher men than he - a woman who'd played him with one hand, stripped him of all dignity and dismissed him after cruelly wielding the crop, jerking the bit, and raking him down with her spurs.

She was never more beautiful or ravishing to behold than in moments like these, totally alive, skin crawling with sensation, eyes snapping and smoldering, every sense exquisitely attuned, her smile expanding into something more unpleasant whenever she struck an exposed nerve. As far as she was concerned, Anthony - by even pursuing her - had asked for it. All men did. They lost their minds (and when she was through, usually quite a bit more) over her type of sexually aggressive woman, their male pride demanding that they try to 'break' her as if she were some kind of wild mare they could ride into submission or tempt with their various sugar cubes. And how she played them! In the beginning they were all convinced that she was what they wanted, positive they were making great progress during the early stages of the relationship when she was still pliant and accommodating. It was only later that they discovered she'd never been broken at all - what a ridiculous notion! She'd merely enjoyed the first hot blush of romance (which she thought sweet) for what it was worth, meanwhile carefully cataloging all pertinent strategic information during the heady, unguarded time when her 'conqueror' was busily patting himself on the back. Well, she got bored easily and they all found out sooner or later who was riding whom. Few were intelligent enough to walk away before she made them crawl. Make no mistake, she liked the idea of 'men' and found their pricks quite satisfying. She even liked specific, individual men...until they were exposed as mortal - for which she never forgave them.

Remaining seated on the easy chair directly across from

Anthony, Cheri angrily twisted and untwisted a strand of her silky, walnut brown hair, her eyes burning black with ire, wanting nothing more than to scorch a hole through the scanty piece of fabric he'd chosen to hide behind, wishing she could unleash a searing death ray of incineration upon this soft and frightened little boy who'd so belatedly discovered that you can't step off a speeding freight train without getting hurt.

And wasn't it interesting how these affairs so often worked out? Anthony certainly wasn't as smug anymore, was he? She'd taught this one well - he wouldn't forget the whip. There was no doubt about who wore the pants and who spread, no mistaking who cinched up the saddle and climbed aboard. This was the reason she started fucking! Power. Complete domination of the male. She'd won Anthony's unconditional surrender. If she so desired, she could drive Anthony home right now, screw him, then take whatever it was she wanted from him - and he'd be grateful! She could 'borrow' his car and credit cards, go out partying 'with the girls,' bed down anyone who appealed to her, knowing full well the entire time that Anthony would be sitting back at the apartment waiting to profess his undying love and devotion to her.

Except she was finished with him. There would be no more of his threats and accusations and crying after tonight. Even if his worries were valid, where in the hell did he get off demanding explanations every time she was out of his sight for more than ten minutes? So what if she occasionally allowed her soon to be ex-husband the pleasure of remembering how awesome it was to sleep with her? (Billy was very nearly worshipful by this point - living alone didn't suit him well at all.) And Anthony dared cry 'foul?' Didn't he remember that old maxim, 'he who lives by the sword dies by the sword?' It didn't help that this new guy at work, Kurt, was endearing himself to her with his persistence either. He'd had the balls to ask her out in front of Anthony! (She hadn't helped Anthony's confidence any by hesitating momentarily before eventually saying, 'no.')

Initially she'd been flattered and amused by Anthony's devoted attention but his behavior had rapidly become intolerable. As one of the plant engineers at her place of employment, he had access to the heating and air conditioning systems. Cheri had recently discovered that he was taking advantage of this access to spy on her from vantage points in the ceiling!

He had been nice enough to her, though, in the beginning of their affair and she hated to dismiss him before deciding who she was moving onto next since nothing makes a new beau cockier than feeling like he took his girl away from another guy. Oh yes, that swelled up their egos. She liked offering them that little treat - they were such fun to be with as they strutted about in their supreme moment of overweening glory.

Poor Anthony. He'd made the fatal mistake of letting a woman know he was hooked. He was no longer a challenge, merely a trophy. Now here he was cowering in Cheri's mother's chair, hiding underneath a coat - and nearly ten years older than Cheri to boot!

The whimpering continued. Cheri realized it was fully possible that he was having a nervous breakdown but the tightly drawn lines of anger around her eyes and jaw did not soften. He was a weak, spineless, son of a bitch and he'd get what he deserved.

"Anthony," she commented scornfully. "Why don't you cut out this sickening charade and get the hell out of here? Go back to your stupid little wife and your nice, safe house and maybe things will be better for you in the morning, ok? Maybe someone can read you a nice little bedtime story before tucking you in for the night, wouldn't that be nice?"

He ignored her. This Cheri couldn't take, having no patience whatsoever. Up and out of her chair like a pot of water unexpectedly boiling over, hardly realizing what she was doing, she found herself on her feet trying to yank that sorry coat off his head. Anthony heard her coming, though, and prepared himself. No matter how hard she pulled, he clung to the coat tenaciously - she couldn't get it away from him! This made her so furious that she belted him three times across what she assumed was his head.

"Christ, you make me sick!" she screeched, breathing heavily from the exertion. "You will never, ever touch me again, do you hear me? We're through! I want you out of my life right now - go back to your dim-witted wife, you asshole!"

If he heard, he didn't let on.

An hour later they were in her car driving north on Route 82 toward Cheri's apartment. Anthony sat white-faced and ramrod straight, statue-like, resembling some sort of stricken pagan deity fallen from grace and being carted off to the village dump.

Back at her mom's house, Cheri had finally announced that she'd be waiting for him in the car whenever he was ready to go, 'freezing to death, since some asshole has my coat.' She went to the car. After a few minutes, he followed.

Anthony stared into the night, unflinching even as the dazzling beams of oncoming headlights glared into his unprotected eyes, briefly illuminating his frozen, death-mask pallor. Cheri ignored him entirely. It'd been coming for weeks...the incessant questioning about her whereabouts, the jealous rages, his black despairs. Then his wife found out that Anthony was cheating on her. He had always prided himself on being a good father (he had an infant daughter), a fine provider and an upstanding husband. Now he was fast sinking into the 'quagmire' of adultery, or so he cried piteously to Cheri.

His final unraveling had come about during the past 24 hours. First, he'd informed his wife that he'd decided to move in with Cheri, only to belatedly discover that Cheri refused to have him and, in fact, was openly contemptuous of him.

That merely set the stage for his getting fired from his well-paying, long-standing job at the plant. Anthony and Cheri had gone out at lunchtime to discuss their rapidly disintegrating relationship. Caving in to the tension, Anthony had foolishly gotten very drunk. Upon returning to the building, noticeably late, he had been summoned by his supervisor. Comment was made regarding the time and his steadily decreasing job performance - a fact that seemed attributable to his letting 'personal' matters, for example his current ill-advised affair, take precedence over his work responsibilities. Anthony, outraged by the rebuke, exchanged angry, drunken words with a supervisor who didn't like him in the first place. A brief scuffle followed during which Anthony ended up punching out some glass windows in the lab (cutting his hands rather badly in the process). He was promptly fired and the police summoned. When they arrived, however, he was already gone. Cheri's supervisor (a much more sympathetic fellow and one highly appreciative of Cheri's outstanding work record) told her to take the rest of the afternoon off and get Anthony out of the building before the cops arrived.

So they left. But Cheri was not in the least bit pleased by any of this. She was tired of this big baby. It had taken a little while to find out what he was really like but now she knew and she was finished with him.

The problem was, he had nowhere to go. He was afraid to return to his estranged wife and Cheri - his revered lover of late - had rejected him as inadequate.

For her part, Cheri thought it utterly disgraceful that he'd come this unglued. She'd known that the soft, pompous crybaby would crack as soon as they started playing hardball, she'd just not expected it would come about this completely. It was inexcusable. And the bastard wasn't even that bad off! He'd probably land a higher paying job in a matter of days (air conditioning and heating specialists in incredibly high demand, as always) and he still had his night job teaching at the community college. His oatmeal-brained wife would take him back in a minute. That spineless, dry-holed bitch would turn belly up the moment he came slinking home. How any self-respecting woman could forgive this ultimate insult – infidelity - Cheri couldn't understand but she knew Anthony's wife would welcome his return. She was too old and tired to find another man.

Turning onto Cheri's street, they took a quick left up a long, dirt driveway, the car bouncing heavily as it negotiated the rocky, eroded grade. Passing a large barn, Cheri wheeled her car to the right and parked in front of her building (a once luxurious stable that had long since been carved into three splendid, albeit antiquated, apartments). Her husband had found the place a few years ago, right after they had Melanie. It was funny - Cheri originally hated the place. 'It's too far out in the sticks!' she'd complained. But now she cherished the privacy and delighted in the peaceful, rural surroundings. She and Melanie remained after Cheri had given Billy the boot.

As she pulled into her parking space she found herself almost wishing she'd find Billy waiting there. Despite his numerous faults and selfish stupidity he'd at least never acted like this! It was stomach-turning. Why did men think that crying and begging could help at the end? It was shameful weakness and only solidified her disdain. Billy had cried and pleaded at the end too but crocodile tears were different, no matter how freely they flowed. He'd at least taken his lumps and ultimately laughed it off (even if his laugh grated terribly on her nerves, making him sound exactly like the incurable dunce she'd decided he was), conducting himself with a certain sense of warped dignity despite the fact that she'd hung his balls up on the wall too.

But Anthony's car was the only one in the parking lot and Cheri remembered that Billy had Melanie this week and wouldn't bring her back until Sunday. ('Just as well,' she decided, 'since I TRULY can't stand to spend even ten minutes with him anymore.') He hadn't been around as much since Anthony had practically moved in.

She was so preoccupied with these thoughts that she was genuinely surprised when Anthony spoke.

"Are you going to let me come inside?" he asked in a tremulous tone, close to tears again, trying to engage her eyes so she could see how devastated he was. He wilted and crumpled immediately as she turned her withering stare on him. It didn't shut him up, however.

"Cheri, I love you...please! For God's sake, I'll do whatever you want - I promise. Doesn't that mean anything to you?"

The last words were almost shrieked out as a gut-wrenching wave of fear tore at his insides. He broke into choked sobs. Cheri was as remorseless as death's own angel. As far as she was concerned he'd made his absolute final mistake when his wife discovered their affair and he'd been stupid enough to consider, out loud, in front of Cheri, the advantages of returning to the domestic fold. He'd only been trying out the words and by that time Cheri had long since determined that she was going to have to dump him anyway (having already signaled her availability to a candidate or two). But she decided right then and there that Anthony was going to pay for his insensitive comments. It didn't matter that he'd ultimately decided to stay with her. Of course he would, they all did! What mattered was that there had been a lapse in the unswerving devotion she demanded.

"Yes Anthony - it does mean something to me," she replied icily. "It means I'm going to have to take two aspirin before I go to bed and I won't get to shower until tomorrow morning since it's so late, ok? Now crawl over to your car and get the hell out of here or I'm calling the police. It's over. We're through. Go on now...run to mommy - oh, excuse me, I mean your wife."

With that, she exited her vehicle and walked over to her doorway. Anthony tried one last time. She heard him get out of the car as she entered her apartment.

"No, Cheri, please don't do this to us! Can I call you later? Can't you - "

She slammed the apartment door behind her and locked it before proceeding directly to the bathroom where she stripped off all her clothes. Examining her reflection in the mirror, she took the two aspirin she'd promised herself much earlier in the evening. Grabbing her book off the kitchen table (a voracious reader, devouring books by the dozen, she found it impossible to sleep without reading for at least five or ten minutes) she headed upstairs to her bedroom. Climbing under the covers, she paused and listened. After a few more seconds she heard his car start up. Another minute went by and then he left.

Once the sound of the disappearing auto faded away she felt better. In fact, she actually felt pretty good. It never failed to amaze her - guys were always the ones who broke down and begged for mercy when the shooting started. She hated to see it happen although she did everything she could to precipitate it. Once proud and cocksure, they always looked so pitiful when it came to slipping away into the night with their little tails pulled up tight between their legs.

Putting her book aside, she went back downstairs to the telephone. She dialed Anthony's home phone number. His wife answered on the first ring.

"Hello?" She sounded worried and whiny.

"Yes. Hello. This is Cheri Melvey. Anthony just left my place and should be home within a half hour. If he's not, call the police and have them check the Mid-Hudson Bridge or something but don't have them come here because he won't be with me."

Cheri fully intended to hang up at that point but Anthony's wife, anxious for information, held her on the line by quickly interjecting, "Why? I mean, is he all right? What happened?"

Cheri was amazed - it was as if Anthony's wife didn't realize she was talking to the woman who'd been fucking her husband for months now - the woman who'd had her gratefully eroticized spouse on his hands and knees begging Cheri to let him stay! There was no doubt that Anthony's wife was going to be glad to have him come home again.

"We were out at lunchtime. Anthony had a few drinks too many and when we returned to work he had an argument with his supervisor. It got out of control. Anthony punched out some windows and was fired. His hands were cut so I took him to my mother's house to clean him up. I just sent him home. Oh, and you know how he wanted to move in here with me? That won't be happening. I told him I never want to see him again and I meant it."

"Oh, thank you! I was so worried -"

Cheri shook her head in disbelief and hung up. It wasn't worth the effort to insult Anthony's wife any further. Opening the refrigerator, Cheri took a sip of Diet Pepsi, put the bottle back on the shelf and closed the door. Turning off all the downstairs lights except the one over the stove, she made sure the front door was locked and then hurried up the creaky wooden stairs to her bedroom.

She set her alarm fifteen minutes early so she'd have time to take a shower in the morning before work. Crawling into bed again, she picked up her book. This was a good one - a true life story about a serial killer who'd brutally murdered a whole slew of young girls in Oregon, Colorado and Florida before getting caught. It was spine-chilling. He'd jammed the broken end of a jagged bedpost into the vagina of one of the victims! How in the name of God did people get to be that evil? When she felt herself drifting off she put the book down, reached up to turn off the light and then immediately fell asleep. She was twenty-one years old.

II

Memorial Day Weekend

May 1980

The Shamrock

I have to laugh, despite myself, now that I finally 'get it' - and so what if I'm indebted to the rainy night, the goddamn moonstruck fact of May or the thought provoking quantities of blackberry brandy I've been putting away all evening? What's important is this - that which appeared senseless, upon further examination reveals itself as making perfectly good sense indeed!

Earlier this afternoon I finished reading a book about a rock climbing enthusiast from Manhattan who took to murdering strangers with his ice-ax. Admittedly, that fact alone was not sufficient to arouse much interest in regard to a city where more than a thousand inhabitants annually meet a roughly similar fate. But there was something about this account that stuck in my mind, causing me to absentmindedly reflect upon it for the better part of today. This man would go out prowling the streets after sunset, haunting the less traveled byways and residential districts. Well-dressed, smiling serenely, he attracted no suspicion whatsoever, his nasty little instrument of dispatch handily concealed beneath his stylish and expensive overcoat. When opportunity presented itself in the form of a solitary, unsuspecting pedestrian on an otherwise deserted street, the murderer would approach the victim from the front, walking briskly, as if late for a dinner appointment, eyes politely averted, bearing and countenance deferential, keeping scrupulously to his own side of the sidewalk - at the last moment perhaps exchanging a nod of restrained acknowledgment with the fated party. Stepping past the (by now) sufficiently reassured citizen, the killer would suddenly wheel about with athletic and practiced grace, whip out his ice-ax and send it splintering it through the back of the poor unfortunate's skull!

Why? The gratification, it was painstakingly explained, came in the form of a raging emotional catharsis and coalescence the killer and victim invariably experienced following the moment of impact. The executioner first underwent a wicked, scalding instant of fierce and entirely unrepentant exhilaration triggered by his unimaginable success in contacting this other person so completely, so conclusively - the two of them now and forever accomplices, having plundered and despoiled the vault of sacred existence itself, both staring on in stricken and horrified awe at the heretofore incomprehensible spectacle of life humbled and reduced to naught, its very substance bleeding away impotently on the dirty and non-porous sidewalk. This grisly undertaking forged an unassailable bond between them - the killer overwhelmed by the magnitude and scope of their brazen audacity, the victim sacrificing so much more than any earthly lover could. Their bloody communion finally induced a rapturous ecstasy as he - the assassin - reveled in their accomplishment...the eternal merging of two into the repository of one.

As can be seen, there was no malice, torture, or sadism involved. No hatred, no desire to see fear, be cruel, or intentionally prolong another's suffering. The killer did it for the intimate contact it provided with another human being and, ultimately, to grapple with the fact of their shared humanity!

I laughed initially at what I then considered the utter lunacy inherent in the author's attempt to even make a stab at rationalizing these murderous actions. I'm laughing now because I finally get it - I understand all too well! And if this starts to sound like the illogical rambling of a seriously deranged mind, well, they're out there everywhere, aren't they? Just examine the headlines - who can be determined out of control before it's too late to do anything except clean up the mess? How long before self-protective irrationality, cog resentment or unfocused anger carries one over the yawning precipice? When do you, as a still functioning, but potentially deranged individual concede the point? (You say you've stifled a thousand murderous impulses - great! Can you stifle the next one or are you suicidal instead?) And isn't this subject further confused when we examine all the monumental achievements in art, literature and history attributable to frenzied minds poised on the brink of murder, madness, or self-annihilation? What makes a Van Gogh, Nietzsche or Hitler lucid one moment and beyond the pale the next?

I'm sitting here in The Shamrock, a neighborhood bar, watching some local youngsters play pool. It's quite late as I stare at the back of one blond boy's head, vividly picturing the effect of crashing weighted, sharpened steel (say, an ice-ax) through his eggshell frail cranium - slashing a curved, deadly spike into that vulnerable looking high spot right THERE on the crown of his skull, stabbing him still and causing God only knows what kind of trauma to the soft gray pulpy matter underneath...ending it all in one fractured, blessed instant. I can't get it out of my mind! I harbor no malice, only compassion and omnipotent love. How much could he feel? Stunned incomprehension upon impact, reel, sway, drop... spreading wooziness, wet and warm swimming sensation, final awareness of friends and strangers clustered about, disorientation, loss of the picture, a reluctance to close his eyes - cessation.

My method of contacting and protecting! What else can preserve their easygoing carefree ways as childhood ends? Do they need to be protected? Oh sure, look at them...it's fine for those that can cope, but at how stiff a price? Don't get me wrong - life IS blessed! But what about the ones that never seem to adjust, the ones who never seem to figure it out, the lonely ones life breaks with casual and chilling disregard?

I'm observing them now...kids - children practically! - swaggering about and guzzling their beer in an unconscious parody of 'adult' behavior. They aspire to be adults. But do they know what that means? The dictionary says first, 'adult - pertaining to mature life, a person who has attained maturity.' But the very next entry gives it all away - 'adulterate" (...to become adult?) "- to make IMPURE by admixture of other ingredients, to CORRUPT.'

Watching them drink and laugh and flirt and bluster has affected me very strangely tonight, I admit. It's so sad to think that these innocent, laughing young babes will soon be cast out into the bullring. How many healthy responses are there? (Pass the ice-ax, please.)

The blond kid has his back to me. The game room is packed to the rafters with his raucous compatriots. It's loud as hell in here (which I love) and the jukebox is blasting out some top-notch, hard-driving, kick-ass rock 'n' roll. I've already invested two dollars worth of quarters so far and there's plenty more where that came from.

The 'kid' just sank the last low ball for his side (he's teamed up with his buddy, Sammy, who I chat with from time to time) and now he's going for the eight ball and game. All his friends crowd around and watch closely, giving him a moment of relative calm as he concentrates intently, grimly measuring the lay. The drama and tension build...this is getting ridiculous! Our protagonist is taking on mythic overtones in my mind as he sternly surveys the scene; a wholesome, all-American comic-book hero standing there in his crisp, white painter pants and Bunyun-esque, 'great north woods' style flannel shirt. He leans down over the table and without further hesitation - pop! The cue takes the eight down the green...an impossible shot - but it goes in! Everybody rushes over and starts pounding him on the back in intoxicated glee, yelling and hollering uproariously. The 'kid' beams proudly as the losers file by to shake his hand.

"Just luck," one of them shouts good-naturedly.

"Yeah, your BAD luck 'cause now you owe me a beer!" the winner acknowledges, winking cheerfully, turning to watch the table as the next set of challengers rack up the balls. It's a frizzy-haired lad, baggy clothes draped over his bony frame, teamed with an attractive, lively young girl I recognize...why? I watch curiously as the two of them exchange an affectionate, pre-game embrace. Red-faced and flushed she steps up to the table with an air of brisk confidence and professionally appraises it. Now I remember - she used to be the 'kid's' girlfriend! During the relatively short time I've patronized this bar, those two have ALWAYS been together, groping and fondling each other in some dark corner. This is a new development.

The 'kid' looks more than a shade taken aback - he must still care about her though, because he seems overly determined not to pay any attention to his ex-girlfriend, laughing a bit too boisterously, swaggering a bit too cockily as he carouses with some fellow ruffians huddled around the pinball machine while waiting for the break. It certainly doesn't affect his game, however. He and his buddy annihilate the newcomers in a matter of minutes. The girl and the chump accept defeat graciously, smiling all the while, staring deep into each other's eyes, oblivious to the crowd and the hecklers as the eight ball finally disappears down a side pocket. Putting their arms around each other, they exchange a last drunken kiss before exiting the bar through a side door that leads out to the parking lot. The 'kid' watches her every step of the way.

And you know, I did see her glance his way once during the game - a gentle, lingering gaze of unmistakable fondness. But that didn't stop her from going out into the parking lot in the arms of another guy, did it? And, geez, for a moment I thought - Oh, God! This is the exact kind of maudlin, sentimental thinking that led me to my current understanding of the ice-ax murderer.

An ice-ax - it's perfect! So direct, so constructive, lets you get right to the point. In fact, if I had one now, I'd like to think I'd sneak out into the parking lot and plant it in the first suitable skull I could find - maybe yours? That's the thing you have to be careful of, alone, at night...not only should you worry about those that hate - you better stay the hell away from us that love!

***

Out in the unlit parking lot a persistent and uncomfortable cold spring rain continues to fall, the resultant puddles soaking my feet thoroughly as I splash to my car. It's late, it's wet, I'm tired and I'm annoyed (once I get in, the interior light doesn't work and I can't tell which key goes in the ignition). I'm holding the key ring up against the sweating windshield hoping for a stray glimmer of light when I realize that someone - or something! - is alive and moving in the rear seat of my darkened car. An icy wave of fear punches through my nervous system and paralyzes me. Afraid to turn around, expecting to feel steely claws or a razor-sharp blade biting into my flesh, I do nothing and freeze incredulously. Satan - I knew he'd be coming for me! A man's voice originating from directly behind my right ear cuts through my panicky fog.

"It started raining harder and nobody else came along, except to go in the bar, so we decided to wait for you in your car. I hope you don't mind too much."

"We don't want to be pushy or anything but we were hoping to take you up on your very generous offer."

The second voice is that of a young woman, the first a guy in his late teens or early twenties.

I slump down in the driver's seat, hands reflexively gripping and twisting the steering wheel as my brain instructs my heart to stop the needless violent pounding. Turning sideways in the seat I can see them - the same two hitchhikers I'd given a lift to on my way out to the bar. It'd been getting dark and starting to drizzle so on the spur of the moment I offered them the refuge of my apartment if they needed a place to stay for the night. I'd already had half a load on by then anyhow and after they politely indicated their intention of trying to catch another ride I promptly forgot about them.

And at this moment I'm not in the most altruistic of moods - what in the hell kind of people are they? Am I going to end up getting ripped off or stabbed to death in the middle of the night? (This ice-ax stuff has me a little paranoid, perhaps.)

My eyes slowly adjust to the dark and I can see them more clearly. The girl is about 18 or 19 with long, blond hair and a plump, good-natured moon face. She's wearing an army fatigue shirt and dungarees and looking more than slightly bedraggled from roadside living. The guy might be two or three years older. He's got tousled, dark brown hair and either long sideburns or a lousy excuse for a beard. He's wearing frayed and faded blue jeans and the ubiquitous (at least in this neck of the woods) flannel shirt. They both look tired and sleepy and harmless enough. It's either take them in or dump them out on the side of the deserted highway for what will undoubtedly be a wet and miserable night.

"Uhh..." I respond finally, trying not to sound too unenthusiastic as I ponder my options, "yeah, no problem. You guys have a sleeping bag, right? I only just moved into my place and don't have any furniture yet. But the offer is still good if you don't mind a little hardship."

The girl speaks up immediately. "Oh no, that's great! Thank you very much, we really appreciate it. It's kinda wet out there. I'm Ellen and he's Lonnie."

"Nice to meet you Ellen and Lonnie," I reply. "I'm James."

Lonnie doesn't say anything and I still feel kind of antisocial myself, so without further comment I concentrate on starting up my car and heading for home. Crunching slowly over the dirt and gravel parking lot, we turn right at the road and head off down the shiny black ribbon.

Within fifteen minutes we're bumping our way up my landlord's ill-maintained excuse of a dirt driveway, past the barn and into the courtyard fronting my modest apartment.

"This is it."

"Great."

Once inside I direct them to the 'guest' room. It's an easy room to keep ready for visitors because there's nothing in it. The rest of the apartment is similarly spartan (which actually makes for a refreshing and invigorating abode).

I retreat to the central living room which is the biggest open space in the place. The walls and ceiling consist of beautifully varnished, three-inch wide, hardwood strips - a stunning feature.

I remember there's a large, unfinished bottle of Lambrusco in the refrigerator from the evening I moved in here.

"Hey, you guys want to join me in a glass of wine before calling it a night?" I holler to Lonnie and Ellen.

"Yeah, sounds good," they chorus.

My kitchen is a tiny, cramped walk-in space barely big enough to turn around in. It has a big window at its far end that opens out onto a lush, green hillside. At night, cool breezes blow in through that window, ventilating the apartment quite nicely.

I pour some 'festival' size glasses of wine and wander out to the living room to turn on some music. This had worked out well too - I can play my stereo as loud as I want (and sometimes I've GOT to let it rip!) because my next door neighbor works nights and the girl at the other end of the building is far enough away that it doesn't seem to bother her or her daughter.

The two youngsters wander in, sit down, pick up their glasses of wine and start telling me about how the girl's mother doesn't want them to get married so they're going to Boston for a few months to save money living with his family. Then they're heading out for the west coast. (Or, at least that's what he says...she looks skeptical).

"Is that right?" I inquire. "I've hitchhiked out that way before. Once with my ex-wife and once with another girl. You've probably already discovered that a guy and a gal together make the perfect hitchhiking combination because he gives her protection and she gives him respectability."

"We've had pretty good luck so far, I have to admit," Ellen seconds, "until tonight, that is...but you've been nice enough to get us out of the rain, so that worked out pretty good too."

We chat a while longer, finish our wine and by then it is clear that my guests are struggling to stay awake. I suggest that we call it a night so we can get an early start in the morning. They gratefully accept my suggestion, get up yawning and shuffle off toward their bedroom. I shut off the lights, plunging the living room into complete darkness and sit by the front window in one of the few chairs I've scrounged up.

Cool, sensual night breezes drift into the room from outside. I can hear the trees rustling, the chirping of a few bugs and a trickle of water running out of a drainpipe. The rain has stopped. I sit there for some time, relaxed and content. Then I go to bed - or to be more accurate, I walk to the other bedroom and crawl into my sleeping bag. There's no furniture in this room either. I stretch out comfortably on the black tile floor, entirely content with my unadorned, monastic quarters. They're appropriate for someone in my emotional and spiritual condition. I fall asleep trying to decide exactly what my emotional and spiritual condition is.

Holiday

I awake to a bright, sunny morning. Out my bedroom window I can see a languid blue sky with only a few swirls of cottony white clouds remaining from the previous day's rain. The birds are chirping wholeheartedly and the world has been washed sparkling clean. It's going to be a hot day, although at this early hour a refreshing and cool morning breeze still circulates through the apartment.

Throwing off my sleeping bag and pulling on my shorts, I pad out to the front room to survey the scene from the night before. It only takes a moment to straighten up - some albums to be returned to their sleeves, a few glasses to wash in the sink and I'm finished. Knocking on the door behind which the travelers are sleeping, I inform them that it's time to rise and shine.

Opening the refrigerator, I find some bacon and eggs. Another moment's search turns up a fresh Florida grapefruit. Putting a frying pan on the stove, I turn on the burner and commence whipping us up a first class breakfast. By the time my guests emerge from their bedroom the smell of bacon frying has spread throughout the apartment.

"Did everyone get a good night's sleep?" I inquire solicitously. "Oh, and by the way, there are some towels and washcloths in the bathroom if you guys want to take a shower before we get going."

"That'd be great!" Ellen quickly responds, giving Lonnie a look as if to say, 'This is non-negotiable.'

He shrugs and replies lackadaisically, "Fine with me - I could use one too."

By the time Ellen finishes her shower, the first breakfast plate is on the table, the food piping hot and ready to be devoured. I sit down and join her. She's hungry and while Lonnie takes his shower she makes short work of her bacon, eggs, toast and grapefruit. A few minutes later Lonnie joins us and duplicates her bravura performance at the table.

The two of them offer to help clean up but I suggest that they grab their sleeping bags instead and get organized for departure. I'm washing the dishes when I hear the sound of a car door opening outside. Instantly I zip over to the living room window and check it out. Yep, it's my neighbor on the end...just who I was hoping to see! Hollering to Lonnie and Ellen that I have to get something out of my car I hurry out my front door into the early morning sunshine.

Cheri is putting some picnic supplies inside the hatchback of her white Ford. She's wearing a pair of cut-off shorts and a skimpy halter top. We've had a couple of good conversations over the last two or three weeks since I've moved in - nothing planned but on more than one occasion we stayed up late and talked into the wee hours.

Nonchalantly stepping out into the driveway, I stretch mightily and feign inattentiveness while yawning. My plan works - the second she sees me she calls out.

"James, hi! I thought you were going to the Jersey shore for the weekend. What happened?"

She's so friendly! I turn to her as if I hadn't noticed she was out there.

"Oh, hi. No, I decided to stick around and enjoy Memorial Day up here."

"Great!" she responds enthusiastically. "Maybe you'd be willing to do me a big favor then?"

She turns on the charm and pans me with one of those damsel in distress looks, all smiles and bounce and legs and I know damn well what favor I'd like to do for the both of us.

"Sure, what?" I reply helpfully.

"I'm supposed to be bringing an ice chest to this picnic I'm going to and I made the mistake of filling it with ice before putting it into the car," Cheri explains.

"Yeah, so?"

"So now it's too heavy for me to lift. Would you put it in my car for me? And oh, geez, I almost forgot the beer!"

With that Cheri turns and dashes back into her apartment. She's already dragged the cooler as far as her doorway so I walk over to inspect it. Before I can hoist the ice chest, though, she returns with three six-packs of Genesee Cream Ale.

"Here, let me help you with them," I volunteer, taking the six-packs out of her hands. We bend down together and begin stuffing bottles in the ice. We're only inches apart and up close like this I'm mesmerized - she has beautiful brown eyes, lips the color of strawberries and an absolutely flawless, creamy white complexion. She catches me staring and knows she has my full attention.

"So really, what are you doing today?" she asks, smiling quizzically and startling me out of my investigation. She shakes the lovely dark hair off the back of her neck and we're so close I can see little beads of moisture on her temples from the bustling about she's doing getting ready for her Memorial Day picnic. She has on a delicate and secretive perfume. The fragrance is intoxicating.

'We live next door to each other,' I tell myself. 'Take your time...there's no rush!'

"I'm going out to a big flea market at Stormville airport," I answer. "A buddy of mine from out that way has been telling me for weeks that it's one of the 'can't miss' events of the summer, so I thought I'd check it out. As a matter of fact, I've got to get going soon. What are you up to today?"

"Well," she answers, "I was telling you. We're all going up to Lake Taghkanic for a picnic. Kurt is bringing his sailboat. It'll be fun."

A sailboat. ('That bastard! Why don't I have a sailboat? No matter, I'm making progress with his babe, sailboat or not,' I tell myself).

"Genesee Cream Ale?" I comment, changing the subject, critically examining one of the green and white bottles. "I've never heard of it before, any good?"

"Sure it's good, why else would I buy it? In fact, it's about the only kind of beer I'll drink. They make it upstate."

She looks at me and smiles conspiratorially.

"I'll tell you what," she continues. "Since you've been so much help to me, give me one of those six-packs. I'll put it in the refrigerator and we can drink it together later, all right?"

She grabs a six-pack and starts back into her apartment.

"Hey, that's not necessary," I protest, albeit none too vigorously. "You don't have to do that. What about your picnic? Just put a bottle aside for each of us."

"Don't worry, I want to do it," she reassures me, smiling warmly and touching my arm lightly. "I do!"

The apartment swallows her up again. I hear her refrigerator door open and close. A picnic. That means she could be home by dinnertime. I'll make a point of returning to the ranch by then myself. Cheri comes hurrying out again with her pocketbook and some final odds and ends.

"Oh, I've got to get going too," she laments. "I can't believe how late it's getting."

I lift the ice chest and carry it over to her car. It's not heavy at all. She could have managed it easily herself. Now it's my turn to smile. She notices.

"What's so funny?"

"Oh...nothing," I reply innocently.

At that moment my front door opens and Lonnie and Ellen troop out with their belongings, the two of them blinking in the bright sunlight.

"Got to run - see you later," I say. "Leave some room for a Cream Ale, ok?"

Cheri holds my eyes steadily as I voice my request. I look directly at her. Another big smile escapes her. Then she turns away so I can't see her face.

"Sure. Thanks for the help - and don't buy too much junk at the flea market," she calls over her shoulder as she climbs into her car, starts the motor and waves a cheerful goodbye before putting the vehicle into gear and disappearing around the corner of the barn on her way down the driveway.

***

'Is this the perfect way to kick off Memorial Day weekend or not? Cheri wants to stash away a little bit of her boyfriend's beer to share with me later on? Yes sir, things are looking

GOOD.'

My spirits, already high, soar higher still. What a beautiful Saturday morning! All traces of last night's rain are gone as the sun climbs into a pure blue cloudless sky. Although the hour is quite early and the dew still wet on the grass, it's clear that it's going to be a hot one. Good thing I remembered to set the alarm and get up early - Wesley's mother had warned me that I should get to the flea market before the heat and crowds made the place unbearable. And here it is, barely nine o'clock and I'm already on the highway. Not bad - and we're at the intersection I'm looking for.

"Hey guys, I'm going to drop you off now," I tell my passengers. "It's real close to that bar where we met last night. Stay on this road about another ten miles or so until you get to Pawling then catch highway 22 south to Interstate 84. That'll take you into Connecticut. After that, you're on your own."

"This'll be great," Ellen answers. "Do you think we'll have any trouble getting rides out here?"

"Oh no, not in the daytime. Lots of people travel this road. You'll be out to Pawling in no time."

Rolling up to the intersection, I pull off onto the side of the road and brake to a halt.

"Hey, thanks for all the hospitality, man, we appreciate it," Lonnie assures me, shaking my hand hastily, then sliding out the passenger side door.

"Yeah - thanks so much," Ellen echoes, clambering out of her seat to join him. "You made it a fun evening for us - not to mention getting us out of the rain."

"My pleasure - best of luck to you two."

Ellen's door slams shut, I put the car into gear, wave goodbye and head down the road toward Stormville airport (site of the renowned Memorial Day flea market). I commence a leisurely, scenic cruise down some of the loveliest country roads in America, motoring mile after mile past bucolic fields and grassy meadows. All about me gentle, wooded hills rise up like green shouldered sentinels guarding the way to the heart of paradise.

But no matter, it's all lost on me - my mind has returned to the topic which I know will haunt me all day long.

'Hmmmm, what time COULD I realistically expect Cheri to be home, assuming she's spending the entire day at Lake Taghkanic with this boyfriend of hers?'

***

The flea market is a spectacle - thousands of people milling about under joyously blue skies amid brightly colored tents and tables piled high with assorted wares, everyone in search of the ultimate geegaw, caught up in a bargaining fever that traces its heritage to the fabled ancient bazaars of Persia and Baghdad. But it's not until I find myself eagerly purchasing three (barely) scratched albums and two striking but utterly useless Menorah candle holders - I'm Catholic! - that I realize how contagious (and expensive) this fever can be.

So I go home before I break the bank. And no, Cheri hasn't returned yet - how could she? It's barely noon when I return to my apartment. She and her boyfriend probably haven't even gotten TO the lake yet. I sit around for about ten minutes before realizing that if I don't do something to distract myself, I'll probably go crazy. So I decide to take a run, hoping to pound the thought of a certain mesmerizing female out of my mind.

A lazy air of serenity pervades the peaceful surroundings and my mind drifts aimlessly in a trancelike state as I slowly jog up to the vantage point I seek on top of Waterbury Hill. The hot sun and windless day have me sweating profusely and gasping for breath by the time I reach my destination but when I get there the toil and effort are forgotten as I absorb the splendid view.

To the west lies a magnificent overlook of the entire Hudson valley. Gentle, rolling hillsides sweep down toward the flatlands in a series of undulating ridges that fade into the mist far away at river's edge. Beyond the Hudson another series of low hills culminates abruptly in the steep blue wall of the Shawangunk range, western boundary of my kingdom.

To my east, only a short hike away, looms Clove mountain, grim and impassive. Its unmanned lonely fire tower pokes above a tree line of stunted pines and gnarled oaks. It served as a lookout over all the surrounding fields, forests and hills in the days before air surveillance rendered it obsolete.

The beauty up here is in the solitude - there's nothing except me and the wind and empty fields. I can see for miles and miles in every direction. I feel like I'm literally on top of the world! It's when confronted with nature on this grand and majestic a scale that it's easiest to feel the presence of God, the master architect. The frantic, racing machinery between my ears is momentarily stilled and humbled, my grandiose schemes and plots temporarily forgotten as my soul drinks the view in.

How small we are, how big the world? What span of time since these hills were thrust up from the ground beneath some prehistoric sun? Enough time for a rivulet to carve a path through a monolithic block of stone, resulting in a majestic river like the Hudson. This is geology working on a scale measured in billions of years. What a fraction of an instant our time is in comparison. Scale. Perspective. And despite the grandeur, an overwhelming sensation of intimacy. ('Is that you out there calling me, God?')

Speaking of intimacy, I do have a shot at intimacy of another sort if I play my cards right, don't I? If only she leaves that picnic early. (Ahhh...the whir and clatter of my mental machinery starts up once again!) It's time to descend from these Olympian heights to seek out some action with my fellow mortals.

> "Comes a time, when you're drifting...
> Comes a time when you settle down."

> "In the field of opportunity, it's plowing time again."

> "Motorcycle Mama, won't you lay your big spike down?"

> "It's gonna take a lot of love...to get us through the night."

> - Neil Young, "Comes a Time" (album)

Down in the lowlands things remain as I left them (no sign of Cheri) except it's turned into one of those hot, lazy afternoons when even the birds are too drowsy to sing. After enjoying a cold, refreshing shower I settle in to watch time creep by at a sluggish pace. Books, records and napping all fail to distract me - with every hint of an outside noise, I catch my breath and listen carefully for evidence of her return but Cheri does not reappear.

The sun is starting to sink when I begin preparations for

my dinner, deciding on 'outdoor cafe' style dining for obvious tactical reasons. By the time I get around to lugging my 'cafe' (table, two chairs, plants and bird-less birdcage) outside, a refreshing breeze has kicked up causing the tall, stately pine trees in the courtyard to swish appreciatively. Down by the pond I can hear the ducks and geese, suddenly restless, quacking and honking to each other above the soothing sound of water splashing over the dam. I enjoy an excellent plate of broiled steak, fried tomatoes and fresh corn beneath the trees, washing my meal down with a glass of chilled lambrusco.

The time comes to carry the dirty dishes inside. Dumping them unceremoniously in the sink, I'm reaching for the faucet when I hear the unmistakable sound of a car coming up the driveway. My heart freezes in my chest as I listen intently. Is it...?

Yes! Her car whips by my front window and disappears in the direction of her normal parking spot. Cheri is home and the night is still young. But an alarming thought - did she bring the boyfriend home too? I can't tell from my vantage point. Ears pricked, I can only hear the sound of a car door open and then slam shut. Next, the tap of footsteps followed by scratching noises as she fits her key into the front door of her apartment. The scuffling of her footsteps recedes as she moves into her living room - and why didn't she close the front door behind her? Her stereo comes to life and the air is filled with the bright sound of guitars strumming, harmonica's blowing and Neil Young singing songs of buoyant romance from his latest album, 'Comes A Time.'

I scurry outside, anxious to be positioned before she emerges, wanting to appear composed and collected when she does so, my stomach in knots, however, at the prospect. She has to have seen the table and chairs - if she comes out again that means she's coming out to see me.

I pretend to resume reading as I take my seat. Scarcely have I turned a page when I look up to see Cheri strolling toward me, long, exquisite legs exposed to their utmost advantage, her cutoffs cut ultra short, two open bottles of Genesee in hand.

"Hi, neighbor. About ready to try one of these?" She hands me a cold beer which I accept eagerly.

"Whoa...uh, hi! What are you doing back so soon? How was the lake?"

"Oh, boring. I was glad to get out of there. Too many people, the place was a zoo. Mind if I join you?"

"Not at all. Help yourself."

She plops her beer on the table, sits closer to me than I would have expected (Oh God! I'm getting delirious from the fragrance of her perfume) and regards me quizzically.

"Two chairs? Expecting somebody?"

"Oh no, no..."

"Why the two chairs then?"

It'd be so much easier to think of a clever answer if I could take my eyes off the smooth curve of her youthful cheek and the delicate pink of her lips, still wet from her last sip of beer.

"Wishful thinking, I guess. And see, it worked out to my advantage."

Diverting attention from the bravado inherent in that last remark, I cock an eye at the bottle in my hand and guzzle a long swig of the Cream Ale. Cheri watches me expectantly.

"Ahhh - nectar of the Gods!" I conclude with gusto. "A toast to Genesee Cream Ale and the good neighbor policy."

I offer my bottle. Laughing, she clinks hers with mine and we both enjoy another healthy swallow.

"What's the birdcage for?" she asks, missing nothing.

In a burst of inspiration I take my half-full Cream Ale, rise to my feet, finish my beer in one gulp, wipe my mouth on my sleeve and then insert the bottle (a pretty little thing with a flashy green and gold label) inside the empty cage, nestling it unsteadily on a perch.

"There," I say, admiring my work and clapping my hands together gleefully as I sit down at the table again. "THAT'S what it's for."

"Kind of weird. I don't get it," Cheri comments, furrowing her dark eyebrows skeptically.

"This way the memory of our drinking Cream Ale together will never escape me," I blurt out impulsively.

I cross a line with that one and we both know it. Reckless, I stare at her, awaiting a reaction. She blushes, momentarily flustered by my forwardness. Regaining her composure, she returns the stare.

"Isn't it funny though...how sometimes the hunter is actually the hunted?"

Smug, satisfied with the repartee, she grins wickedly, raises her bottle to me and drains it. A jolt of ecstasy hits me as the wonder of my present reality sinks in. Oh lust, the hunt! There's no turning back now. An electric charge crackles in the air.

"Oh, and by the way," she continues boldly, "why don't you come on over to my place? I'll show you my..." (she pauses, smiles suggestively, and then slyly continues) "album collection! We can have another beer too - I'm ready, if you are."

Laughing merrily, she beckons toward her front door and then, confident I'll follow, gets up, turns on her heel and provocatively strides into her apartment.

***

Cheri's offer to show me her album collection is clearly a ruse. Oddly enough, it nearly backfires. Once inside the dim, cavernous hall of her apartment she points me toward her stereo while getting us each another Cream Ale. Examining her records, I come across another Neil Young album that I like and innocently request that Cheri play a cut off it. Cheerfully acceding to my wish, Cheri remarks that the album I've chosen belonged to her soon to be 'ex' husband, Billy. She chooses a tender, bittersweet tune, laughingly prefacing her selection with the comment that she played this song whenever Billy was around in the last days before their separation:

> "Lover, there will be another one
> Who'll hover over you, beneath the sun
> Tomorrow see the things that never come today.
> When you see me fly away without you
> Shadow on the things you know
> Feathers fall around you
> And show you the way to go...
> It's over."
>
> - Neil Young, "Birds"

As the last melancholy strains fade into the background I ask, "You played that FOR Billy? Kind of morbid or cruel or something like that, isn't it?"

"Oh yeah, that's the point. I can be a real bitch but it's still a good tune! I love that song. Although, I don't think Billy much cared for it by the end."

She starts to get up to change albums but I interrupt her, "Wait! Let it play - the next song makes me think of you."

Seconds later an up-tempo barrage of crashing, heroic guitar chords rings out, sweeping aside the fatalism of the previous number, building dramatically to an exuberant conclusion:

> "I got something to tell you,
> You made it show -
> Let me come over, I know you know,
> When you dance, oh, oh, I can really love!"

- Neil Young, "When you Dance I Can Really Love"

And so it goes. Before long we're swilling beers left and right, ferrying album after album to the turntable. It's all great fun but somehow we're getting sidetracked from the reason we came inside. Or maybe we've seized on this distraction precisely because we know why we've come inside and are afraid of making a wrong move and blowing the whole thing. One way or another we've squandered the original sexual charge that carried us this far. Making matters worse, we've finished off the beer too. It suddenly dawns on both of us that our golden opportunity is in grave danger of being lost. We could be reduced to mere 'neighbor' status once again.

"Can I make you some tea?" Cheri improvises.

"Tea?" I echo blankly.

"Yeah, tea. Comes in little bags - you put them in hot water and presto! You drink it. Do you want me to make you some?"

This is an unexpected development. I search for some hidden

meaning behind the question, but of course, there isn't one. Then, the light clicks on. (She wants me to stay!)

"Yeah, that'd be nice. Sure, I'll have some. Are you a big tea drinker?"

"No, not really," she calls over her shoulder, heading into the kitchen to rummage through various cabinets in search of a tea bag.

"About five foot seven, maybe a hundred and fifteen pounds...there are bigger tea drinkers out there than me, I'm sure," she jokes.

This is what we've been reduced to? An hour ago we were smoldering with passion and now we we're a jumble of nervous jitters. This evening will be a terrible waste, a blown opportunity of immense magnitude if we don't make physical contact. As aggressive as Cheri is, it's clear she's still old-fashioned enough to want me to make the first overt physical move. The time for talk is over. Cheri is starting to look a little discouraged and tired.

The water boils, the tea is served and we sit across the coffee table from each other listening to yet another album, conversation at a bare minimum as we conserve our energy.

"Can I kiss you?" I suddenly interrupt, out of the blue, gazing into her eyes, bending over the table to within a few inches of her face, surprising even myself with the words I've uttered.

She regards me with some degree of confusion, uncertain as to her options. I take her hesitation as consent and kiss her full on the lips, holding her by the shoulders. She doesn't try to pull away, returning my kiss eagerly. Soon my hands are running up and down her body and we find ourselves tumbling to the floor, pressed tightly against each other. Cheri surreptitiously drags her hand across the front of my jeans, letting her fingers linger. The torture becomes exquisite as she applies enough touch to drive me wild, but not enough to permit release.

"Oh, my God," she breathes, "it's so big!"

Rolling onto her back, she pulls me up on top of her. Biting down hard on my lips, she wriggles beneath me and works her hands over me with a magician's touch. But right as I start to believe 'this is it!' she pushes me away, eyes dilated wide by the sexual fire burning inside her.

"No, we have to stop!" she gasps. "We shouldn't be doing this. If we go any further I won't be able to...stop."

She doesn't sound convincing at all so I kiss her again. She puts her arms around me, sinks into my embrace and returns the kiss wholeheartedly. I remount her and the rhythms pick up where we left off. But she only lets it go on until she senses that I'm getting close to the point of no return. Nearly biting my lip off, ramming her tongue down my throat one last time, she pulls away again and looks me in the eye.

"We really have to stop...I'm serious!"

I absorb the news silently, unable to believe she means it, nonetheless giddy, happy and delighted beyond belief. There's so much time - we live next door to each other!

III

Paradise

Late Spring 1980

Getaway

'A change in seasons is good reason for pleasing!' Quite often James found himself humming this mindless little ditty as spring sprung. Every aspect of life appeared to him as fresh and full of potential as the tender green leaves and shoots hastily redefining the world around him. It had been a long, hard, cold winter but now icy, frozen hillsides yielded to shady, inviting forests and snow blown, windswept tundra gave way to grassy, fragrant meadows.

In jarring contrast, Cheri, at this particular moment, was experiencing no such wide-eyed glee. Instead she slumped, morose and brooding, in the passenger seat of James' Pontiac as the vehicle eased out onto the Taconic State Parkway.

'Why did I ever agreed to go on this stupid trip?' she fretted. 'Oh sure, it sounded great - a weekend at the Jersey shore. When was the last time I got to go to the ocean for some sun and fun? But it's never that easy, is it? I can't believe how guilty I feel! This is the end for me and Kurt."

Even though she'd realized all along that her growing attachment to James must inevitably lead to a conclusion of her relationship with Kurt, she'd never directly confronted the fact until now. Kurt ostensibly knew nothing of her budding romance with James and remained a fixture in her life at work, playing cards with the gang at lunchtime, always available despite the fact that Cheri had been evasive the last few times he'd asked her out. For whatever reason (Cheri suspected a swollen ego that was too arrogant to conceive of potential rivals) Kurt believed her alibis and the two of them drifted along without incident, Cheri fortified by the knowledge that she had a safety net if things didn't work out with James.

But the end of this idyll was fast approaching. Just prior to closing time today Kurt had asked her out to a movie this weekend and he'd been unwilling to accept her breezy put-off.

"Oh, sorry Kurt, I'd like to do something with you this weekend but I'm going to be in Jersey," she groped for an excuse.

"Oh, is that right? Jersey, huh?" Lights were finally blinking on in Kurt's head.

"Yes, that's right, Jersey," she bit off sharply. "What of it?"

Kurt absorbed her comment in wounded silence. He tried to stare her down. Cheri regarded him with icy impatience. Finally he broke off his gaze. Her bluff had succeeded despite the fact that her heart was pounding furiously and she was certain her cheeks were bright red with guilt.

"You and your folks have relatives in Jersey, don't you?" Kurt weakly offered, clinging to a lifeline, unsure of himself for the first time since Cheri had known him. It suddenly dawned on her - he was afraid of losing her! She felt an unexpected surge of sympathy and suppressed a wild, irrational impulse to blurt out the truth and ask forgiveness. But he'd left her too easy an out and reflex took over.

"Yes, we do," she calmly replied, with enough annoyance to keep him on the defensive.

"I guess I'll see you on Monday," he glumly concluded.

"I guess so…" Cheri relented, weakening.

His dejected expression hurt her worse than any words he could have spoken in anger. He appealed to her mutely, his eyes red and teary with emotion. She met his stare and turned it away once again. And suddenly he knew. It was that simple. She could outmaneuver him all day long but he knew that she was seeing someone else. And such was the power she held over him that he accepted even that indignity. He still wanted to be with her. But she offered him nothing further in return and finally he walked away, shoulders slumped in defeat.

And now, hours later, that incident was driving her crazy with remorse.

'And who the hell is this guy I'm with?' she admonished herself. 'Do I really know him well enough to drag my kid down to his parents' house for the weekend? What are they going to think if they suspect we're sleeping together?'

She cast a suspicious glance toward James, half expecting to unmask some lecherous ogre. It was somewhat of a surprise to see the same pleasant, cheerful person she'd taken such a liking to over these past few weeks sitting behind the driver's wheel happily minding his own business. Cheri squirmed in her seat, torn between accepting her chosen fate or screwing up enough nerve to ask James to turn the car around.

James, not entirely stupid, knew by the oppressive silence that things were touch and go. It wasn't until the moment he watched Cheri pack her bags in the trunk and then arrange Melanie in the back seat of the car amid some pillows and toys that he'd allowed himself to believe that Cheri was going with him to New Jersey.

'But hell,' he reasoned, 'I'm ahead of the game until she asks me to turn around. And the farther we get the less likely she is to ask. I just need to keep cool and not pressure her,' he cautioned himself. 'This is not the time to get overconfident.'

But he couldn't conceal the fact that he was ecstatic.

'I can't believe I've got her for a whole weekend at the beach!' he rejoiced, taking a sip of cold beer, tuning the radio to a rock station and sitting back to enjoy the scenery and his good luck.

Cheri too leaned back and took a sip from her beer. Idly contemplating the view, she momentarily succeeded in pushing her problems out of mind. The woods pressed against the shoulder of the road and she could see dogwoods and tulip trees in full bloom, their pink and white flowers contrasting nicely with the tall pines and leafy hemlocks that served as a backdrop. Steep hillsides and sheer rock walls stared her in the face as they negotiated the treacherous curves of the Taconic State parkway. The radio caught her attention and she found herself listening to songs that reminded her of other summers, other drives, other romances. It wasn't the specific tunes that were affecting her as much as it was the mere act of riding along in a car with the windows down and the music playing. They were going to the beach! She began the slow process of relaxing. If she could keep herself distracted like this she'd be all right. It just took a little practice. There! Wasn't that a pretty lake they were driving by? It occurred to her that she'd made a decision by not making a decision. A quick stab of remorse pricked her conscience - Kurt, poor Kurt! But she was going to the beach.

***

Day settled into the wistful, melancholy calm preceding nightfall. All the picnics, ballgames, outings and excursions were over. Deep shadows reclaimed the playing fields and parks, a soft breeze picked up, mothers called their children home and screen doors slammed shut behind them leaving the world quiet and at rest.

The car descended from the hills and entered the vast complex of interstates, parkways and expressways that funneled vehicles into the suburban sprawl surrounding New York City. The actual flow of traffic, however, diminished considerably as they approached the metropolis. Rush hour was over and increasingly James, Cheri and Melanie had long stretches of highway to themselves as they sped southward.

Cheri felt better with each mile they traveled. This was a time of day that appealed to her intrinsic moodiness. She felt recharged and reinvigorated as nightfall approached - the workday was done, an adventure was underway, she was going away for the weekend!

There was one final bad moment as they neared Peekskill. Kurt had recently interviewed for a job there and it brought him to mind one last time. But as the cauldron of conflicting impulses bubbled to the surface, Cheri experienced a cathartic sort of pain that passed quickly and left her feeling purged of the anxiety that had plagued her all afternoon.

'Goodbye, Kurt!' she declared to herself, still uncertain as to why going away with James for the weekend made her feel so guilty. 'I'm having a good time with this new guy. Maybe if you'd paid more attention to me and not been so quick to respond to your ex-wife's every beck and call you might have seen it coming and done something about it. But it's too late now.'

She snuck another glance at James to see how he was coping with her sustained silence. She smiled, watched him studiously peer straight ahead through the windshield, head bobbing in time to the songs on the radio, bemused smile on his face as he occasionally sipped his beer.

'The cocky son of a bitch! Look at him - he thinks he's got me right where he wants me. He's on top of the world,' Cheri reckoned.

It occurred to her that he had every reason to feel that way.

***

Speeding along the eastern bank of the Hudson in their final approach to 'the City,' they rounded a curve and dramatically encountered the Metropolis. Directly in front of them, plainly visible through a gaping rent in the trees, loomed the George Washington Bridge. The three of them marveled at its monumental proportions as the parkway shunted them toward the span's massive stone footings. High overhead, white globes of light glittered at regular intervals along the taut suspension cables. The iron skeleton was lit up like a carnival midway on a hot summer night, steel superstructure illuminated against the onrushing purple backdrop of evening. Endless rivers of headlights streamed across its stately arch, the forbidding structure perched above the river like a modern day colossus.

A moment later they were beneath the bridge, staring straight up at its tangled network of interlaced girders and beams. Then, breaking free of its shadow, they found themselves cruising down the battle-scarred West Side Highway, crumbling docks and wharves to their right, warren of high-rises, tenements and city streets to their left. And dead ahead lay the most stupendous assemblage of concrete, steel and glass the world has ever known. No descriptive word has ever been more aptly chosen to describe these monumental structures – skyscrapers!

The West Side highway carried them as far south as the cruise ship berths at 53rd street before depositing them with a sudden decelerating whoosh in the honking, beeping, teeming heart of Manhattan. All around them a frantic, reckless demolition derby was in progress as cars, taxis and buses dueled heroically from traffic light to traffic light, disregarding risk and ruin, competing ferociously to gain the slightest advantage in their respective races across the hopelessly snarled concrete canyons of midtown. Time after time Cheri closed her eyes in anticipation of collisions that, miraculously, never quite materialized, contending vehicles veering away at the last possible millisecond, the collective group behaving like a school of fish changing direction in perfect, mindless synchronization as they flowed around obstacles and hindrances.

And the pedestrians! Swarms of individuals lost in private reveries overflowed the city sidewalks, spilling out into the streets, darting across intersections, dodging cars and each other as they doggedly charted their way cross-town.

"Watch out!" Cheri blurted in alarm as a traffic light turned green and James, head rapidly swiveling from side to side as he absorbed the sights and sounds, stepped on the accelerator to keep pace with the surge of vehicles surrounding him. Alerted, he promptly hit the brakes and managed to avoid running over a slow-footed individual who had not yet fully cleared the intersection. This elderly gentlemen angrily brandished his cane, sharply rapping the front fender of the Pontiac, mouthing some unintelligible insult before continuing on to the relative refuge of the sidewalk.

"Jeez, ok, ok! Can you believe this guy? What is he, pissed off because I almost clipped him?" James grumbled, unperturbed.

"Please be careful," Cheri pleaded. "This place makes me so nervous. I can't stand driving here."

"No problem...I've got it knocked," James confidently replied as they raced forward another block to the next traffic light.

"Besides," he continued, "we'll be out of here in a flash. I just wanted to sample the City atmosphere on the way down to my folks' house. I love visiting this place but I can only take it so long and I guess it's been about long enough. I'm gonna cut over to the river and catch the Lincoln Tunnel. We'll be cruising down the Jersey Turnpike in five minutes."

"Good. My nerves can't take much more of this," Cheri emphasized.

"Ooops, damn! That was 42nd street," James groaned.

"So?"

"That was our turn-off to the Lincoln Tunnel. Oh hell, no biggie. We'll swing around the block and catch it again coming from the other direction."

Of course, this being Manhattan, it proved maddeningly impossible to 'swing around' quite that easily. They ended up traveling several blocks further out of their way before James could negotiate the proper sequence of turns to counter the maze of one way streets and get them headed in the right direction. But no matter, only slightly frustrated by the delay, James eventually got the car pointed north. And this time he didn't miss his turn. At 42nd street he hung a hard left and shot down the block. He was momentarily unencumbered by traffic...an unexpected opening. Finally, freedom to drive! He mashed the pedal and zipped past two lanes of stalled traffic on his right before hitting yet another red light. But something was wrong.

'Why is everyone else over there jammed up in those two lanes while I've got this one completely to myself?' he mused.

The answer came to him in a jolt of pure adrenal terror as a torrent of honking vehicles suddenly came rushing straight at them. He was in the WRONG lane - on a two way street. He was going west in an east-bound lane!

"Oh, my God!" Cheri gasped as the reality of their precarious situation dawned on her.

There was nothing James could do except flinch as oncoming cars sped directly at them before swerving crazily aside at the last moment upon realizing that some lunatic was camped in their lane. He couldn't merge into the right-hand lanes until the light changed to green on that side and allowed traffic to unclog.

'Oh please, you filthy whore of a light, change!' he pleaded, not risking a look Cheri's way, afraid to see the expression on her face. Second after agonizing second crawled by as they sat there trapped like rats for all of Manhattan to observe. Car after car negotiated the obstacle they represented without catastrophe. And then, just as James began to believe they were going to escape unscathed, another distraction materialized out of nowhere. Two men, gesticulating wildly, were approaching him on the driver's side of his car.

"Oh, Christ, what in the hell do these guys want?" James muttered, picking them up in his peripheral vision, his attention still riveted on the unchanged traffic light.

"They're cops," Cheri informed him, her voice devoid of emotion. "They want you to pull over."

Cops! They were at his car now. A dark-haired officer with a mustache knocked his night stick angrily on the hood and gestured to the far side of the street.

"Pull it over there!" he hollered, his partner stopping traffic long enough to create an opening for James to maneuver the big Pontiac into a relatively protected spot near the corner on the opposite side of the street.

James suddenly remembered the beer he and Cheri had in the car.

"Quick," he hissed, "shove that six-pack under the seat!"

Cheri scrambled to hide the beer but with a sinking feeling James realized that even a cursory inspection of the car would reveal its presence. Then, out of nowhere, he remembered that his inspection sticker had expired.

The mustachioed officer walked up to the open driver's side window and bent down to examine the occupants of the car. Melanie regarded him with a two-year old's wide-eyed wonder.

"Cop," she enthused. "Cop!"

The officer - a relatively young guy with a big hooked nose and black, bushy eyebrows to match his expansive mustache - was not amused.

"Shut it off," he ordered.

That's when James recalled the latest mechanical problem the Pontiac had been experiencing. It ran fine but once it got hot he couldn't shut it off or it wouldn't start again until it had twenty or thirty minutes to cool down. A minor enough problem if you weren't in any particular hurry, but he hardly expected, no matter what else happened, that these cops would let him sit here blocking the crosswalk and traffic on one of Manhattan's busiest streets for a half hour without calling a tow truck. And what would that cost - hundreds of dollars? It would all be academic since he only had about thirty dollars with him anyway.

"Officer," he tried to humbly explain, "if I shut this car off I won't be able to start it again for -"

"SHUT IT OFF!" the other policeman, a big, red-faced, hostile looking fellow bellowed from behind his partner.

James shut it off.

"License and registration," Mustachio ordered, irritation evident in his voice, along with a degree of boredom now that he'd surveyed the occupants of the car and realized they didn't have any hardened criminals to deal with.

James handed over the requested documents and waited for the verdict in silence. The officer concluded his inspection of the papers and returned his attention to James. Cheri and Melanie regarded the officer hopefully as he glanced at them again before speaking.

"I don't understand a guy like you," he began in disgust. "What in the hell do you think you're doing? You must be out of your mind."

He shifted to a tone of exaggerated, exasperated calm. "You've got a BABY in the car, for chrissakes, and here you are driving like an idiot! So tell me -" (here he glanced at the license to get the name) "James, what's the story?"

James took a deep breath and answered in the most deferential tone of voice he could muster.

"I'm from upstate, officer. I made a mistake - I thought this was a one-way street. There was nothing coming this way when I turned the corner and -"

"42nd street! Come on, James," the officer interrupted, "it's the busiest street in Manhattan. You didn't realize it was two way traffic?" he spluttered in disbelief.

The policeman shook his head unhappily, unable to believe he was dealing with such a moron. He stepped away from the window as if afraid that James' stupidity might prove contagious. Then he noticed the expired inspection sticker.

"Ahhh, James, what's with the inspection sticker?" he asked sternly, bending down to look at him again through the window.

"I...let it expire, I guess," James responded weakly, speaking in the voice of a man who'd lost all hope. Even HE was embarrassed, fully aware of how utterly pathetic his performance had been to this point. He stared miserably through the windshield. He could almost imagine the officer pulling out his service revolver to perform a roadside execution, ridding society of the menace James represented.

But instead the officer shook his head in exasperation, shifted his gaze to include Cheri and Melanie (who were both looking at him in wide-eyed wonder) and then stepped away from the window. He stared at traffic, lost in thought, for 20 or 30 seconds before turning his attention to James again.

"Ok, James, I'll tell you what...you could be in one hell of a lot of trouble right now, you realize that, don't you?"

"Yes, sir," James meekly replied.

"But I'm gonna give you a break," the officer continued, sounding annoyed with himself for even considering such a ludicrous idea. "I'm only going to issue you a ticket for having an expired inspection sticker. And then I want you to get the hell out of here, ok?"

James looked at him with a blank expression, waiting for the catch, unable to belief he was getting off that easy.

"Now don't screw me over on this, James," the policeman continued, writing out the ticket as he spoke. "I'm giving you a break, right? Make sure you pay this ticket or we'll find your ass."

"Yes, sir," James replied, "Thank you very much, sir!"

"One last thing," concluded Mustachio, handing James the ticket through the window. "Sign where I've indicated, please."

James signed, the cop tore off his copy of the ticket and handed it to him.

"Ok then, get out of here...and be careful! You've got a nice family - try not to kill them," Mustachio remonstrated. Then, as an afterthought he added, "By the way, do you know how to get out of here?"

"Yes, sir, I do. I'm taking the Lincoln tunnel - there's a sign for it right over there. I make a left at this next corner."

The policeman nodded and almost reluctantly, it seemed, turned away, walking to the sidewalk where his partner regarded the car and James with narrowed, suspicious eyes.

Anxious to get while the going was good, James turned the key in the ignition and held his breath, praying that the Pontiac had cooled down enough to restart.

It hadn't.

James turned the key again. Nothing. The vehicle was dead. His pulse rate started climbing. So close to freedom and now this!

"Is something wrong?" Cheri inquired nervously. "Let's get out of here before they change their minds."

"The car won't start again until it's cooled down longer," James woodenly informed her.

"Cooled down longer?" Cheri's voice cracked under the strain she was experiencing. "But, James, how long will that take? We can't sit here on the wrong side of the street blocking the intersection forever - they'll have us towed!"

"I know, I know. But believe me, the car won't start until

it's had more time to cool down."

He snuck a glance at the policemen. They had both turned their attention back to James and were regarding him curiously.

"Oh God, I can't believe this," James muttered, turning the ignition key one more time. Nothing. He sank into his seat, whipped, glancing over at Cheri. She didn't look happy.

"Well, do you see what I mean?" he asked. "Isn't the city a blast? You can't have fun like this just anywhere."

Inexplicably, Cheri found herself laughing, quietly at first, but then louder and louder, the pent up emotion and tension demanding release.

"You can't believe this?" she finally managed to gasp. "YOU can't believe this? 'Let me show you the City,' he says to me. Well, here we are! And aren't we having a good time trapped on 42nd street waiting for the police to tow us away?"

Cheri couldn't continue as another fit of laughter overcame her.

Melanie, encouraged by her mother's apparent good humor, piped up conspiratorially, "Bad cops...those were bad cops, weren't they mommy?"

"Oh, God no," Cheri gasped. "Shhhhh! They're good cops. It's this fool we're riding with that's bad. They should lock him up!"

She deteriorated into another spasm of laughter, "Mother of God, I can't believe this. I'm sorry, I'll get myself together in a minute," she apologized.

James snuck another look at the sidewalk. The police were still there, watching. James tried the key again with the same lack of result.

"It's got to cool down on its own," he lamented.

"Oh wait," Cheri interjected, still giggling hysterically, "why not take some of your beer out there to pour on the engine? That might help cool it down. And while you're at it, maybe you could offer some to the policemen too. That might be about the only way to keep them from towing your car to the city lockup."

James let out a deep sigh, opened the car door and stepped into the street.

"I'm going to pop the hood and pretend like I'm accomplishing something useful," he told Cheri. "Stick around," he added sarcastically, "the fun's not over yet."

He glanced over at the officers and gave what he hoped they'd interpret as a reassuring nod, before lifting the hood and staring down at the recalcitrant engine. Halfheartedly jiggling the spark plug wires, he toyed with the distributor cap. At least out here there was a comfortable breeze - he'd been sweating profusely in the car over the past few minutes although he hadn't realized it until now.

"What's the problem?"

James startled, looking up to find Mustachio standing next to him.

"Did you check the wires to the distributor cap? The battery and starter are good, aren't they?" Mustachio continued, not sounding angry at all.

"It starts fine when it's cold but once it gets hot, if I shut it down it takes a few minutes to cool off before it'll start up again. But it always comes around," James added hastily.

"Yeah, you know my brother-in-law had a car like this," Mustachio laughed, "a real a piece of shit! It wouldn't start when it was too hot or cold."

The cop was acting downright friendly, discussing the problem with James like they were buddies hanging around in the neighborhood garage. Looking sidelong at him, James realized they were probably close to the same age.

"I usually don't shut it off unless I don't have anywhere I have to be in the next half hour or so," James offered.

"It's got to be your battery cables!" Mustachio suddenly declared. "Yeah, the damn battery cables...they get all corroded and then when the car is hot they won't hold a charge. You had them replaced anytime recently?"

"Ahh...no, I haven't." James leaned over the engine, grabbed the battery cables and twisted them to see if they were loose or if any corrosion was noticeable. They seemed fine.

"Looks ok. I think I'm gonna give it another shot now - it'll probably start up this time."

"Well, good luck," Mustachio sympathized. "And be careful on the tunnel approach. It's kind of tricky. You have to merge left."

"I'll be careful," James assured him. "And thanks for everything."

"No problem."

And with that, Mustachio sauntered back over to the sidewalk where his partner had been joined by what looked like - judging by the additional gold on his shoulder patch - a sergeant or lieutenant.

"Ok, baby, it's now or never!" James cajoled, easing behind the steering wheel. He looked at Cheri, crossed his fingers, pumped the gas pedal once, and turned the key.

The Pontiac roared to life. They were safe! He and Cheri both whooped with joy as James clunked the car into drive and whipped it out into the street before the officers had a chance to reconsider. Thirty seconds later they were swooping down the entrance ramp to the Lincoln Tunnel.

"Merge left, he said," Cheri cautioned.

"Piece of cake," James declared, feeling his beleaguered confidence returning.

"Ready for another beer, Mr. Reckless Driver?" Cheri inquired as he steered them down into the tunnel's mouth.

"Sure am. Whew-ee, man, did we luck out?" James commented.

"What do you mean, 'we'?" Cheri teased. "If it'd come to that, me and Melanie would have gone over to Grand Central Station and caught the next train home. You're the one that'd be locked up downtown."

She was laughing, having a good time. He made an obscene gesture at her with his middle finger.

"Very funny, very funny," he acknowledged.

They were far inside the tunnel now, speeding across the river bed in a series of - essentially - large coffee cans welded together far beneath the surface of the Hudson. The white interior tiling and overhead fluorescent lighting reminded James of public restrooms. The roar of traffic was magnified a hundredfold by the close quarters and an 18-wheeler barreling along inches behind James' rear bumper, ruthlessly enforcing its own version of the speed limit. Claustrophobia became a factor as James raced to get out of the tube, childhood nightmares of cracked ceilings, cascading water and submerged vehicles more than adequate to hustle him along.

But just as James' blood pressure began climbing into the danger zone, the tunnel opened, traffic surged forward and blessedly there were stars overhead once more.

A hairpin curve remained to be negotiated as traffic poured out of the hole in the ground on the Jersey side.

James alerted Cheri, "Keep on eye out your window...we get a great view of New York City around this turn."

Slowing almost to a complete halt to negotiate the banked curve, at first they could see nothing over the concrete restraining wall due to the steep pitch of the road surface. Halfway through the turn, however, the banking began to level off and suddenly - as if by a magic trick - an unforgettable panorama of Manhattan appeared before them. Row upon row of glittering skyscrapers stood stacked shoulder to shoulder like bejeweled foot soldiers in parade formation lined up along the edge of the Hudson.

"Hard to believe we were over there a few minutes ago and drove under all that water to get here, isn't it?" James asked Cheri.

"It really is."

And that quickly, the view disappeared, terminated abruptly by a wall of rock as the highway veered inland, routing them towards the notorious Jersey turnpike.

Immediately they encountered another wild scene, easily as amazing as Manhattan in its own perverse way. The blasted corridor of land occupied by the Jersey turnpike carved its way through perhaps the most polluted, tortured, industrial wasteland in America, an ugly, stinking byproduct of progress. No matter what direction they turned the effect remained the same - astounding scenes like something out of Dante's inferno, flames shooting high into the sooty sky as oil refineries burned off flammable gases produced in the production of petroleum products. A byzantine labyrinth of piping, storage tanks, valves and ducts stretched before them for miles like a cancerous growth run completely amuck, each refinery competing with the others to cover the most possible acreage with tangled, twisted tubing.

And the lights! As far as they could see, horizon to horizon, billions of pinpoints illuminating the darkness - in neat ordered rows where streets and houses predominated; in jumbled, chaotic anarchy where power plants and refineries proliferated; in luminescent, shimmering arteries where streams of headlights flowed over the landscape and in white, beaded strings of pearl and ruby where high tension lines, steel support towers and their attendant blinking aircraft warning lights snaked over the countryside.

The earth in this part of New Jersey doesn't even exist anymore - it has been paved over with concrete and asphalt or transformed into a disgraceful open sewer. A wretched, oil-soaked dumping ground for toxic wastes and garbage, the whole mess is huddled around 'the Meadowlands,' a vast swamp where, amid the reeds and cattails, poisonous sludge and effluvia ferment a mutant chemical mix which will doubtlessly someday reap its hideous revenge upon mankind.

In the sky overhead, shrieking jetliners hurtled through the atmosphere at thirty second intervals, frequenting nearby Newark airport. Black exhaust trails spewed out behind the planes which were adding their fair share of pollutants to the dismal, noxious pall already generated by the belching smokestacks and crowded highways below.

They were driving along at a steady 65 miles per hour, absorbing the mind-boggling scene, when Cheri suddenly wrinkled her nose distastefully.

"What's that horrible smell?" she asked.

James took a deep breath and picked the odor up - a pungent, stinging, nauseating stench.

"Oh, that?" he laughed. "I forgot to tell you about this part of the trip. I'm sure you've heard of the famous Jersey aroma. People come here from all over the world to catch a whiff of the exotic fragrances that mysteriously arise from the earth here and are carried on the breeze for all to sample. This is where the French perfume designers come to get their new ideas."

"Oh, my God," Cheri cried out piteously. "It's getting worse! I can't stand it."

Searching about desperately, she seized her open beer bottle and held it under her nose, breathing in the smell of brewed hops and grain in an attempt to block out the ghastly odor emanating from the slaughterhouses, chemical plants and refineries.

"Does that help any?" James inquired, grinning, amused by her innovative tactic.

Refusing to abandon the life-saving shelter of her beer bottle, Cheri merely nodded in the affirmative and continued sniffing.

James rolled his window down all the way and breathed in the night air.

"Ahhh...there's no place like home," he proclaimed. "Welcome to New Jersey!"

Wildwood

Where the sun, the sea, the sand and the sky all came together, God thought to take mercy upon man and created that harbinger of paradise known as 'summer at the beach.' The bracing smell of saltwater carried on an ocean breeze, the soothing crash of waves breaking on sandbars, the guilty pleasure of dozing at noon while the sun slowly broils oiled flesh, then, revitalizing plunges into the invigorating surf. These elements all combine to provide harried, working souls with the most effective balm known to man – a day at the beach.

And yes, the fleeting impermanence of the enchantment makes each such outing all the more memorable, so evanescent the sensation of escape, so illusory the mood. Three short months of summer to capture it, experience it, savor it and then the harsh reality of winter returns to the northern climes once more.

Yet people are not easily satisfied, even with God's best work and so the enterprising citizens of these beach communities took it upon themselves to 'improve' upon the experience. After all, what good is a day in paradise without some taffy from the boardwalk and a few souvenirs to tote home?

Wildwood is the kind of place God would have created had he

known man better. Wildwood is dedicated to the philosophy that summer at the shore is one orgasmic, monster blowout of a party. The fun starts on Memorial Day when the shops along the boardwalk throw open their doors to kick off a new season, then picks up momentum throughout the gleeful, anticipatory days of June when the schools let out and the tribes gather. Roaring exuberantly on into the joyous Fourth of July festivities, the party gathers steam and then races at full throttle into the magical days of July and August when the sun shines high overhead and time ceases to have meaning. Finally, a crescendo is reached on Labor Day weekend with a concluding orgy of parties, picnics, parades and partings. This last round of merrymaking marks perhaps the most bittersweet holiday of the year, signaling as it does the end of the season, the closing of the boardwalk and beach towns. There is nothing left to do then except return to the tiresome routines at which mere mortals labor so unenthusiastically all winter long.

But no one can conceive of such foreboding thoughts as Easter paves the way to Memorial Day and the opening of the beach and boardwalk! The exhilarating days to come lie ahead uncounted, the approach of summer beckoning like a magic carpet ride promising new adventures, new excitement, new discoveries and growth. Vacationers pour into this seaside resort from Canada, New York, Pennsylvania and the entire eastern seaboard. It's a mere two hour bus ride away from Philadelphia, a virtual summer home for its suburbanites and the natives of New Jersey who flock to it unabashedly. Who wants to miss out on the good times? The entire town is jam-packed with people bent on enjoying an unparalleled summer long festival of food, fun, drink and dance. Where is the rival to Wildwood's wonderfully garish boardwalk with its crowds packed shoulder to shoulder, reveling in their escape from the suffocating heat of the concrete jungles, delighting in the refreshment offered by the cool ocean breezes, clutching prizes, streaming along the wooden planks blissfully lost in the carnival atmosphere? Neon slashes of red, green, yellow and blue light up the night, earsplitting shrieks pierce the air as thrill seekers risk life and limb riding diabolically conceived mechanical marvels on antiquated piers that defiantly jut out over the very ocean itself. Who can forget the fevered cries of the barkers touting their rides, their games, their arcades, their booths, their snack stands? And don't leave out the food! Pizza, hot dogs, salt-water taffy, ice cream, custard, pork rolls, hero sandwiches, submarines, cheese steaks, onion rings, sugary fried dough, sausage and peppers, fudge!

Come daybreak there are beautiful, unsullied beaches to recuperate on and shops and boutiques enough to satisfy those incapable of relaxing but all that is peripheral to the lifeblood of Wildwood. This hot vital fluid runs after dark in the nightclub and bar district stretching for block after block in the white-hot, incandescent heart of the city. Here there is a stretch of rip-roaring nightclubs of every conceivable stripe with the frenzied partying continuing well on into the wee hours of dawn. This is why people come to Wildwood - to get blasted out of their minds, waking up hours or days later with little remembrance of what or when or where or how, uncertain as to the establishments frequented and 'refreshments' consumed, the old friends lost and new ones gained. The town and its transients lose themselves each summer night in a high-voltage, 'there is no tomorrow' search for the sublime. Nothing is more uplifting, cheerful and exuberant than a beach town in summer!

***

They came to a causeway leading over the last stretch of marsh and open water between them and Wildwood. Ahead of them they could see the incandescent glow of the city silhouetted against the black backdrop of night and the Atlantic ocean. All around them cars streamed toward the resort. The highway abruptly began a steep ascent and Cheri and James found themselves atop a bridge overlooking the inlet that separated the barrier island from the mainland. Gazing down, the two of them could see marinas and docks and countless pleasure boats and fishing craft clustered around the harbor. Descending from their vantage point they immediately found themselves immersed in a massive traffic jam, part of the crowd caught up in the frenzy of summer's biggest ongoing party.

James and Cheri's progress slowed to a crawl as they joined an endless parade of cars inching their way through the downtown city streets, windows open, convertible tops down, T-tops stashed, everyone creeping steadily towards the pulsating beat of the nightclub district and the action. Down here the lights were so bright it could have been mid-afternoon instead of night. Music blared out into the streets from every open car window and barroom door - loud, raucous rock 'n' roll, jaunty rhythm and blues and hip-shaking dance music. Throngs of people milled about on the streets walking, talking, partying, laughing, stumbling, hollering, kissing and cursing.

As James and Cheri crept up to one intersection, the door to the 'Penalty Box,' a well-known drinking establishment, flew open. Three bouncers in white and black striped referee shirts came flying out struggling with a crazed long-hair who - despite the odds and his scrawny physique - gave as much as he got, flailing away wildly at his oppressors. The whole bunch of them spilled out of the club's front door like Hollywood cowboys ejected from a local saloon to continue the action out in the gutter. Spectators gathered and cheered wildly, urging on the underdog as traffic came to a complete halt and everyone watched the entertainment. The contestants duked it out for another minute or two, the bouncers gradually wearing the skinny guy's resistance down, ultimately pinning the feisty little warrior to the pavement and holding him there until he submitted, exhausted, but unbowed, still cursing up a blue steak. The bouncers left him in the care of some friends, dusted themselves off, exchanged a few high fives and went back into the bar looking for another 'bad' hombre to subdue.

On the street the crowd calmed down again, satisfied that they'd gotten their money's worth, the spectators turning back to the business of getting high, partying and checking out each bar and club and band and all the girls and all the guys and what better way to spend a Saturday night in the summer?

It was time for James to turn off the main drag and begin the daunting search for a parking space. With remarkable luck they immediately found someone already packing it up for the evening. Grabbing that spot, they locked up the car and eagerly stepped out into the festival night.

The boardwalk was only three or four blocks away, the crashing and banging of the rides, the screams of the riders, the smell of popcorn and cotton candy putting an excited, anticipatory bounce in James' and Cheri's footsteps as they joined the pilgrimage of pedestrians making their way toward the ocean.

Emerging from a side street, they climbed a wooden ramp and found themselves entering a vast mob shuffling up and down the oceanfront promenade. It was impossible to see more than five or ten feet in any jostling, shoving, jam-packed direction. A riotous blur of lights, loud noises, animated faces, bright colors and powerful odors bombarded their senses.

"Oh, this looks like so much fun!" Cheri enthused. "I only wish we brought Melly with us."

"Don't worry, I'm sure she's sleeping peacefully. Her day at the beach tired her out. She went down without any resistance," James noted.

"I hope she doesn't wake up and cause any problems for your parents," Cheri worried.

"Relax, my Mom and Dad raised four kids. I think they can handle a two-year-old."

"I guess you're right."

Cheri and James joined the press and walked the boardwalk, looking out over the placid ocean. The two of them luxuriated in the hot, sticky night air, enjoying the occasional light breeze that swept in off the waves, watching the moon beam cheerfully over the gentle swells. Cheri was beautiful and vivacious, wide-eyed and excited, taking everything in. She scrutinized the passersby as intently as an FBI agent searching for a fugitive, surveyed the game booths like a gambler intent on betting his life savings and examined the menus posted outside of each restaurant like a condemned prisoner deciding upon a last meal. After vigorously debating the merits of various eateries with James, she finally settled on a funnel cake, daintily breaking apart the dough with her fingers, the white, powdered sugar getting all over her hands and face, her eyes sparkling mischievously as she dug in, made a mess and didn't care. There was no need for James to ask her if she was having a good time because it was all there on her face for him to see.

Eventually, however, the time came when the boardwalk began shutting down for the evening. They came out of the haunted house where Cheri had screamed and squealed with the best of them and realized their special night was almost over. The bumper cars were stacked away in darkened corners of their rinks and the lights on the carousel were turned off. The previously fanatical arcade hawkers paid them no mind, focused instead on counting up their take and calling it a night.

Without any particular intent, Cheri and James discovered one last ride still open. It was a roller coaster type affair affectionately named 'The Wild Mouse.' This contraption was built on the end of a pier, its tracks and railings extending far out over the very ocean itself by way of an additional thrill. Its imposing, intricate steel support structure loomed far overhead in the night and as they approached, the toboggan-like cars came blasting and clattering down from above. The shrill, hysterical screams of passengers pierced the air as the ride rocketed along the rails at a blistering, neck-snapping rate. James turned and looked at Cheri. She knew what he was thinking.

"Looks like fun..." he appealed, hope undying, trying desperately to get her to agree to go on this one last ride. Cheri was deathly afraid of heights and she'd rejected all his previous attempts to get her on one of these devilish machines. Now though, he looked so forlorn that she could feel her resistance crumbling. She studied the ride carefully - long enough for him to realize that she was seriously considering it.

"Oh, come on!" he cajoled. "What do you think can happen? They're all safe - if they weren't they'd close this place down in a second."

He had a point there, didn't he?

"Can't you go ahead and ride by yourself?" she equivocated. "I don't mind waiting..."

"It's no fun by yourself," he answered, turning away from her glumly, dejection written all over his face.

The wind, stronger out here over the ocean, blew through his hair and he looked, for an instant, like every suffering 10-year-old who'd been told 'no' by his parents one time too many at the amusement park. Her heart went out to him as he turned away in defeat, starting down the pier with the full expectation that she was following behind him.

Cheri, though, remained rooted in place, staring guiltily at the mechanical monstrosity. She cast a skittish glance at the web of tangled iron girders high overhead and had to turn away as her stomach churned unhappily. She couldn't go up there!

Directly in front of her the car they'd observed negotiating the track eased to a halt in the loading ramp. Four die-hard stragglers disembarked. Two of them were teenage girls. 'Must be the screamers,' Cheri decided, noting also that they didn't appear to be suffering from any obvious injuries. The attendant scanned the pier for any last takers before shutting down the ride for the evening.

Almost without realizing what she was doing, hearing her disembodied voice float out into the night air as if it belonged to someone else, Cheri called out after James, "Wait!"

He turned around and looked at her questioningly.

"I'll ride it with you," she stated.

The moment the words were out of her mouth her stomach began a violent series of sickening flip-flops.

"You'll go up there with me?" James queried, uncertain he heard her incorrectly.

"I don't like the idea...but if you want me too, I will."

"You're sure?" he pressed, burdened by guilt now that his tactics had borne fruit, weighing the pros and cons of Cheri's unexpected change of heart. "You don't have to ride it if you're going to get sick or anything," he stalled. "I don't really want to go on it that bad."

"You goddamn liar. Let's do it now before I change my mind."

Indecision paralyzed him as he gazed longingly at the 'Wild Mouse.'

"Oh, c'mon, let's ride it," she cajoled, walking up to him and surprising him with a tender kiss planted flush on his lips.

"All right, let's go!" he agreed enthusiastically once she let him catch his breath.

Delighted with his good fortune, James rushed over to the ticket booth and purchased their tickets. With all the enthusiasm of Marie Antoinette sidling up to the guillotine, Cheri made her way down the loading ramp to the beckoning attendant. They were the only riders. The attendant took their tickets and led them to ('Oh no,' Cheri gasped,' not the front!') the front seat.

"Oh, Mother of God, what am I doing?" she wailed, sliding nonetheless into the car. There was nothing between her and certain death except a waist-high, thin steel bulkhead - she could see right over it! James wrapped his arm tightly around her as the bored attendant banged the restraining bar in place.

"If these rides are so safe, why do they need all this padding?" Cheri questioned anxiously, observing the thick cushioning surrounding her.

"It's for comfort...this way if you feel like taking a short nap during the ride you have something soft to lean on," James teased.

"Oh, sure!"

Cheri could feel herself shaking all over, a phenomenon she attributed partly to the rapidly cooling night air and partly to her rapidly escalating horror. It was too late to get out! She could taste the fear in her mouth.

"Oh, my God," was all she could manage, "oh, my –"

Her words were cut off as the car lurched forward with a loud bang and clatter. They were on their way! The track went dead ahead for a short distance and then straight up toward the stars. Cheri's eyes were drawn hypnotically to the top of the incline.

"We're going all the way up THERE?" she yelped, a note of hysteria creeping into her voice. Her hands were sweating profusely as she clung to the safety bar in desperation. The whine of a motor straining to haul their car to the top of the incline was nowhere near as loud as the sound of her own blood pounding in her ears. How high were they going? Her legs and knees felt like jelly. They were nearing the top and she snuck a quick glance around.

The view was breathtaking. The entire night was laid out at her feet in a riot of light and color. From this dizzying perch she could see all of the boardwalk and the town behind it as well. The ocean stretched away to the dark horizon in front of them. She was looking DOWN at Ferris wheels, roller coasters and a host of other contraptions. People on the pier were merely small dots. Cheri almost forgot her fear of heights as she gazed in amazement at the stupendous scene – it took an involuntary wave of dizziness and vertigo to remind her of her predicament. Swiftly she turned her attention to what lay immediately in front of them and unexpectedly found herself staring straight up into the heavens. They were at the summit!

Their car teetered momentarily on the edge of the precipice, rocked forward and began a free fall. No fear Cheri had ever known prepared her for the horror she now experienced plummeting from the heavens like a kamikaze dive-bomber on a suicide run. Her neck was snapped back involuntarily and a horrendous banging and shaking battered her as the forces of gravity took their revenge and pinned her helplessly against James. She could hear him whooping with joy as he clutched her firmly. Her stomach had been left at the top of the summit and she felt a gaping, empty hole in her gut where it belonged. She braced herself for the impact of the inevitable crash but it never came - instead, they bottomed out effortlessly and shot forward toward the end of the pier where a hairpin turn was the only remaining barrier between them and a plunge into the ocean itself!

Relentlessly they picked up speed, rocketing toward the abyss, hitting the curve at full speed...would the rails hold? All Cheri could see was water - they'd broken free of the ride! But no, the car whipped sideways, her head snapped left, and a back-breaking reversal in direction sent them hurtling toward the boardwalk. In rapid succession they careened through three, four - five! - viciously banked curves, the track crazily rising and falling beneath them the whole while as Cheri's insides fought to maintain their proper place in her body. She closed her eyes but almost passed out as she experienced the black, swimming dizziness her brain was engulfed in. Reopening her eyes she found herself speeding toward a twisting, spiraling turn. Halfway through it the track dropped out from beneath them again, leaving her stomach flying solo somewhere high overhead.

The loud clattering of the cars had deafened her to the point that she couldn't hear herself screaming or James hollering. All she could do was hang on for dear life, absorb the pounding, and hope it would be over soon. Around and around they whirled in a nightmarish tumble, the din overwhelming, the lights blinding, the banging intolerable, the sickening lurches and drops unending. James held her tightly, but not so tightly that he himself couldn't hang onto the safety bar. Cheri found herself wondering how they could possibly make machinery durable enough to withstand this incessant pounding and abuse. It had to break!

Then, just like that, it was over. They ricocheted around a last turn and were suddenly smashed forward against the front of the car by the unexpected application of the ride's hydraulic brakes. Regaining their composure, they found themselves cruising up to the disembarkation platform as if nothing out of the ordinary had happened. The tired attendant unlocked their safety bar, pulled it out of the way and they were free.

Cheri staggered to her feet and clambered over James' knees to get on solid ground as quickly as possible, James following close behind her.

"Hey, look!" he yelled, distracting her from the sudden urge to punch him.

"What?" she snapped.

"The Hell Hole is still open. It spins you around in this giant barrel until everybody is stuck against the wall by centrifugal force and then they drop the floor away and - ooofff!"

She nailed him with a sharp elbow to the ribs, catching him by surprise. He rubbed his rib cage and stepped out of range.

"Does that mean you don't want to ride it?"

"You won't ever get me on one of these stupid rides again as long as I live, you conniving son of a bitch!" she vented.

"Oh, come on," he teased, "are you telling me you didn't have one of the best rides of your life on that thing? It was great!"

"If you ever want another 'great' ride with me, I'll give it to you in the bedroom, ok? But I am not getting on another one of these death traps again - EVER!"

"You big baby!" he called after her as Cheri turned and walked away from him, heading down the pier toward the boardwalk.

"What's the matter, can't take a little name-calling?" he hollered, scurrying after her, hurrying to catch up.

"No, it's not that," she replied sweetly over her shoulder. "It's just that, judging by your last remark, I can see you don't have any interest in doing any 'riding' when we get back to your parents' house tonight."

"Wait, that's not what I meant! You wouldn't stoop that low to make a point, would you?"

Cheri crouched down as low to the ground as she could get without falling over and then burst out laughing.

"Oh, wouldn't I?"

James grabbed her with both hands and turned her face toward his. They stared into each others' eyes as the cool ocean breeze blew through her hair and sent discarded wrappers and paper fluttering across the nearly deserted pier.

"You're a beautiful woman," he whispered to her in his most conciliatory manner, showering kisses on her forehead, cheeks and unyielding lips. Arms folded adamantly, she resisted his advances.

"Bullshit!" she retorted, breaking away. "You're only worried that you're not going to get laid. And you're not."

The oldest tactic in the book, it still never failed to have the desired effect. The rueful expression on his face showed that she had him where she wanted him. But Cheri was in a good mood too, thoroughly enjoying herself even while maintaining this pretense of anger toward him for tricking her into riding the Wild Mouse.

He stared at her uncertainly.

"Come here," she told him.

He stepped over to where she stood waiting for him next to the railing. Kissing him lovingly she let her hand slide down to the front of his jeans and softly applied pressure. With her free hand she reached up behind his neck and pulled him closer. Kissing him eagerly, she pushed her tongue past his lips before he was aware of what she was doing. She held him another twenty or thirty seconds before breaking off the kiss.

"How's that for forgiveness?" she asked.

"I love you," he told her for the first time.

"I love you too," she replied without hesitation.

"I guess that means we're making some progress," he offered.

"I guess it does," Cheri seconded.

"Thanks for coming here this weekend...it means a lot to me."

"I'm having a great time. I'm glad you asked me to come."

"Just about now, I'd rather make you 'come'," he joked.

"Well then, let's get back to your parents' house and you can, if nobody is up."

No one was up.

Not so Fast

Cheri was sunbathing on the concrete apron in front of her apartment, wearing her skimpiest cut-offs and a T-shirt, as James pulled up the driveway. It seemed as if his day at work had lasted longer than usual, an effect he attributed to residual fatigue from the travel filled weekend.

Concealing his self-satisfied smile, James got out of the car and casually strolled over to where Cheri lay absorbing the warm sun. Her book had been cast aside and she squinted up at him as he approached.

"Hi," she smiled, "how're you feeling today?"

"Good. A little tired, maybe, and you?"

"Great - and oh, by the way, thanks very much for the flowers you left on my doorstep this morning. They made for a very nice start to the day. But how on earth did you find time to pick them? We got in so late last night."

James had picked the flowers 'late' - around midnight, in fact. It was easier than it sounded, though, because the flowers were sprigs of apple blossoms he'd spotted in a tree along the driveway. No need to downplay his romantic efforts to Cheri, however.

"You're welcome. But hey, I know it was a big day for you today, how'd it go?" he inquired with undisguised interest, flopping down on the warm concrete beside her.

"It's done," she answered quietly, "it's over - I'm officially, legally divorced...it's hard for me to believe."

She looked at James almost as if seeing him for the first time, her thoughts wandering away into some region inaccessible to him.

He stared back, commenting finally, "It's got to be tough going into a courtroom and ending your marriage in front of all those lawyers and strangers. How'd Billy take it?"

She smiled faintly. "Oh, he tried his tricks up to the last minute. He was late, of course, and the judge ended up calling a recess at noon because of it. So Billy asked if he could buy me lunch - can you believe it? He's going to buy me lunch after not paying a dime of child support the whole six months we've been separated?"

"Did you go?"

"Yeah, I don't know why - it was stupid, I know. Anyway, we go to lunch and he gives me the whole, 'are you sure you know what you're doing?' routine, asking if I've thought about the effect it's going to have on Melanie. So I say, 'No, Billy, I only spent eight hundred dollars on a lawyer and took the afternoon off work to come down here because I DIDN'T know what I was doing, you moron! Why the hell didn't you think about Melly when you were running around partying every night and not holding down a job?'"

"You said all of that to him?"

"No, of course I didn't. I told him I knew what I was doing and that the marriage was over. So we return to the courtroom and the shit starts crying in front of the judge and everyone is looking at me like I'm some kind of bitch - which I am, I admit without apology. I then stand before the judge and tell him all the things Billy did to make me want a divorce. Billy had a list of things he was accusing me of too. He decided to be a total loon and sue me for divorce at the same time, for what reason I still have no idea. And then it was over, except..."

Cheri stopped and laughed ruefully. "You won't believe this, you really won't."

"Try me."

"The son of a gun has the balls to ask me for a ride to work. So, like an idiot, I say, 'ok.' On the way he asks me to stop by his house so he can change into his work clothes. We get there, he invites me in, disappears into his bedroom and then comes out in his underwear looking ridiculous and tries to put a move on me. I couldn't believe it."

James was silent as Cheri paused. She realized immediately that he was jealous. She experienced a moment's contempt for men in general - how could they be so vulnerable and obvious? She let him think about it for another moment and then, realizing she had something else to tell him which wasn't going to make him any happier, she let him off the hook.

"Oh, come on, don't be silly, nothing happened. I let him kiss me, just to see what it would feel like after getting divorced and hey, it didn't do anything for me. I knew then that we were finished. I told him to put his clothes on and I left."

"I didn't say I thought anything happened," James responded stiffly.

"Good, because nothing happened," Cheri emphasized, suddenly tired of the whole subject and of Billy and James and Kurt and everything that had to do with men and women and love and hate. But she had one more task to complete before her work with James was through for the evening. She approached it with a mixture of dread and resignation.

"Oh," she began as an aside, "I ran into Kurt at the courtroom - a friend of his works there..."

She watched James tense up instantly but he waited for her to continue without interrupting. Cheri felt as if she were already screwing up the delivery of her message. It sounded like she was apologizing for something when, in fact, she wasn't. Was she? She tried to regroup and appear more nonchalant.

"He's taking me to the movies tonight. I didn't tell him 'no' because he reminded me I'd promised him I'd go see this movie with him before. I..."

Stuck in mid-sentence she watched James' face turn cold and emotionless. She had to hand it to him - no vulnerability there! She felt guilty as hell for the second time today and this made her really furious. What did all these selfish bastards want from her? They didn't own her!

"See, Kurt's a big horror movie fan," she awkwardly explained, "and we made a deal that when 'The Shining' came out we'd go together..."

As soon as the words were out of her mouth she knew she'd blown it big time. Watching the expression on James' face crystallize into pure anger and hostility, Cheri recalled that only a week ago she'd promised James she'd take him to go see 'The Shining' with her. They'd been kidding about how he didn't like scary movies and now she knew he was remembering that conversation and hating her guts for it.

Looking at James' stony countenance Cheri wondered, fleetingly, if perhaps she'd made a serious tactical error. 'What if he goes inside and calls up his little twat, Angela, and I end up blowing this whole thing because of Kurt, who I don't even care about anymore and who just happened to catch me at a time when I didn't feel like arguing?' she second-guessed herself.

It was too late now, though, to do anything about it. The lines were drawn and she fell silent, feeling utterly miserable. She'd gotten divorced today. She needed time to think and she knew already that the night was going to be a disaster too because now she'd spend the whole time feeling guilty about upsetting James.

'What more does he want?' she marveled. 'Kurt's actually the one I'm cheating on if we want to get technical about this. Who in the hell does James think he is, getting mad at me after I spent the entire weekend with him?'

Her thoughts were interrupted, however, as James soundlessly rose to his feet and without any further ado matter-of-factly stated, "Yeah, well, I guess I better get supper going."

Not waiting for a reply, he turned and walked into his apartment.

'You son of a bitch,' Cheri thought to herself. "You selfish, cold-hearted son of a bitch!"

But it didn't diminish her opinion of him at all - quite the contrary.

***

Once inside his apartment, James silently and methodically cursed himself, 'You goddamn flying asshole! Why, why, WHY do you insist on getting involved with these flighty women that can't make up their minds about who they want to be with? Why not find a nice, level-headed, sensible girl who will reciprocate your affection and attention? Why go for the ones that drive you insane with jealousy?'

That spasm of anger vented, James drifted into a state of genuine confusion.

'What does it mean? I know Cheri likes me - she spent the whole weekend with me at my parents' house, didn't she? But then she turns around and does this - what a heartless bitch! She's always telling me, 'Oh, me and Kurt are going straight downhill, it's all coming to an end, I can't stand him anymore,' but that doesn't stop her from risking everything with me to see him, does it? 'I have to go see the movie with Kurt because I PROMISED him months ago!' Ha! What kind of sucker does she take me for?'

James calmed himself somewhat by methodically preparing his supper - chopping carrots, green peppers, onions and red cabbage for a salad, breaking apart a head of lettuce, occasionally shaking his head in disbelief as he reflected on his gullibility and capacity for self-delusion. There he'd been, all weekend long reveling in a fool's paradise, merely setting himself up for this crushing turn of events.

They'd had so much fun over the weekend. Why couldn't he even have a few days to enjoy the afterglow?

'Ok, fine, I don't really care all that much, do I? Maybe I'll just give Angela a call tonight, or that new girl at work, Susan. And if Cheri wants to run around with some broken-down, has-been son of a bitch, let her.'

He turned his stereo on and poured himself a glass of lambrusco.

"Hell, yeah, that's what I'll do - I'll never speak to Cheri again. I'll act like we don't even know each other, that'll show her!'

He mulled over his statements and then laughed out loud.

'Listen to the insulted little juvenile mind at work here,' he berated himself. 'The poor girl gets divorced today, risked ruining another relationship to spend the weekend with a man she barely knows, has three guys tugging at her simultaneously and here I am banishing her to hell permanently for what? For simply taking her time in deciding what she wants to do? Is she my prisoner, that I can insist she not date anyone else when we've barely known each other a month? Don't I have any confidence that the more she sees of me, the less she'll want to see any other guys?'

Unconvinced, he returned to preparing his dinner. Peeking out his window and seeing that Cheri had retreated inside her apartment, James set up his table and two chairs on the concrete pad in front of his apartment, determined to see his rival face to face when he arrived.

***

A few minutes later, Cheri reappeared. Striding over to James' table, she plopped down on his extra chair without waiting for an invitation. She knew it was unfair coming out here to try and make him feel better when she'd already ruined his evening. This could almost be construed as rubbing salt in the wound. She also knew that Kurt was not going to be pleased when he pulled up and found her cozily chatting with 'the neighbor.'

But sitting inside her apartment, watching James eat his dinner alone had gotten to her. She had to talk to him.

"Hi...how was your meal?" she innocently inquired.

"Fine, just great," he answered evenly without looking up from the story he was reading.

"How's the book?"

"Not bad."

"You're a real ball of fire tonight, aren't you?" she pressed, refusing to be dismissed.

James looked up. Was she taunting him now? If she was out here to mess with his mind, he was willing to get nasty.

"How do you mean?" he countered belligerently.

"Well, you don't seem very interested in talking or anything. Is something bothering you?"

He stared at her in disbelief - why was she asking him such a dumb question? Why not drop the whole subject and leave him in peace?

"Something bothering me? What are you talking about? Why would -"

"Oh, bullshit!" Cheri interrupted. "Look, I'm sorry about this thing with Kurt coming up, ok? I don't know why I agreed to go out to the movies with him tonight, I really don't. It's going to be a miserable evening but when he asked me out, I didn't have the energy to say 'no' and argue with him about it."

She sounded sincere. James suddenly felt a wave of guilt flowing through him. This poor girl had been divorced today and here he was, the guy supposedly in love with her, doing his best to make her feel lousy.

"Hey, ok, look, I'll try and understand," he replied. "I'll take your word for it - if you say nothing is going to happen except you're going to see a movie with a guy you don't care about anymore, then that's good enough for me."

Cheri raised the stakes.

"You don't have to take my word for it. If you tell me not to see Kurt tonight, I won't go."

She looked at him across the table, her eyes meeting his. She was so beautiful! Her vulnerability disarmed him completely. She looked terribly sad and unhappy.

"I won't ask that," James finally responded. "If this gets to the point where I can't take it anymore then I'll have to make a decision, right? Simple as that. I don't know what else you and I can possibly say on this subject."

They both sat there quietly reflecting on his response. The longer they sat, the harder it was to break the mood and start up a dialogue again. The evening had grown quiet and cooler. The sun was going down behind the hills to the west, its last rays falling flat, the peculiar lighting capturing and bathing everything in a pale, yellowish glow, like an old-time photograph. The moment seemed timeless and eternal as they sat there watching the deepening shadows. James listened to the waterfall at the end of the road and observed the deep, rich green of the lawn on the hillside below them, speckled with yellow dandelions. Overhead he spotted a bat darting and flitting about as it hunted above the rooftops and trees for its evening repast.

Cheri finally broke the awkward silence.

"James, Kurt and I are through. We have been for some time. I thought he'd just go away or something, I guess, yet to my surprise, he hasn't. I've tried to tell him it's over at work but he always interrupts me. However, I did promise that I'd go to this movie with him and he remembered. James, I love you. I know that."

Expressionless, James absorbed her comments. Was she trying to placate him to assuage her guilt? A sharp stab of twisting pain knifed through his abdominal muscles. She'd said she loved him but...

"Look," James started, "I - "

They both froze, hearing the crunch of gravel as a car began the long, bumpy trip up their treacherous driveway. Feelings of anger, hopelessness and despair welled up in James as the sobering, eye-widening truth of what was about to happen next took shape in his mind. A blue Volvo suddenly appeared before them and turned sharply into their courtyard, cruising to a halt in one of the two parking spaces under the big pine tree in front of Cheri's place.

"James, can we meet at your workshop for lunch tomorrow at noon? Please?" Cheri asked.

James looked at her, stunned.

"Sure," he heard himself say.

The door of the Volvo opened and Kurt stepped out. He looked first, curiously, at James, sitting outside at his dinner table. An unmistakably hostile expression crossed Kurt's face when he realized Cheri was sitting there too. Without flinching, James stared murderously at Kurt.

Kurt turned to look at Cheri who met his eyes for only the briefest of moments.

"I'm about ready," she stated, getting up from the table.

James watched as she walked down the sidewalk and disappeared into her apartment with the enemy.

***

James' bedroom was as quiet and dark as a tomb. Squinting in the direction of the luminescent clock he could barely read the time - 12:35 a.m. A car had just pulled up the driveway and stopped in front of the apartments. A sudden surge of confusion, anxiety, hope and despair swirled through his mind as he waited, stomach knotted miserably, trying to ascertain whether it was Cheri returning home. A car door opened - he heard a man's voice...

'Oh, Jesus Christ, no,' he prayed silently, 'Please don't let this happen! I won't ever talk to her again if she takes that bastard inside and sleeps with him. I swear to Christ that'll be the end of it!'

Now he could make out a woman's voice and the sound of footsteps - but the car engine was still running...was there hope? Was Kurt going to leave with nothing more than a perfunctory goodnight kiss?

James listened closely, the open bedroom window only a foot or two away from where he lay despondent on the second hand mattress he'd recently obtained at a yard sale. Ears straining, he tried to pick up some kind of a clue as to what was going on but he couldn't quite make out what they were saying.

'Damn it! What's happening out there?' he groaned, lifting himself to his elbows in the hope of hearing more.

He recognized the man's voice...and flopped down on the mattress with a sigh. He knew what was going on. The guy with the apartment between James and Cheri worked second shift. He'd come home to change clothes, leaving his girlfriend out in the car. Now they were leaving. James listened as the driver's door slammed shut, the car slipped into gear and the vehicle crunched down the long driveway. Then it slipped beyond hearing into the night.

It was only James and the dark and the clock and the silence again.

'I can't take this,' he muttered. 'I can't take this kind of relationship.'

He could feel his pulse racing, his chest tightening, his breathing coming faster than normal. And why? Because some flighty girl he'd been unfortunate enough to fall in love with had decided to see some other guy?

James returned his head to his pillow, knowing full well that it was no use - sleep was absolutely out of the question. But what else could he do but try? He'd already read Joan Didion's 'Play it as it Lays' in one sitting, a grim little tale about terminal depression, madness and suicide. The ending of the story was so gloomy he'd read the first fifty pages of Tolstoy's 'The Cossacks' hoping for a change of pace, successfully losing himself in nineteenth century Russia for a little while. It'd still been early when he'd laid that book down, 9:30 or 10:00 P.M. at the latest, but he'd read all he could stand for one night. He'd hoped he could simply nod off and be out of his misery until morning - although what relief morning might bring, he couldn't imagine.

After Cheri left with Kurt, James became utterly morose - awash in self-pity and sorrow. He went out for what was intended to be a long walk but soon found he was in no mood for burbling brooks and the smell of apple blossoms on a warm summer breeze so he quickly aborted that enterprise. Back at the homestead, the T.V. reception resembled a cloud of electric snow, so there wasn't much distraction available from that quarter either. The thought of playing his guitar or listening to records left him cold. He was beyond relief. All he could think about was Cheri out there with Kurt. Was she laughing at the thought of James sitting home alone? Was this some sort of power trip designed to maximize her leverage on him? Or was she so heartless that none of James' misery mattered to her at all?

Taking things to a logical conclusion, didn't this mean everything between James and Cheri was over? How could they go on? James couldn't stand another night like this. Why had he gotten so emotionally involved with Cheri this fast? Why hadn't he kept dating Angela or seen some other girls?

That part was simple. It was because he knew Cheri was 'the one.' There was no doubt in his mind. And that thought only increased his dejection. He wanted Cheri fiercely, jealously, unreasonably! Why? Because he loved being with her, laughing with her, talking to her, watching her, touching her, thinking about her. Because he felt like a merciful and loving God had arranged a meeting between them, expecting them to take advantage of a once in a lifetime opportunity to find true love a second time.

He realized that this was perhaps an antiquated notion - one woman and one man destined only for each other. After all, how could that be? But James believed in that notion. And as he lay there he recalled the exact moment he was convinced God had chosen to intervene on his and Cheri's behalf.

A few months earlier, James had looked at an apartment downtown. It was in a great location near Vassar College, the rent was cheap and he had a good buddy who lived in the complex. The landlady said it was his for the taking. Returning later with Angela to show her the place too, James told the landlady he'd go to his bank in the morning to get the deposit and first month's rent.

When James arrived the next day with the money, however, the landlady told him she'd rented out the unit to someone else. In retrospect, James realized bringing Angela with him the night before was a mistake. The landlady had pointedly warned James and Angela that overnight 'guests' were not allowed.

Yet the very next day at work, Larry told James about the place for rent on Oswego Road. It was the apartment complex where Cheri lived. If the first landlady had kept her word and rented James the room near Vassar College, he never would have met Cheri.

But the landlady hadn't kept her word and James once thought he'd known why. But now he wondered if perhaps he'd been hopelessly superstitious to imagine for even half a second that God had intervened on his and Cheri's behalf.

James lay there totally defeated, staring at the ceiling of his bare room, unable to sleep, unwilling to think, yet incapable of shutting her out of his mind.

'Oh, Lord,' he whispered, 'why doesn't she come home? Enough is enough! Please, just let her come home...'

Another sharp pain sliced through his abdominal muscles. How was he going to live this close to her, seeing her lovely, long-limbed body, her laughing face, her dark brown hair, knowing she was no longer his? How could he endure watching the door close behind her as she disappeared into her apartment with another guy when James knew what joy it was to follow her up that steep flight of stairs to the dark bedroom at the end of the corridor where she slept naked beneath the covers every night?

He sat bolt upright and raged at the shadows, 'That's it, we're through! What kind of heartless bitch would let me suffer like this if she loved me?'

His mind made up, he slumped down into his covers again. He'd been as good to her as he knew how to be. They'd had fun, lots of it and they'd shared intimate, tender moments. If she wanted to play games with him, so be it. She could play her games with someone else.

'There - that ought to do it!' he declared to himself triumphantly.

But it didn't.

***

1:45 a.m. and she wasn't home. James' eyes had long since adjusted to the dark and his virtually empty room lay around him like a mute testimonial to his equally empty life.

'Oh God, please let me sleep! Close these eyes and make this nightmare end.'

He lay on his pillow trying to regroup. Where was she? She'd never been out this late since he'd known her. Inexplicably he felt tears welling up in his eyes.

'What is wrong with me?' he groaned. 'This is not normal. Two months of romance shouldn't cause this.'

Then he heard it - footsteps. Footsteps coming up the driveway at this hour? Yes! They were getting closer and closer. Who could it be? He fought back an overpowering urge to peek out his bedroom window - what if it was Cheri and she saw him? Then she'd know how much this was getting to him. He couldn't let that happen. But why would she be out walking at this hour?

Then it occurred to him - maybe Cheri and Kurt had parked near the end of the driveway so James wouldn't spot their car. Maybe they'd walked up, hoping to be discreet. It sounded as if the footsteps had gone over near her apartment too, hadn't it?

'Those sneaky bastards!' James seethed. 'I'm not about to play this ridiculous game any longer - I've about had it with uncertainty and indecision.'

He sat up and peered furtively out his window into the darkness. There was nothing to be seen.

Hesitating another moment, he decided, 'Why not take a stroll to the end of the driveway? And if I find that blue Volvo parked there, I'm through with that bitch, finito!'

He rolled out of bed, the soles of his feet slapping on the cold tile floor. Scrabbling around with his hands he found his clothes and pulled them on haphazardly. It wasn't until he cautiously opened the latch of his screen door and stepped out into the cool night air that he reflected on what an incredibly strange thing he was doing. Here he was at nearly two o'clock in the morning searching for a blue Volvo when he couldn't see five feet in front of his face. The moon had disappeared, clouds had moved in and there was a heavy mist blanketing the fields around the apartments. He stared long and hard at the windows of Cheri's place, both upstairs and downstairs, but if she and Kurt were inside, they'd disguised that fact quite well.

'Boy, they're awfully sly, aren't they?' James considered. 'Probably hopped straight into bed. To think that someone would go to these extremes - sneaking around in the middle of the night to deceive me. What kind of fool does she think I am?'

There was no doubt in James' mind that he was going to find the Volvo as he turned and set off down the driveway, moving cautiously since he couldn't see very well and he knew the path was full of rocks and gullies.

'I'm not going to break an ankle over her - no way!'

He was getting near the end of the driveway. The trees pressed in closer here, occasionally scratching his face and outstretched arms as he groped his way toward the street. Then he saw it - the Volvo! Parked right where the driveway intersected Oswego Road. Just as he suspected. He actually experienced an unanticipated spell of exhilaration and relief upon making the discovery.

'Well, that about wraps it up, I'd say. It certainly shows what kind of two-timing bitch I'm dealing with, doesn't it?' he mused, making his way closer for an absolute confirmation. Then, with no slight amount of shock, James realized that this car wasn't a Volvo at all.

'What? It has to be...'

He peered closer - light from a nearby porch was reflecting off the chrome, illuminating the hood ornament. It was an Audi, not a Volvo. He felt another jolt of exhilaration and near joy. She wasn't a lying, sneaking bitch after all. This wasn't Kurt's car!

James also realized with a start that if anyone saw him creeping around looking into cars in the middle of the night, they'd assume he was breaking into them. He stepped away from the Audi as quickly as if he'd placed his hand on a hot oven.

'Maybe I should check along Oswego Road, that way there'll be NO doubt in my mind,' James ruminated.

Another disturbing thought cropped up. How could Cheri explain to Kurt why they had to park this far away from the apartment? James let out a deep sigh and shook his head silently as he realized how absurd it was for him to be here by the duck pond at this hour of the morning searching for a car he was not going to find. Dejectedly he turned and trudged up the long driveway to his apartment, stopping momentarily to stare wistfully at her place again - no lights, no signs of life.

Then he was struck by another idea. What if, when James had dozed at around ten o'clock, Kurt had dropped Cheri off and James had missed them? After all, he'd probably slept an hour or so.

'That's it!' James exulted wildly. That would explain

everything. Cheri had likely gotten home at ten-thirty or so. Maybe she and Kurt had fought because Cheri had told him about James and maybe Kurt got pissed off and left. Of course! Cheri had probably not come over to tell James because she didn't want him to know she'd lost a strategic chip on the game board. She'd unveil the fact that she'd dumped Kurt to score some point on James at a later time. Let her. She could score a thousand points if she was done with Kurt.

'How dumb can I be?' James wondered. 'She's upstairs in her apartment tucked in beneath her blankets.'

With a considerably jauntier step, James yanked open the front door to his own apartment and went inside, shedding clothes left and right, hopping into bed, pulling up his covers and basking in a warm blur of happiness, contentment and fatigue.

'What a relief! Now I can finally get some well deserved sleep.'

As as started to doze, he heard a sound that pulled him back oh, so reluctantly, toward consciousness.

No doubt about it - a car was making its way up the driveway.

'Christ,' James thought, 'that bum next door home already? If he brings his girlfriend in and they turn on the stereo or television I'll never fall asleep.'

Another vague dread began to gnaw at his mind but reflexively James suppressed it.

The sound of the engine was loud and right outside his window. Then, abruptly, it shut off. He listened intently as he heard two car doors open and close. A knot of fear and anxiety clenched his gut.

'That goddamn guy better not plan on partying all night long or I'm going to kick his ass,' James tried on for size.

A woman laughed and a man said something in response. James felt his blood freeze and turn to ice...it was Cheri. His mind reeled in shocked disbelief, 'No, this can't be. Cheri's already asleep inside!'

The pain in his stomach and chest was so excruciating that he propped himself up on his elbows to try and assuage it.

Footsteps - it seemed like the thousandth time he'd listened to footsteps tonight! - crunched across the gravel and made their way to the concrete walkway in front of the apartments. Keys clinked and James remembered how odd looking Cheri's house key was - big and square. James heard the sound of a door being yanked open, slammed shut and then locked from within.

It was already bright and sunny when James went out his door the next morning to go to work. Ah yes, it was a beautiful day! The birds were singing, the dew was wet on the grass and the sky was as blue as the Volvo parked outside Cheri's front door.

***

The knot in James' stomach tightened each time he looked up at the clock. What difference did it make if Cheri showed up at lunchtime or not? The situation couldn't be clearer. She was a two-timing, cheating bitch and he was through with her.

Yet, despite his intent, with increasing frequency he found himself sneaking sidelong glances at the timepiece on the wall as the long morning at work wore on.

Why had he agreed to this farcical meeting? Why not concentrate on stilling the dull, throbbing pain that spilled out of the gaping hole where his heart used to be? Revisiting the past wasn't the answer. Looking to the future was the only way to accomplish the necessary repairs. He needed to put this unfortunate interlude behind him.

So what time was it now, anyhow? 11:10 a.m. Less than an hour to go...

At high noon, blood pounding in his veins, he took a deep breath and walked outside for the showdown. Stoically seating himself on the hood of his car, he wrapped his arms around his knees and watched the road. What choice did he have but to play out the final act of his and Cheri's sorry little affair? Why not have the satisfaction of hearing her try to lie her way around the incontrovertible evidence? At least this way he would have the satisfaction of seeing the expression on her face when he told her they were through.

The sun blazed high overhead, turning the parking lot into an oven. Wave after wave of blistering heat rose up off the asphalt. Sweat ran down his back and trickled out from under his armpits as he waited impatiently. The metal hood of the car burned his skin wherever it came into contact with his flesh. Not even a hint of a breeze offered respite as minute after minute ticked by. What else had he expected? Of course she wouldn't have the guts to show up and face the music.

He'd been brooding so intently that it wasn't until her car was literally bearing down upon him that he realized he'd stopped paying attention to incoming traffic. And now here she was, parking her car and getting out. She'd taken him completely by surprise! Why that mattered, he didn't know.

"Hi," she offered tersely, her eyes narrowing in anger as she registered his accusatory expression.

"Hi," he acknowledged coldly, meeting her stare.

A studied pause followed. She looked exhausted.

"We didn't do anything," she told him bluntly, the lack of emotion in her voice somehow making her statement all the more convincing. This was the part where he was supposed to be able to tell that she was lying, right?

"Oh? And that's why you were out until 2:30 in the morning? That's why his car was still parked in front of your place when I left to go to work today?"

Dangerously exasperated now, her eyes burning holes into his, Cheri replied, "Look James, if I didn't care for you as much as I do, I'd tell you to fuck off because I don't like the tone of your voice and I don't have to answer to you. Since you ask, though, we had to go all the way to the Fishkill drive-in to see the movie. It turned out to be the second picture so we had to sit through both movies and the intermission. That's the reason we were so late, ok? Do the math - first show at dark, around nine o'clock or so, second show starting after intermission at around eleven-thirty, feature movie over at one-thirty, me and Kurt at my apartment by two-thirty. But I didn't come here to try and convince you of anything. You believe whatever the hell you want to believe."

She stared at him until he glanced away uncertainly. Then she continued. "James, I came here because I like you an awfully lot and I know last night freaked you out. I'm sorry about that. I didn't mean for it to happen. But nothing went on between me and Kurt."

Her tone softened, some of the anger having bled away.

"It was strange because I remember the first time the two of us went to that drive-in. Halfway into the first show we were both so worked up that we rushed home and jumped into bed. But last night we watched both pictures without saying more than five words to each other. When we returned to my apartment, Kurt asked if he could crash there for what was left of the night. I told him he could sleep on the couch and I went up to bed alone. He was gone when I got up this morning."

James absorbed all this in silence. He was in trouble now because he had no idea what to think. But worst of all, despite what he'd been through the previous evening, he found himself believing her!

But what if she was lying and he was so gullible he couldn't tell?

Cheri stared at him defiantly, asking no favors, waiting for his response.

"Cheri...look," James began weakly. "I know I'm not helping things any by forcing you to choose between me and Kurt right now. I'm sorry but I can't stand the thought of you being with anybody else."

He got down off the car and put his arms around her, hugging her tightly to him. She responded in kind.

"Things are happening so fast..." she whispered, her head cradled against his chest. "I only got divorced yesterday, you know?"

"I know," he replied. "I know."

IV

Paradise (Not Lost)

Summer 1980

Fireworks

There's considerable confusion when we arrive, which is to be expected with a mob this size. The boardwalk in front of the casinos is jammed with humanity and before long the party-hungry throng pours down the steps onto the beach. Since this is the inaugural Fourth of July command performance, the security people are nervous and unsure about exactly how to keep the rapidly swelling, increasingly unruly crowd from overrunning the fireworks staging area. Their backs against the ocean, the beleaguered staff calls to mind Custer's men grimly awaiting the final onslaught, swallowed up in a sea of Indians.

We wandered by the staging area when we first got here. I looked over the tubes and frames used for launching the fireworks and was surprised to see that the technology was probably not that far advanced from thousands of years earlier when the Chinese first ignited gunpowder packed in hollowed out bamboo tubes, inventing firework displays to the enduring delight of festive peoples everywhere.

Initially the casino security staff let the crowd hang out by water's edge but soon afterward they herded us behind the little cabanas the hotels assembled on the sand for the enjoyment of their paying guests. Cheri and I marveled at the neatly organized rows of brightly striped, multi-colored canvas tents. They looked so theatrical! Sitting there on the sand like that, they couldn't help but call to mind the Middle East and 'Tales from the Arabian Nights.'

As an appetizer, the casinos provided a full orchestra to entertain the guests. The musicians set up on the beach and were playing when we arrived. The conductor led them through a number of spirited, classical favorites before they concluded with a rousing version of the 1812 Overture. After the orchestra members packed up their woodwinds, strings, brass and percussion instruments, nothing happened for the next hour or so.

Now the crowd mills about in excited anticipation, darkness settles in and increased rowdiness is evident as people around us overindulge in various recreational refreshments. This, of course, makes the job of the cops and organizers trying to maintain some semblance of order that much tougher and they begin to buckle under the strain. We're sitting here comfortably when suddenly some yahoos with bullhorns and badges appear, gesturing angrily, bellowing orders intended to get everyone up and moving again. At one point they threaten to cancel the fireworks performance if everyone doesn't vacate the beach and retreat to the boardwalk pronto. This is clearly an absurd expectation. If they don't hold the show there will surely be a riot! Thousands of spectators lay sprawled out on the sand in various states of repose. There is no way to shoehorn these legions up onto the equally jam-packed boardwalk which is groaning under the weight of the hordes of people continuing to arrive, all lured by the promise of an 'unprecedented' fireworks extravaganza.

Crowd anticipation gives way to crowd irritation and the

mood becomes decidedly surly. It's been dark for an hour - when is the damn show going to get started?

"Oh, Melanie - look at all the pretty lights. Do you know what they are?"

Cheri points past the breaking surf into the darkness where hundreds of lights bob crazily about. Melanie stares curiously in the direction her mother indicates but draws a blank when it comes to identifying the source of the illuminations.

"They're boats, baby. They're here to see the show too," Cheri explains.

A vast armada of pleasure craft is assembled on the water - yachts, motorboats, sailboats - as everybody tries to take advantage of the free show. Staring out at the glowing swarm clustered in the middle of all that dark ocean is disorienting - it's like being perched atop a mountain peering down at a city illuminated in the night.

"Maybe we should go up on the boardwalk?" Annie - a dear high school friend of mine who accompanied us here tonight - suggests anxiously, observing the crush of people surrounding our blanket. I think the crew on the sand next to us is making her particularly nervous - four scruffy looking dudes in full biker regalia (black leather jackets, buckled boots, bandannas and ripped blue jeans) who are laughing uproariously while taking serious slugs from a Jack Daniels bottle they're passing around in a brown paper bag.

"Christ almighty, Annie, we're staying here - it's just as crowded up there and we'll never find a place to sit," Chip - Annie's long-suffering boyfriend - exclaims.

I'm glad Chip said it because I have no intention of moving - we've got a great spot! We're on the beach, lying comfortably in the sand on our blanket with a nice ocean breeze keeping us cool. I can't imagine being any more content than I am at this moment with Cheri and Melanie at my side enjoying the evening festivities. Neither of them seems the least bit disconcerted by the crowd or our proximity to the launch site. Annie has been like this since we were teenagers growing up together. She'd never go up front at concerts either, uncomfortable in the scrum of bodies pressed closely together.

Chip looks at me and says, "Hey, James, what do you think, brother?"

"I'm perfectly happy right here," I reply.

Annie can be tough on Chip at times but it never seems to bother him.

"We're really too close, don't you think?" she tries again.

No one responds so she appeals directly to Cheri. "Maybe we should go? I don't like all of these people."

Cheri looks at me for a sign. I glance at Melly. She's sitting wide-eyed and excited like any two-and-a-half year old would be in similar circumstances. She doesn't know what in the hell is going on but she damn sure likes the idea of hanging out on the beach at night with all these people. My inattentiveness to Annie's plea is a signal to Cheri that I have no intention of leaving.

"Well...it's really not THAT bad here," Cheri equivocates, trying not to appear unsympathetic to Annie's request, but at the same time indicating that she isn't going to be of any help in getting us off the beach.

Annie glances about unhappily. She's a close friend and I don't want to see her upset, but I know from long experience that she ALWAYS complains about things like this and if everybody simply ignores her griping, she'll have a good time. Right as it appears Annie's ready to force the issue, Melanie speaks up.

"Why are all of these people here now?"

She's perplexed by the fact that it's night and her only previous experience with beaches has been swimming and sunning on them during daylight hours.

"And why doesn't everybody have their bathing suits on?" she follows up with.

"At nighttime you can go swimming with your clothes on," I offer, straight-faced. "That way you won't get cold in the water when the sun's not out."

She looks at me to gauge the seriousness of my comment and then turns to stare at the waterline to see if anyone has gone in fully clothed. No one has. She smiles coquettishly but doesn't comment directly. She knows how to play the game. What a woman this one will grow up to be!

"Well, why don't WE go in now?" she asks innocently, playing her trump card.

"You can," I comment, "but at night you have to watch out for the great, big, mean old KILLER SHARKS that come to the edge of the beach hunting for supper. Boy, do they love snatching up little kids for dessert!"

Cheri intervenes. "James, stop teasing her! Melanie - we're here to see fireworks, not to go swimming. People don't swim at night in the ocean."

"Oh yes they do," Chip teases. "And the good thing about swimming at night is, you can take all of your clothes off. You don't even need a bathing suit."

"Chip, you pervert! Don't tell that to a little girl," Annie scolds, although she has lightened up and seems slightly amused. "She'll be trying it herself and you'll get her into trouble."

"Killer sharks?" Melanie wonders aloud, liking the idea already. "What are killer sharks?"

"Oh, they're terrible creatures with sharp teeth and mouths that open as big as garage doors," I offer. "They swim in the water at night looking for little –"

"James! You're the one who gets to sit up with her tonight if she can't sleep," Cheri tersely informs me.

"All right, all right," I reluctantly concede, giving Melanie a good show of my teeth, lips wrinkled balefully, my exaggerated, silent snarl capped off with a sudden molar-rattling chomp.

Melanie isn't the least bit disturbed, however – she loves the idea of monsters and things that go 'thump' in the night. She makes the same face at me. Grabbing her by the neck, I roll her over on the beach a couple of times to teach her some respect. Cheri intervenes when sand starts flying in every direction as Melanie flails about wildly in an attempt to regain her equilibrium.

"Ok, James – now you've got her all wound up!" Cheri protests. "I hope you plan on enjoying a long evening entertaining her tonight."

Looking at Cheri, I'm seized by an overwhelming desire to touch her. She looks beautiful every day but something about the beach accentuates her attractiveness and appeal to me. It's an irresistible combination of factors – her brown, silky hair tumbled and disheveled by the sea breeze, her eyes sparkling happily under the boardwalk lights, her seductive figure casually sprawled on the blanket, her easy laughter and beguiling wit each outdoing the other when it comes to captivating me.

She willingly slumps into my arms once I maneuver close

enough to grab her. We hold each other tightly, kissing tenderly.

"I love you," I whisper.

"I love you too," she responds warmly.

We kiss again. Melanie comes over and snuggles next to us. We pull her up against our bodies and the three of us settle down propped up against each other.

We're lying flat on our backs on the cool sand staring straight up at the glow reflecting off the belly of the sky from the boardwalk lights when the first rocket screams up without warning, taking the startled assemblage by surprise. Our ears follow the sound of the rocket's invisible flight as it shoots up higher and higher and higher and then WHOOSH! A blinding flash of color. Right on it's heels - BANG!!! The firework explodes in a shimmering display of incandescent gold, glittering emerald and brilliant yellow.

The crowd cheers wildly. Melanie looks as if she's seen a vision of God. Brave as she is, however, she hasn't yet decided if this is a God of mercy or destruction, so she wedges herself in tightly between her mother and me.

Cheri smiles reassuringly at her daughter, then sweetly at me, before we all turn our attention to the heavens. The show is courtesy of one of the big Atlantic City casinos - a heartfelt 'thank you' to the gambling enthusiasts who line the card tables day and night, tossing the dice, spinning the roulette wheels, jacking the slots and filling the casino's till with incredible, unbelievable, nearly obscene amounts of cash. To their credit, when it comes to celebrating their windfall, the casinos spared no expense. The fireworks amassed for this extravaganza are enough to humble the arsenals of entire nations. From our vantage point I can see the handlers scurrying about in their white, fireproof suits orchestrating their pyrotechnic tour de force.

BAM! BAM! BAM! BOOOOOMMMM!!!

The detonations are like thunderbolts from some violent summer storm ripping apart the fabric of the sky. The din and uproar are deafening once the handlers warm to their task and start setting off entire orgiastic volleys of ordnance at a time. Overhead, electric pinks, fluorescent greens and sizzling crimsons rain down toward us in continuous, eye-popping cascades. The sheer number of simultaneous discharges makes focusing irrelevant, the rapidity of the eruptions creating a strobe-light effect on the beach, multi-colored lightning bolts flashing too frequently for overwhelmed retinas to separate. Eyes can't contain all the color, the splendor, the excitement - THIS is one helluva Fourth of July celebration!

Now, though, we have problems. The security men should have been heeded. The crowd is way too close to the exploding bombs and projectiles. From out of the heavens a heavy rain of fiery particles begins to fall, flames burning brightly as large pieces of paper and cardboard from detonated shell casings come drifting down into the throng. The fireworks display was designed to explode over the water but a stiff inland breeze has disrupted those plans. Meanwhile, more and more salvos shoot up into the night. The handlers seem to have gone berserk, remorselessly discharging fusillade after fusillade, refusing to relent even in the face of the obvious danger to the spectators.

BOOM!!! BOOM!!! CRACK!!! BAM!!! BAM!!! BOOM!!!

Large, acrid clouds of sulfurous smoke settle like a low hanging fog on the beach. It's impossible to make out anything more than dim figures scurrying about frantically in the murk as the intensity of the bombardment grows unabated.

FIREWORKS

The beach takes on the look of a battlefield, Okinawa maybe, or Iwo Jima. Cries of dismay and alarm ring out as the burning particles find targets and continue to fall wholesale out of the sky. And, apparently, what has gone up until this point was merely a warm-up because now they start letting off the fireworks in earnest.

BAM! BAM! BAM! BAM! BOOOOOOMMMM!!!

Overpowering shock waves slam into us, pinning us to the beach like bugs under a sheet of glass.

"Oh, my God, we've got to get out of here!" Annie shrieks, fear gaining the upper hand on her emotions.

At that precise moment a large piece of burning cardboard falls straight toward us. Startled, I hurriedly push Melanie and Cheri out of the way. The casing lands next to us, smoldering until I throw sand on it, extinguishing the flames. All about us a steady silent rain of ash and debris falls. It's like we're at Pompeii as the volcano erupts! The smell of burnt powder attacks our nostrils, breathing becomes difficult, coughing and hacking can be heard from every quarter. Eyes tear uncontrollably, making a bad situation worse, hindering our ability to discern from which direction the next fiery projectile might fall.

"Chip, I want to get out of here NOW," Annie howls. "Let's get up on the boardwalk!"

She jumps to her feet, bleary-eyed and staggering.

"What's wrong with you people?" she shrieks, angry and embarrassed. "This is fire, we can get burned to death down here - we've got a baby with us!"

Melanie is lying on my stomach, my arms folded over her for protection as we lay there in the thick smoke. She's stunned and mesmerized by the events of this evening. Above us discharge after discharge of explosives continues the dazzling display of firepower and artistry. Occasionally Melanie lets out a slight whimper, following any particularly ear-splitting clap of noise and thunder, but mainly she remains immobile, absorbing the scene without comment. Occasionally she turns to examine my face, assesses how I'm taking things, then, reassured, returns to her vigil.

I look over at Cheri. She smiles warily at me, keeping one eye skyward at all times. I can't help it - I start laughing and can't stop. All about us people are running for cover like we're attacking the beach at Normandy on D-Day but there's no place to go! The boardwalk is absorbing a far greater proportion of the debris than the beach because the wind is blowing inland forcefully. The people up there are so jammed together they can't get out of the way of whatever chances to fall upon them. Our location isn't ideal, I reason, but it's not as bad as up on the planks. Enough people have abandoned the beach that we have all the room in the world to dodge the occasional flaming shell casing coming our way. There's really no danger as long as we keep our eyes on the heavens to ensure that no fiery surprise lands in our laps.

Knots of people continue to scramble by holding blankets and articles of clothing over their heads, casting fearful glances skyward, as if being pursued by some terrible monster. That's what this scene reminds me of now - a Japanese horror movie! It's as if some 1950s B movie sci-fi creature is emerging from from the sea and the military, despite this intense bombardment, can't repel it.

"Run for your lives - Godzilla is coming! Hurry, faster!" I holler.

Annie regards me with disgust. I can't breathe anymore I'm

giggling so uncontrollably. And it must be contagious - Cheri is also doubled up with laughter watching the spectacle of all these grown people racing about panic stricken. Annie glares at us.

"You're out of your minds! I can't stand this - I'm getting out of here. Chip, let's go," she orders.

There's no mistaking her tone of voice. She's leaving with or without him. She turns and starts for the steps leading from the beach to the boardwalk. Chip catches up to her as she nears the top of the stairs. Together they push their way into the chaotic mob.

Overhead another barrage of thunderous crashes reverberates loudly, pushing us down into the sand once again. Night turns into day and it seems as if the battle of Armageddon has begun. In the glare we can see the beach littered with burning debris, smoldering wreckage and discarded items of clothing. Down by the waterline the fireworks madmen are still enthusiastically launching yet another earsplitting thunderclap, darting about under a ghostly cover of sparks and smoke.

BOOM! BOOM! BOOM! BOOM! BOOM! BOOM! BOOM! BOOM! BOOM! BOOM! BOOM! BOOM!

It's out of control - this has to be it, the crescendo! Explosion after pounding explosion splits open the sky. The field is lost as the triumphant handlers outdo themselves, launching assault after mindless assault upon their hapless and stricken victims, letting loose one last mind-shredding, crashing orgasm of light and noise. The prostrate bodies on the beach jerk and shudder involuntarily, as if held in the iron grip of a collective grand mal seizure.

And then it's over, the most stupendous fireworks display

I've ever witnessed. We lay on the sand as limp and lifeless as discarded rag dolls. A loud, roaring echo rings in my ears long after the sound of the last explosion fades away.

By the time we finally get up, brush the sand off our backs, make our way shakily to our feet and stiffly climb the steps to the boardwalk, much of the crowd has dispersed, melting away into what's left of the evening.

Chip suddenly appears at the railing in front of us. He reaches a helping hand down. Stepping up onto the boardwalk we see Annie seated at a bench nearby.

"Well, some fireworks show, huh?" I ask.

"Hell," Chip snorts disdainfully, "they probably had a bigger one than that at Mellsville High School tonight."

"Oh yeah, right," I retort sarcastically.

We make our way over to the bench.

"You ok, Annie?" I ask her gently.

"Just a little worse for the wear," Chip comments cheerfully.

"My eye is burnt," Annie informs us calmly, slightly chagrined, but sticking to her guns.

"C'mon, Annie, you'll be all right," Chip cajoles.

"A big piece of paper that was still on fire came down and hit me in the face, Chip, if you don't mind. You couldn't care less, though, could you?" she bitterly retorts.

"Oh, baby, that's not true and you know it," Chip reassures her. "That's not true at all!"

Hilltop Vista

On a devilishly hot, sticky and uncomfortable afternoon in the Hudson Valley, Cheri and I hike our way, nonstop, up the face of a nearly bald hillside near the township of Poughquag. There are no birds in the sky as even they are smart enough to avoid exertion during the hottest part of the day. The grass - just weeks ago lush green, dewy and moist - rattles beneath our feet, burnt brown and lifeless by the unrelenting tyranny of the implacable, fiery tormentor above.

The ascent seems interminable, our brains buzzing and swimming in the shimmering heat. Lungs suck in superheated gulps of hot air and sweat pours down our faces, itching and burning chafed skin. Overhead, there's only a clear blue sky, no clouds in sight, the sun white hot with nary a trace of a breeze to cool or soothe our aching limbs. Leg muscles begin to rebel, calling attention to themselves via twitches and spasms that threaten to become full-fledged cramps.

But when it seems we can go no further, I look up wearily and see our destination is within reach! The pinnacle lies before us. Another sustained push and we're there.

Throwing myself down on the ground, my sweat-soaked T-shirt cools, almost imperceptibly, against the earth. Cheri collapses next to me and we lay there like two broken dolls carelessly tossed on a trash heap. And then, some measure of relief! Here at the summit, a slight current of air is moving across the hilltop. We lay here exhausted, utterly spent.

Eventually, normal breathing resumes and the worst of the sweating subsides. Muscles recover and begin to protest against the discomfort of the various stones and twigs poking into them where we lay on the hilltop.

It's not until I sit up that I remember why we hiked all this way. Because of some farmer's design, or nature's caprice, there's not a tree or bush within two hundred yards of the hill's summit. The entire, perfectly rounded, symmetrical crown is without interruption. Except for a thick carpet of ankle-high clover, grass, and small wildflowers, the arena is ours, and ours alone, a stage without props. It's almost too perfect, an abstraction created by nature, all non-essentials ruthlessly stripped away, resulting in a seamless, uninterrupted hilltop union of earth and sky.

For 360 degrees the view is unbroken, a vast panorama opening up around us, sweeping to the horizon in every direction. We stare out at a storybook kingdom of patterned fields, contoured hillsides, thick forests and stately mountains that rise above the flatlands like a flotilla of ships sailing serenely across a placid sea. Far in the distance small puffs of white clouds float in the sky. From our vantage point all the world seems well-designed and ordered, as if some great craftsman has heeded every rule of form and composition in executing this harmonious, achingly perfect sweep of creation.

Cheri and I stand up and wander absentmindedly across the hilltop, separating, taking in the scenery that appeals to us individually. It's as if solitude and concentration are necessary to absorb all that is offered for our viewing pleasure. Sounds are distant and muffled, increasing the sense of solitude. We drift away from each other and soon find ourselves separated by a considerable distance. We stay apart for some time, carried away on our own private slipstream of consciousness as we contemplate the magnificent spectacle.

In due time, however, the spell is broken and with inexplicable urgency I anxiously look for Cheri. My search carries me toward the summit and it's with great pleasure that I discover Cheri has the same idea. Our paths intersect at the crown of the hill.

Coming together, we put our arms around one another and embrace silently - words inadequate to convey the bliss we're experiencing.

Our embrace lingers and the touch of her supple, young body against my tired, sore muscles is a panacea, a gift from the Gods. Her fingers knead and massage my neck and shoulders, loosening the kinks, exorcising the fatigue. She lightly works my lower back, her hips swaying against mine as we lean against one another and rock in the gentle breeze. Rubbing more firmly against her, I drop my hands from the small of her back to grip her firm buttocks, taking her belt loops in my thumbs and using them to pull her ever closer against me. Our mouths meet in a hungry, exploratory union, conveying all the thousands of messages a kiss can convey.

Above us the sky remains pristine blue as a few cotton balls of cloud drift by lazily. I hold Cheri tightly and begin to feel a warmth inside of me that cannot be ascribed to the sun. Her shirt already has two buttons open, exposing her delicate neck, and my kisses seek out the tender flesh below her collarbone as she willingly allows my lips to explore her salty skin. Directing my search ever lower, loosening a third button in the process, my pursuit carries me to the soft delight of her breasts. She leans back, closes her eyes, pulls my head gently to her chest, inviting me to continue my investigation of her body.

Standing proudly erect, unashamed, giving pleasure and taking pleasure, her hands work now on the long bulge in the front of my pants. She unzips my dungarees and reaches in to close her fingers around me. Taking my cue from her, I release the snap on her pants and begin to pull the material down, inch by inch, taking my time, enjoying the progressive exposure of her nakedness. As her jeans finally fall free from the curve of her ass, I drop to my knees and gently taste her sweetness. I'm nearly drunk on the intimacy and perfume of her presence as she stands over me like a naked goddess, every aspect of her body perfect - a classic beauty: tall, slender, with upturned breasts, well-defined hips and long, lovely legs.

We're ready. She strips off her shirt, laying it on the ground. Her laughing eyes meet mine and I smile self-consciously before her all-knowing gaze. She reaches over to me once again and kisses me hungrily, forcing her tongue deep inside my mouth. Sinking down onto her shirt, she pulls me on top of her. The increased area of skin contact between us expands our pleasure correspondingly, surprising us as we lay in the grass, oblivious to all else, concentrating only on each other.

With a shudder of pleasure, I slide all the way in. Cheri catches her breath, almost as if surprised to suddenly find me inside of her. Then, like a champion athlete she warms to the task, taking in deeper and deeper gulps of air, clutching and pulling, pushing and bucking as we work harder and harder, still under control, still taking our time, my back arched as she digs her fingertips into me, forcing me in ever deeper. Soft moans come out of her now, noises that never cease to amaze me. It's almost like I'm not there anymore, she's going away somewhere I can't follow, but no matter, I've got somewhere to go too. Pinning down her upper body with my chest, leaving only her hands free, I brace myself. It's time...

"Oh yes, oh yes," she groans, "That's it...yes!"

Cheri, trapped beneath me, bites hard into my shoulder, both of us locked in rhythm, no pretense of resistance, jamming ourselves together. I feel myself filling up. She feels it too and with one last spasm of wild, unabashed joy, the two of us reach for heaven together.

Afterwards, we lay blissfully content, side by side, gentle and affectionate, indolent and happy. Far above a hawk spirals on an updraft and another breeze wafts by, cooling down our overheated bodies. It's summertime and all the world lies at our feet.

V

The Unraveling

Winter 1980

Winter

It should be said from the start that I think winter was largely responsible. I mean, who can survive month after month of cold, snow, sleet and gloom without some kind of emotional impairment? Darkness in the morning, darkness in the evening. Night after night, the same T.V. shows, the same dinners, the same people, the same fights.

When I look back over the events that transpired, I have to say that I don't think the fault was hers or mine or the child's. Instead, I blame winter. Hell, it's even been documented! Researchers have discovered chemical reactions humans undergo when exposed to sunlight - reactions that result in mood elevation, buoyant feelings, joy! And what reaction does the sunless dark of an Alaskan or Scandinavian winter evoke? The highest depression, suicide and alcoholism rates in the world. So I sit here hoping that the damage isn't irreparable, that spring will return with its sunny days and warm nights. We can spend time together outdoors again, like we used to. Time for healing our wounds, time for fun, romance - after all, we met in the springtime...

I sit here in the dead heart of winter, assessing the damage, wondering about our chances of making it to a better day, trying to comprehend exactly what's happening to us as this accursed season grinds on in its grim, remorseless way and we come to despise each other, not so much because of who we are but because of who we failed to be. That's the maddening thing - I can't really get my mind wrapped around our problem. It's not anything we've said or done. It's things unsaid and undone. We missed something, somewhere and we just don't know what it is.

The Chance

Cheri often marveled at how glum and cheerless downtown Poughkeepsie actually was. Why had the fates conspired to deliver her here instead of somewhere else? Was it really necessary that she live out her life in a place where it was dark when she left for work and still dark when she got home? Was the unrelenting cold and chill her unalterable birthright? Had it been written somewhere in the stars that she was to be born in this depression era outpost of crumbling brick and mortar? Had destiny chosen this aging community of sagging roofs, weather-peeled shingles and moldering clapboard specifically for her? How had it been determined that she - Cheri Melvey - would enter existence in this sleepy backwater burg where a century old accumulation of grit and grime had effectively blocked off all paths of escape? Why had she been delivered - a mere helpless baby! - to this godforsaken place where the tides of progress and prosperity had evidently once washed ashore but had long since mysteriously withdrawn? Why had the city's inhabitants been left as stranded and clueless as sleepwalking travelers wandering endlessly through an empty rail station, unable to comprehend the fact that the last train had long since pulled out and connections now were all made through airports?

Add night and a pouring rainstorm (like, say, tonight), the utter lack of human life along the darkened sidewalks, the harsh glare of street lights, the ever-widening puddles and the entire scene resembled nothing so much as a deserted movie set, an abandoned soundstage, the scenery and props convincing, the mood appropriately somber and brooding but the cast and actors inexplicably absent, with no hint as to where they'd gone.

How she'd been ambushed by this foul mood, Cheri didn't know or care. James may have coerced her into attending this lousy little concert but that damn sure didn't mean she had to like it. And to make things as awkward and uncomfortable as possible, they were supposed to meet up with Jay, a bachelor friend of James'. This meant James would drink a little more than usual, get a little louder and more loaded than usual as the evening progressed, eventually getting to the point where he'd start hollering at the band and then, after the 'concert' came to an end, he would undoubtedly be a pain in the ass about leaving early enough to get home at a reasonable hour. Cheri silently vowed 'never again!' as they motored down the arterial, the car's headlights illuminating the rain-slickened pavement.

And why was it taking them so damn long to get there, Cheri wondered with more than a little irritation? James was the most erratic, poky driver she could remember riding with since the days when her father shepherded her around before she got her driver's license. Both of them were prone to maddeningly long lapses of concentration if overly taxed by thought or conversation, the car slowly decelerating as they unconsciously relaxed the pressure on the accelerator. Then, upon coming to their senses (usually when someone in the line of cars behind them lost their patience and started honking their horn or flashing their headlights), they'd step on the gas, jerkily bringing the car up to speed, only to repeat the whole scenario a few minutes later, never able to simply proceed smoothly down the highway like other normal drivers.

It was enough to make Cheri wonder if there was anything to that old saying, 'you end up marrying your parents.' James and her Dad were also equally inept when it came to car repairs. In fact, this new car they were presently driving had been purchased following just such a fiasco. It all started when Cheri's last auto had inexplicably started smoking on the way home from work one afternoon. James nobly offered to look at it when she arrived back at the apartment. Raising the hood, he poked around earnestly a few minutes and then pointed out that, oddly enough, the oil cap was missing. Sticking an old rag in the hole to keep the oil from escaping, he recommended that Cheri simply obtain another oil cap. The next day she'd stopped by her parents' house to show James' handiwork to her father who pulled out the rag, muttered something unintelligible, peered down the black hole, then returned the makeshift 'cap' to its position, agreeing with James' diagnosis of the problem.

Somehow, between James' and her father's handiwork, the unorthodox repair predictably backfired. On her way home from her parents' house the car started lurching awkwardly, losing power and barely creeping over the sizable hills in the area before miraculously getting to her driveway. When James looked under the hood again he found the rag had been partially sucked into the engine by the car's valve action. Upon removing the valve cover, it looked like a hamster had built a nest inside Cheri's motor, the shredded cloth resembling nothing so much as bedding material stuffed away by some overzealous, home-making rodent anticipating a winter of long freezing nights.

Needless to say, the car was a goner. Truthfully, it had run like a dog ever since the day Anthony bought it secondhand from some buddy of his, that much Cheri admitted, but still, it had gotten her to work every day, hadn't it? Before she even recovered from the shock of losing it, though, James gallantly suggested they buy a NEW car together. Cheri, horrified at the thought of a car payment - even with James' help (never mind how she'd be able to afford it if nothing ultimately came of their union) - was paralyzed with uncertainty and despair at that prospect. James, however, dutifully checked out a number of car dealerships that very evening and picked out a reasonably priced, brand new car of which 'they' were now the proud owners. Even the financing had turned out to be relatively easy since her parents had generously insisted on loaning the two of them the money at a 'reasonable' interest rate instead of what the banks were asking.

Now that they had their new car, Cheri had to admit she was enjoying it although it still made her nervous every time she thought about how many payments they still owed her parents.

While Cheri brooded, James put on the blinker light and made a left turn off the arterial onto a narrow side street. Immediately thereafter he made another left and steered them into the parking lot of the 'Chance,' a downtown bar where the concert was taking place. Other than four or five cars huddled under a streetlight near the alley leading to the entrance, the only other sign of life was a huge truck which pulled into the parking lot ahead of Cheri and James. The truck had a big hydraulic lift which Cheri recognized as the type used for emptying out the trash dumpsters found behind businesses everywhere.

The rain was beating down in sheets, drumming on the roof of the car so hard that Cheri couldn't have heard James if he'd been speaking to her. How were they ever going to get into the 'Chance' without getting soaked? And how long was James going to sit here idly waiting behind this truck?

As if in response to her thoughts, white backup lights blinked on in front of them. What on earth was this guy in the truck doing now?

'Can't he see we're sitting here?' Cheri considered in annoyance. Then a moment later she realized, 'Maybe he CAN'T see us here...'

"James, do –"

CRUNCCHH!!! The truck lurched into reverse and rolled right into them, the body coming up and over their hood, violently crushing it before Cheri's disbelieving eyes. James was completely paralyzed as the trash truck stopped and pulled forward a foot or two. Scarcely daring to breathe, Cheri was opening her mouth for air when, suddenly, as if the driver was determined to finish them off, on came the backup lights again.

CRUNNCCCCHHH!!! This time the huge vehicle hit them harder, literally crumpling the hood of the compact car beneath its massive, grinding bulk. It reared over the top of their sedan like some berserk automaton – the two of them were going to be crushed to death!

Mercifully, the driver of the truck finally realized something was very wrong. The backward progress of his vehicle stopped. He pulled forward a foot or two, braked to a halt and then for what seemed like forever, nothing happened. Neither Cheri nor James could find even the simplest of words to say, both of them staring in horror at the extraordinary amount of damage inflicted on the front end of their brand new car.

The rain continued to fall in torrents as they sat there in stunned silence. James recovered first.

"Light a cigarette and give me a hit or two off of it. I've got to go inside and call the police. I don't want them smelling any beer on my breath when they get here."

Mindlessly obedient for lack of any other alternative, Cheri pulled out her pack of cigarettes and shakily lit one. James took it from her outstretched hand and awkwardly puffed on it a few times before returning it to her, opening his door and hopping out into the rain. He disappeared from sight on the driver's side of the truck leaving Cheri alone to try and absorb the enormity of the event that had just occurred.

Tears formed in her eyes as she frantically considered the consequences of these few brief seconds. What would her parents say? Why hadn't James done something? How could they ever pay to get the car fixed? What would the police think? How were they going to get home? How was she going to get to work in the morning? What had she done to deserve this? She hadn't even wanted to go to this stupid concert and look what happened!

James, meanwhile, skirted a vehicle that appeared as massive and impenetrable from the ground as a battleship on the high seas might appear to a canoeist. Approaching the driver's side door, he reached up and rapped on the sheet metal panel. As he waited uncomfortably, the rain poured from the heavens, running off his head and down his collar in driving streams.

Another moment passed before the driver's window slowly rolled down. Shortly thereafter, a head poked through the window and regarded James silently.

"Stay here, ok? I'm going inside to call the police!" James

shouted.

Without a perceptible response from the driver, the window abruptly rolled up again.

Darting to their car, James stared briefly at the mangled front end before pulling open his door. Inside, the overhead light came on, displaying Cheri's stricken white pallor as rivulets of condensation ran down the window behind her in the suddenly claustrophobic interior.

"Hey, I'm going to run inside the 'Chance' and call the cops, ok?" James dutifully informed her. "Take down this guy's license plate number in case he tries to leave."

"Why would he leave?" Cheri nervously blurted out. "What did he say? Why –"

"He didn't say anything. Just watch him. I'll be back as soon as I call the cops."

Without waiting for her response, James slammed the door shut and sprinted across the parking lot, dodging puddles as best as he could, failing miserably for the most part, soaking his feet thoroughly as he disappeared from sight around the corner of the alley.

Continuing his dash to the 'Chance,' James finally reached the bar's entrance alcove. Breathing heavily, he presented his ticket to the door guard who viewed his bedraggled, waterlogged appearance indifferently and waved him inside where the sparse 'crowd' was scattered haphazardly about various far-flung tables. James instantly spotted Jay standing near the stage.

"Hi," Jay offered cheerily as James approached. "What happened to you? Haven't you ever heard of an umbrella? Where's Cheri? I thought she was coming too?"

"She's outside sitting in our crushed car," James explained

casually.

"What? Your crushed car?"

"That's right - a trash truck rammed into us and completely demolished the front end."

"Oh no, that's terrible."

"You're telling me? I mean, we've got insurance and all and it WAS the other guy's fault. We were sitting there behind him waiting at that stupid stop sign where you enter the parking lot. The next thing I know, he backs right into us. But, listen, I've got to call the police, this just happened before I came in."

"Sure, I think there's a phone on that wall near the stairway."

James turned and headed in the indicated direction, Jay trailing along behind him.

"Hey, do you think this is going to make you miss the concert?" Jay asked with obvious concern after a moment's reflection as they shouldered their way past the customers lined up around the bar.

"Well, I actually hadn't given it much thought yet but I guess there's no reason NOT to stay, right? That is, if you could give us a ride home later, since our car's not going anywhere tonight on its own."

"Sure, or you guys can stay over at my place since I live so much closer."

"Nahhh, Cheri'll never go for that," James reflected as they approached the phone.

Inserting his quarter, James dialed 'O' to get the Operator.

"I'd like to speak to the police department please," he politely requested.

"Is this an emergency, sir?"

"Yes it is, ma'am."

"One moment."

Another voice, that of a businesslike, no nonsense male, came on the line.

"Poughkeepsie Police Department, can I help you?"

"Yes, there's been an accident in the parking lot behind the 'Chance' theater. A trash truck rammed into my car and we need a police officer to come by and make a report."

"Parking lot of the 'Chance?'"

"Yeah, that's right."

"Somebody'll be there in a minute."

"Thanks."

Turning to Jay, James regarded him optimistically and said, "I've got to talk to Cheri but we'll probably stay for the show once I get this all straightened out."

"Great!" Jay responded enthusiastically. Having gone to the trouble of procuring the tickets for this evening's performance by Tom Verlaine's band, 'Television,' he was visibly relieved by James' reassurance that he was not going to end up spending the night alone at what Jay hoped would be a classic concert.

Meanwhile, outside, Cheri sat in stunned silence. Since James had left, she'd simply stared wide-eyed at the wreckage of her car's crumpled hood, unable to muster enough effort to write down the license plate of the garbage truck. It wasn't until she heard that vehicle engage its gears that her attention focused once more on the here and now.

Her terrified mind immediately considered, 'Is he going to finish me off?' A jolt of terror rocketed from the tips of her toes to the hair on top of her head as she listened to the driver step on the gas. She shuddered, anticipating the riveting sight of backup lights flashing on again. But this time the truck inched forward and slowly began to pull away from the scene of the accident.

'What the hell,' Cheri wondered in astonishment. 'Is that son of a bitch trying to get away?'

Finally snapping to life, Cheri desperately peered through the windshield and tried to catch a glimpse of the license plate number as the truck picked up a bit of speed.

'Is that an F or an E?' she wondered, urgently wiping away the condensation on the inside of the windshield, succeeding only in smearing it into messy swirls of the sort little children create when introduced to finger paints for the first time.

As she helplessly resigned herself to watching the offending vehicle escape, she saw its red brake lights blink on. What was this guy doing now? Rolling down her window, Cheri stuck her head out into the rain long enough to hear the sound of bottles breaking as the driver leaned over a trash can and threw a paper bag into it.

'Oh, ho,' Cheri instantly realized. 'The bastard's been drinking. That explains it!'

And with that, the truck's backup lights winked on once more. Cheri's heart fluttered fearfully at the sight. Unconsciously her hand felt for the door release as she monitored the vehicle's return to the scene of the crime. For the second time this evening she felt like a bit player in some low budget film. This was the part where the villain finished off the leading lady! But with the incriminating evidence disposed of, the other driver apparently had no intention of leaving the scene of the accident. He closed the distance between the car and his truck to about 10 feet and came to a final halt.

As James sprinted through the downpour back to his and Cheri's car, he saw no black and white police cruiser on the scene and wondered how long it was going to take for the cops to arrive. The damn police station itself was only two blocks away! Were he and Cheri going to miss the concert on top of everything else?

Pulling the driver's side door open, he quickly slid into his seat and slammed the door shut behind him. Inside the car the atmosphere was thick with cigarette smoke, humidity, unspoken fears and nervous tension.

Cheri regarded James dully - they sat together in miserable silence.

"The cops are on the way," James authoritatively informed her, trying to stay calm and composed.

"The guy in the truck pulled over to a trash can and dumped some bottles into it - I'd guess they were bottles of liquor of some sort," Cheri relayed lifelessly.

"We gotta be sure to tell the cops about that but I don't think there's gonna be any question as to whose fault this was, do you?" James considered.

"No, no...I guess not."

Her response took James a moment to decode.

"Whaddya mean, you 'guess' not? Does that mean you think it was MY fault for letting that guy run us over?"

"No, of course not! I mean...oh, I don't know - why DIDN'T you back up?"

"Did you have time to say anything about backing up? No? I didn't think so. The damn truck was on top of us before I had a chance to even think of backing up. And since when is it the responsibility of the driver in the car behind someone to avoid getting backed into? That's bullshit!"

Clearly she'd struck a nerve.

"Ok, ok, already, I'm not saying it was your fault..." she conceded.

"Boy, it sure sounds like you have your suspicions, though," he accused her heatedly, entirely unmollified.

That thought was left hanging in midair between the two of them like a festering cloud of poisonous gas.

"Did you call my father to come pick us up?" Cheri asked.

"No - and don't you want to stay for the concert?" James cajoled. "Jay went to all the trouble of getting these tickets for us and what's done is done, right? I mean, not going to the concert isn't going to fix the car, is it? Jay said he'd give us a ride home when it's over. And besides -"

"Are you crazy?" Cheri blurted out angrily. "NO - I do NOT want to go to any goddamn concert right now, ok? After the police come, I want you to call my father to take me home and then you can do whatever you feel like doing. I never wanted to go to this lousy concert in the first place!"

"Oh, so now it's because I wanted us to go to the concert that all this happened, is that it?"

Cheri sat in obstinate silence, arms folded tightly across her chest, foot tapping ominously. She knew it wasn't exactly James' fault the guy had backed into them, but why in the hell couldn't James have been paying more attention? Why had he pulled up so close to the damn truck in the first place?

"Well, I really appreciate your support on this," James spoke up bitterly. "And, look, the cops are here - why don't you go ahead and turn me in? Why not tell them it's MY fault some drunk truck driver slammed into us when we stopped at the stop sign like we were supposed to?"

"Look, I didn't say -"

James didn't wait to hear her reply. Without another word he opened his door, jumped out into the unrelenting rainstorm, slammed the door shut and turned to meet the police car that was slowly approaching their disabled vehicle.

Sloshing a few steps across the flooded parking lot, James positioned himself on the driver's side of the oncoming cruiser. The police officers appeared to be in no particular hurry as they inched up next to the scene of the accident. As James stood there waiting, rain soaking him from head to toe, the driver's side window of the police car rolled down and a dark-haired, middle-aged officer suspiciously peered out.

"What's the problem?" he demanded unceremoniously.

"We pulled up to the stop sign here behind this guy in the truck and next thing I know, he backs right into us. Oh yeah, and then he pulls forward a few feet, puts it in reverse and does it again! My girlfriend says he threw some liquor bottles into that trash can over there while I was inside calling the police. And -"

"Hold on, pal, I think I've got the picture."

The officer reached up onto the dashboard and put down a sandwich he'd evidently been munching on during the ride over.

'No wonder it took them so long to arrive,' James resentfully considered, 'they stopped to get a snack!'

While James continued to stand there getting drenched, the cop pulled out a clipboard and began writing. After a few seconds it was clear that neither he nor his partner were going to offer James shelter in their car, nor bother with getting out of theirs.

"Hey, look," James finally broke in as water trickled down his back from beneath his collar. "Is it ok if I run inside the 'Chance' again to call my girlfriend's father? We're going to need a ride home."

"Yeah, I'd say so," the cop grunted in assent, glancing indifferently at the evidence before returning to his report writing. "Go ahead, I've got to get a statement from the other driver too, so you've got a few minutes. You also might want to call a wrecker if you've got one in particular you want to work with."

With that, James turned and sprinted across what was, by now, virtually a lake with a paved bottom.

Inside the 'Chance,' a vaguely punkish warm-up band droned out a distinctly unmusical set. James spotted Jay without difficulty - he was standing near the speakers in virtually the same place James found him the last time, hands shoved in his pockets, head bobbing as he absorbed the band's performance.

"Hey, sorry man, but there's no way Cheri'll stay for the concert!" James hollered in Jay's ear as he approached him from behind.

Jay turned to face him. What started out as a welcoming grin disintegrated rapidly into a disappointed grimace as James' words and expression sunk in.

"You don't think there's any possibility, even if I take you guys home? I mean, what sense is there in missing the concert too? After all -"

"Jay, I know! I told her all that but she's real upset about the car and she wants me to call her Dad to come take us home so that's what I'm gonna do."

"Well, all right man, but I hate to see you miss this band 'cause I think you'd really like them."

"I'm sure I would - although they'd have to be one helluva lot better than these guys."

"What? Are you kidding me? These guys are one of my favorite bands! You've seen them here before, haven't you? Agitpop."

"No, can't say that I have...but, anyway, look, I've got to call Cheri's dad and get a wrecker here to tow away the car. I'm sorry we have to miss the show. We'll have to catch another one sometime soon."

"Yeah, well, I'm sorry about the car."

"Thanks, I appreciate it. See ya."

James turned and made his way to the phone.

Although he'd been dreading making this call - not that Cheri's Dad had ever been anything other than friendly and gracious to him - Cheri's father took the news well, despite having some difficulty understanding James' story with the band noise pounding in the background.

"Oh, my God," Cheri's Dad empathized once he finally had all the details, "are you both ok?"

"Yeah, we're fine, although the front end of the car is in bad shape."

"That's why you have insurance, right? And by the way, a good friend of mine owns a repair shop in that neighborhood. You oughta have it towed there. Tell them to take it to Jimmy Rowe's body shop on Smith Street."

"Jimmy Rowe's on Smith Street?"

"Yeah, that's it."

"And if you don't mind, your daughter wants to know if you'd be willing to pick us up," James continued. "My buddy, Jay, could take us home after the concert but Cheri wanted me to call you instead. She wants to go home now."

"Oh, geez, sure! Give me fifteen minutes and I'll be there - you're in that parking lot off the main mall, right? Just behind the Poughkeepsie National Savings bank?"

"Yep, that's the one...we'll be the folks in the crushed car."

"Ok, I'll see you in a few minutes. You sure you're ok? You

don't sound so good."

"Yeah, we're both ok but it's been a rough night."

"Ok then, I'll be right there."

In the parking lot, the police car was pulled up next to the truck. The driver was standing in the rain telling his story to the warm and dry police officers who remained in their vehicle, obviously having no intention whatsoever of getting soaked investigating some routine fender bender collision.

For lack of anything better to do and desperate to get out of the rain, James jumped inside his and Cheri's battered car.

"Your Dad is on the way," James offered, by way of breaking the silence.

"Good," Cheri responded stonily. "Great."

Dick's

Dick Smith's Lounge and Restaurant, part of an adjoining motel complex, was mainly frequented by visiting businessmen looking to unwind after a hard day's work. Recently an entire Hollywood movie crew and their very well-known comedic superstar - the entourage filming scenes on the grounds of a nearby, exclusive prep school - had adopted the Lounge as an informal, after-hours 'hangout.' Word spread quickly and for weeks on end the bar's business boomed with seemingly everyone in town vying to top each other in the quest for 'most sightings of a visiting celebrity.' When the film shoot finally came to an end, crew and cast vanishing as suddenly as nocturnal apparitions fleeing morning's light, it was as if the bar's newfound customer set refused to admit that the party was over, continuing to show up night after night in undiminished numbers, hoping evidently for one last opportunity to brush shoulders (at least on the dance floor) with fame.

On Friday evenings, however, the fashionable English-style pub, with its polished floors, spit-shined cherry wood bar and low-hanging Tiffany-style lamps, had long been renowned by the locals for the swinging 'happy hour' (proper attire required) that commenced immediately following the close of the workweek. This signature event rocked on well into the wee hours of any given Saturday morning, its momentum fueled by potent drinks, well-stocked buffet lines, infectious dance music and the cheery respite it provided from the ever-earlier arriving darkness and increasingly frigid winter nights.

On this particular Friday, as Cheri pulled her newly repaired car into the jammed parking lot, the first thing she noticed was Helen's Chrysler wedged securely into a spot up close against the front of the building, incontrovertible evidence of her early arrival and a sure sign that she hadn't even bothered to go home after work.

'Probably brought her stuff with her and went over to Ginnie's to change so she wouldn't have to deal with Fred,' Cheri considered as she maneuvered her car into a sliver of a space left between the fire lane and crush of vehicles.

Fred was Helen's husband. He wasn't invited to these Friday evening blow-outs either, a topic James and Cheri had been 'discussing' prior to Cheri's departure, his words still fresh and bitter in her mind.

"Goddammit!" James exploded angrily. "I'm supposed to watch you come home from work, take a shower, put on your make-up, wiggle into your sexiest clothes, slip on your stockings and then strut out the door in your high heels without me? What kind of bullshit is that?"

"But you go out with your buddies all the time!" Cheri pointed out for the hundredth time, never once placating James with this line of reasoning. "Concerts, band practice, you name it! And do I ever say anything to stop you? No! So when I want to do something with my friends after work, why is that such a big deal?"

"It's a big deal because it's every Friday night," James

argued. "The one night of the week couples should be out together, you go and spend with everyone else BUT your boyfriend!"

"James, I look forward to coming home and spending every OTHER night of the week with you - but one night of the week I like to do something with MY friends and Friday night happens to be that night. I don't understand where you get off being such a bastard about it," Cheri countered, a touch of irritation creeping into her voice.

"I guess that's because you don't ever bother to put yourself in my position or consider how I feel," he accused her.

"That's not fair, James, not fair at all," Cheri wearily responded. "Look, why don't you call Bobby and go see a band tonight? You know how much fun you guys have doing that," she cajoled, switching tactics, willing to try anything to avoid prolonging yet another of these tedious arguments about the same boring subject.

"Because I don't WANT to go out with Bobby and see a band tonight - I want to go out with you tonight!" James adamantly maintained, his face taking on that angry, flushed look she'd come to know and dislike so much of late.

"Well, James, I'm going out with Helen and Ginnie tonight. I wish it didn't upset you this much but there doesn't seem to be anything I can do about that," Cheri dejectedly concluded, her spirits sinking as she absorbed the body blows of his radiating anger.

"Great, just freaking great!" he raged, finally storming downstairs in frustration, leaving her to dress in blessed solitude.

That exchange had occurred well over an hour ago however and Cheri felt her spirits reviving as she stepped out of her car in the parking lot of Dick Smith's. She heard the music blaring from inside the bar as a couple stumbled out into night, momentarily leaving the door ajar. The sounds of laughter and cheerful voices carried out into the evening and she felt her heart swell with - pleasure! - as she looked forward to meeting up with her girlfriends, having a few drinks, hearing some tunes, doing a little dancing and putting the woes of her troubled relationship behind her. With startling clarity she suddenly realized she was feeling better precisely because she was away from James.

Her heels clacking loudly on the pavement, she hurried toward the building, the gusting wind slashing at her face as she dodged puddles and negotiated the last few steps to the entrance.

"Brrrrr!" she exclaimed involuntarily, yanking open the heavy glass door by its big brass handle, then hustling into the comfort of the interior hallway where a smiling hostess greeted her.

"Will you be needing a table for dinner?" the young girl questioned her loudly over the pounding music. Pulsating lights from the nearby dance floor illuminated the room in a shifting montage of colors and patterns.

"No thanks, I'm meeting some friends."

"What?"

"NO THANKS - I'M MEETING SOME FRIENDS," Cheri yelled as she unbuttoned her coat and walked over to hang it up on the nearby coat racks. Beneath her protective outer garment she was wearing a boldly patterned black and white pullover blouse, tight black skirt, matching stockings and towering heels the guys at work descriptively called, 'come fuck me pumps.'

"Whoa, baby, believe it or not, here I am - a new friend

anxious to meet you," a smiling, well-dressed young guy standing next to her joked as he finished hanging up his own expensive looking leather jacket. Cheri recognized the fragrance of his designer cologne as he turned to appraise her in an open, friendly and respectful manner no attractive, well-endowed woman could possibly resent.

"Oh, is that right?" Cheri remarked with scarcely disguised amusement.

"Sure, look, I'll prove it. Let me help you with your coat," he quickly offered.

"Thanks," Cheri acknowledged, smiling as she noted his stylish shirt and muscular chest.

"My pleasure," he replied. Stepping behind her, he tipped her backwards into his arms, then slowly - suggestively? - slipped the garment off her shoulders.

"Can I push my luck and offer to buy you a drink?" he whispered from somewhere near her ear, the smell of his cologne so strong now as to be nearly overpowering.

"No, thank you, my friends - the ones I've already been introduced to - are waiting for me," Cheri firmly declined, emphatically pulling herself out of his clutches but taking no offense at his harmless hijinks.

"Oh, baby, c'mon, you call them friends? Who was waiting for you at the door? That's right, me! How about a dance later on, once you get a chance to slip away?" he gamely bargained, unwilling to concede defeat.

"Well...maybe later, we'll see," Cheri fended him off, leaving him with some hope, however unrealistic, as she turned away and started into the lounge.

"My name's Randy - I'll be looking for you," he called after her. "I never forget a set of nice legs - lose those other friends and keep your eyes open for me."

"Don't worry Randy, I will," Cheri called over her shoulder, enjoying the first genuinely pleasant moment she'd experienced this evening.

As her thoughts turned to finding her friends, she almost ran smack into Ginnie who was standing directly in front of her with undisguised glee.

"Oh-ho! So you're going to dump your friends and go hunting for young Tarzan at the first opportunity, are you?"

"Oh, my God, you surprised me!" Cheri exclaimed, flushing with embarrassment upon realizing Ginnie had watched the entire episode.

"You're surprised? How about me? And here I thought you and James were the perfect couple, all bliss and happiness –"

"Yeah, right. We were discussing that just before I left, if you know what I mean," Cheri interjected glumly.

"– so you can imagine how astonished I was to find our loyal, domesticated, BORING Cheri fluttering her eyelashes and swooning in the grip of some aspiring Rhett Butler whispering sweet nothings in her ear while removing her clothing," Ginnie continued.

"My coat, not my clothing! And don't you go starting any rumors like that, Miss Busybody. That's all I need James to hear. Where's the rest of the gang?"

"They're behind the bar at our usual table – along with, shall we say, a 'mystery' guest who's been impatiently awaiting your arrival," Ginnie dangled the bait before her in a tantalizing tone.

"Who is it? Tell me!" Cheri demanded, instantly intrigued.

"Oh, no, I can't spoil the surprise – you'll see soon enough."

"You know, it's a sad day when you can't count on your

friends to provide vital information."

"Ain't it the truth? Let me just say...you won't really be ALL that surprised," Ginnie winked. "But -" Ginnie held up her hand, cutting short Cheri's response, directing Cheri's attention to the bar with a discreet nod of her head, "that's only if Romeo over there leaves you alone long enough for the rest of us to enjoy the presence of your witty, charming, PROMISCUOUS company at OUR table."

Turning to follow the path of Ginnie's gaze, Cheri found herself staring once again at the guy who'd helped her out of her coat. Catching her eye, he launched himself into a dramatic pantomime, painfully clutching his heart while gesturing for her to join him at the open bar stool next to him.

Emphatically shaking her head 'no,' Cheri barely contained her laughter, turning to Ginnie and saying, "You know, he's actually kinda cute, isn't he? If -"

Cheri found herself addressing blank air.

'Now, where did she run off to?' she wondered momentarily, before deciding, 'Oh well, let me find the others and see who this mystery guest is.'

Rounding the bar, she stepped onto the edge of the dance floor where numerous absorbed couples were writhing to the uptempo tunes that followed hard on the heels of each other without interruption.

Maneuvering carefully along the picket line of flashing elbows and enthusiastic, if unskilled, flying feet, Cheri gingerly made her way to the other side of the bar, issuing numerous, 'excuse me!'s along the way. Finally breaking clear of the fray, she was relieved to spot Helen seated - as Ginnie indicated - at the big table parked up against the rear wall. No sooner had she spotted Helen, however, then she felt her heart flip-flop in dismay (and...?) as the identity of the 'mystery guest' became clear.

John Lovingood was sitting quietly at the table, peering curiously about the ruckus, ignoring all the noise and partying as he serenely scanned the surroundings, evidently looking for someone in particular. Patiently nursing his drink, he wasn't participating in the spirited discussion that was going on around him. Helen was seated to his left, leaning forward and listening with great interest to Ginnie, who was settling into her seat.

Spotting Cheri's approach, Helen interrupted Ginnie long enough to loudly exclaim, "Oh no, Ginnie...not OUR Cheri! She's practically married, isn't she? She'd never let some big, gorgeous hunk of a stranger sweep her off her feet and into a coatroom without putting up at least SOME resistance."

"Ginnie!" Cheri hollered self-consciously as she slipped past the last few tables between her and her friends. "What did I tell you about starting rumors?"

"But, Cheri, darling - this is no rumor. Ginnie actually saw it all happen," Helen countered sweetly, a self-satisfied grin smugly fixed on her wide-eyed (and red-eyed) countenance. "John, dear, if you have an eyewitness, it's hardly a rumor now, is it?"

From the moment Helen called out, John's attention focused entirely on Cheri. It was clear who he'd been searching for. Welcoming her with a big smile, John grinned sheepishly and agreed, "Well, you've got a point there -"

Cheri, however, cut him off.

"John Lovingood, don't you dare listen to a word this troublemaker says...she's got nothing better to do than get everyone all stirred up over something that didn't happen but I expect a

LOT more out of you."

Cheri fixed him with her most intimidating stare. He met her gaze and held it, literally swelling with pleasure as he happily regarded her, beaming cheerfully as Cheri relented and allowed the slightest trace of a grin to form around the corners of her mouth.

At that moment their harried waitress stopped by the table to take drink orders, giving John a moment's respite.

"Is everybody all right, or can I get someone a refill? I thought you'd be about ready for another one," the girl joked, addressing her remark to Helen while picking up her empty glass.

"What? Little ole me wanting more of that nasty old alcohol?" Helen replied, feigning surprise.

"Can't you bring her a gallon jug or something that'd make this easier for you in the long run? We wouldn't have to keep working you so hard then," Ginnie added helpfully.

"You're probably right, but sorry, our cocktails don't come in jumbo sizes. I take it you don't want another one then?" the waitress asked Helen.

"Oh, no, silly me, I didn't say that. Since you insist, let me have just one more eeensy-weeensy jack and coke, ok?"

"You got it...how about the rest of you?"

"Oh, give me one of those Kahlua and milk thingamajigs," Cheri piped up. "What do you call them, white Russians?"

"Yes, white Russians," the waitress confirmed. "Anything else? No? Ok, back in a flash."

Helen immediately steered them to a topic of more interest to her prurient nature, "Ok, NOW let's return to what Cheri was saying - that was intriguing! Exactly how much 'more' do you expect out of John and will you be performing again in the coatroom so the rest of us can watch this time?"

"Helen!" Cheri burst out in embarrassment. "What is wrong with you? John, don't mind her - the girl is a menace."

"John, dear, support me on this one, you handsome devil, you," Helen shamelessly flattered him, shifting her weight to lean against his shoulder, reaching out to hold his hand as she ingratiatingly reminded him, "After all, I invited you to join us tonight so I'd have at least one friend I could depend on. You won't let mean old Cheri come between us now, will you, sweetheart?"

John blushed as Helen stared expectantly into his eyes from mere inches away, awaiting his reply.

John had recently transferred into the area from their company's home office in Florida. Once upon a time he'd been an aspiring big-league ball player, attending college on a full baseball scholarship. An untimely knee injury put that dream to rest but he remained an excellent athlete, participating in the softball league at work where he had acquired some degree of fame among his teammates and co-workers. Long before they'd actually met him, Cheri, Helen and Ginnie heard numerous stories about the new manager's exploits on the baseball diamond from his teammates in the company softball league who were also regulars at the girl's lunchtime card playing sessions.

It so happened that Cheri was the first of the 'gang' to actually have day to day contact with John at work. Along with her responsibility for updating and maintaining the company's online computer files came the opportunity to work closely with most of the managers and supervisors in the plant. This was how she met John. It wasn't long after she input his initial batch of data and began providing him with regular reports that she noticed him manufacturing excuses to bring her updates in excess of what was strictly necessary to conduct his responsibilities. As his visits became more and more frequent, he also developed the habit of prolonging his stays, chatting amiably with her, clearly enjoying the camaraderie. Soon he began confiding more and more of his personal life to Cheri, detailing the difficulties he and his fiancee were having with the move up north, wondering aloud about their prospects of 'making it.' He complained bitterly about her bitchiness and even went so far as to reveal extremely personal details of what was apparently an unsatisfying sexual union, John being forced to use techniques other than 'normal' intercourse for his fiance to experience orgasm.

Cheri, for her part, flirted and bantered with John the same way she did with all the other cute guys at work. John, though, responded more seriously to her attentions than she'd anticipated. Oh sure, she found him attractive but what girl at work didn't? He kept himself in great shape and even though he was ten years her senior somehow he seemed vulnerable and inexperienced, especially when relating some of the 'difficulties' he and his girlfriend were experiencing.

Cheri's mothering instincts welled up whenever John came dejectedly wandering by, bringing her his latest tale of domestic woe. Knowing the rather significant salary John was drawing (one of the 'fringe' benefits of her position being access to the personnel and payroll files for virtually anybody in the company), Cheri also couldn't help but imagine from time to time how nice it would be to have a boyfriend or husband pulling down an equivalent amount - she and James together were barely making half as much. How much easier life could be with that kind of money when it came to paying off the seemingly endless pile of bills she and James accumulated. Imagine all the things she could buy for Melanie!

But she never seriously considered an affair with John - at least not until it became apparent that he was contemplating one with her. Oh, he hadn't come right out and said it but she knew. And he knew she knew. Cheri felt a sudden flash of angry at Helen for her conniving to have John join them tonight. That little schemer had purposely brought the two of them together without informing Cheri of her wicked intentions!

So now Cheri had two serious problems on her hands. First, James would flip out if he heard about John being here. Cheri had made the mistake, early on, of telling him about John and his personal 'confidences.' Guys being guys, James instantly knew - was it something in her tone of voice? - that eventually John was going to make a move on her. James had harped on this subject for weeks on end and although Cheri had pooh-poohed the idea, in her heart she knew James was right. And here she was - having sworn to James that nothing went on at these get-togethers other than 'the girls' having a little fun after a hard week's work - with an unescorted John sitting next to her. Then, to top it all off, Helen - James' version of the 'devil' woman - was present to stir the mix and orchestrate whatever intrigue might serve to keep her amused for the evening. If James chose tonight to check up on who Cheri's 'friends' were, there would be trouble. But her second problem was more immediate...the way John was staring at her!

Their waitress returned with the drinks and was in the process of giving change when Helen startled her and everyone else at the table by suddenly emitting a two fingered, piercing whistle, then loudly calling out, "Ronny, over here baby!"

Helen's voice rang out over the clamor and refocused everyone's attention on the arrival of yet another of their 'regular' Friday night gang.

Ron Ebersol, all 6 foot 3 inches of his well-proportioned, gymnasium maintained physique on display for the ladies to appreciate, was working his way through the tightly packed crowd, his glasses steamed up after making the transition from the cold outside to the heat inside. Behind his facade of brimming confidence - despite the image he created with his Corvette sports car, showcase home, ski trips and vacations to the Caribbean - Ron had about him the whipped air of a puppy that had been continually punished for something it didn't quite understand. Eager to please, trying ever so hard to make Helen happy, he couldn't seem to shed the aura of depression that seemed to torment him without respite. Wearing a tentative smile, he waved as he spotted Helen.

Nothing offered better insight into Ron's 'curse' than his relationship with Helen. He was head over heels in love with this married women 14 years his junior, very nearly worshiping the ground she walked on, clearly regarding every day stolen from Helen's husband as a gift from the Gods that might be snatched away at any moment. His own wife having left after declaring him 'unsatisfying' in bed, Ron had all his emotional cards out on the table. He was totally dependent on Helen for his mental stability and happiness. And in Helen he couldn't have found a more unstable and confused soul mate. How these two ill-fated lovers had ever crossed paths, only some once-in-a-lifetime diabolical misalignment of the stars might explain. It was clear to Cheri that their affair was doomed from the start, the day of reckoning only a matter of time, no matter how brightly Ron and Helen burned the candle of their romance today.

They'd met in this very same bar, not all that long ago, Helen stopping by on the way home from work one evening to unwind. A few innocent drinks together, some laughs, a couple of dances and then, inexplicably, Ron somehow became the man Helen chose to commit adultery with.

A 'good' Polish girl from Pennsylvania, Helen's facial features and bone structure unmistakably marked her as sturdy immigrant stock, no matter how much rouge and makeup she applied. Still visiting her family religiously, calling her mother on the phone almost nightly, Helen seemed an unlikely candidate to cheat on her husband, yet there she was, throwing herself into her affair with total abandon.

Helen's husband, Fred, was an unassuming, prematurely balding engineer who wanted nothing more than to come home from work at the end of a long day to find his wife fixing dinner, the fire blazing in the hearth, his prized Irish setter waiting by his favorite chair. A 'big' weekend to Fred meant washing and waxing the couple's cars, taking a few spins around the yard of their brand new split-level Colonial home in his shiny John Deere riding mower, firing up his beloved gas grill and then maybe curling up on the couch with Helen to watch a movie for the rest of the evening. A number of years older than his vivacious wife, Fred never quite 'got it,' when it came to deciphering Helen's burgeoning discontent. As she sank deeper into apathy and despair, Fred helplessly responded by sending her off to pick out new drapes, new furniture or new clothes but unfortunately for Fred, what Helen ultimately picked out was a new lover.

To make matters even crazier, this had all come to a head recently, Fred finally realizing something was seriously wrong the Friday night his wife failed to come home altogether.

Angrily confronting Helen upon her return the next morning, he infuriated her to the point that she forgot all about her well-rehearsed and collaborated excuse ('I had too much to drink, passed out and had to spend the night at Ginnie's') and, instead, looked Fred dead in the eye and told him exactly what it was she HAD been up to the last few months. Expecting nothing less than an immediate divorce, Helen stormed out of the house and spent the night at Ron's. By the very next day, however, when she went home to retrieve some personal items, Fred was already a broken man, red-eyed, distraught, wanting nothing more than to know how they could work things out 'together.'

Helen being Helen, she hit upon a novel solution - not wanting to be totally dependent on Ron either, perhaps subconsciously realizing how slim their chances for a permanent union were, she negotiated the best of both worlds. During the week she stayed at home and slept with Fred. On the weekends she disappeared from Fred's world, reappeared at Ron's place and resumed her life with him. Fred, unbelievably (at least, to Cheri) meekly accepted these conditions, apparently rationalizing, 'half a wife is better than no wife at all.'

Ron reached their table and pulled out the chair next to Helen, plainly perplexed and somewhat disconcerted at the sight of his cherished 'prize' cozily snuggled up against an, as yet, unidentified male.

"Ronny will take one of these too," Helen indicated to the waitress who nodded her head in acknowledgment as Helen winked slyly and pointed at her own jack and coke.

"I'll take one of what?" Ron interrupted, too late, as the waitress hurriedly departed.

"Ronny - this is John, one of our favorite friends from work,"

Helen introduced the two of them. "He and Cheri work REAL closely together."

"Helen!" Cheri intervened threateningly.

"Hi, John, nice to meet you," Ron offered tentatively.

"Nice to meet you too," John said, standing up and exchanging a handshake with Ron.

"Hi, Cheri - where's James? Is he going to stop by tonight?" Ron innocently inquired as he sat down.

"James? James who?" Helen broke in, delivering a playful elbow to Ron's side as she comically widened her eyes and stared at Cheri.

"James and a friend of his are going out to see a band tonight so I don't think he'll stop by," Cheri explained.

The waitress returned with Ron's drink and Cheri took the opportunity to drop the subject, taking a long, satisfying sip from her cocktail, the creamy, coffee flavor smoothing out the bite of alcohol behind it.

The topic turned briefly to mutual interests John and Ron shared. As they chatted, absorbed in the details of a recent blockbuster baseball trade, Helen reached over and clinked her glass against Cheri's and Ginnie's.

"To Friday nights and...having a GREAT time together!" she toasted boisterously, very nearly knocking Cheri's drink out of her hand in the process.

"To Friday nights...and, to not having TOO good of a time!" Ginnie seconded, all three of them laughing and sipping their drinks as Cheri found a napkin with her free hand and wiped up the liquor that had spilled out onto the table following Helen's overly enthusiastic effort.

One song ended and another from the D.J.'s apparently inexhaustible supply throbbed to life and caught Helen's fancy.

"Oh, that's one of my favorites!" Helen squealed in delight, leaping to her feet and tugging at Ron's arm. "C'mon handsome, 'shake your booty' with me."

Needing no further prompting, Ron - an enthusiastic and somewhat accomplished dancer (as well as skier, horseback rider and all around sportsman) - leapt up with a big smile on his face to join Helen. The two of them locked hands and made their way toward the dance floor, Helen already gyrating sensuously to the beat. Flinging themselves wholeheartedly into the melee, they were immediately lost from sight.

"I think I'll take this opportunity to call home and remind Jimmy to give the baby her medicine," Ginnie declared unexpectedly. "Anything I can get for you guys at the bar? I'll only be a few minutes."

"I'm ok," John politely declined.

"Ummmm...yeah, could you please bring me another one of these Kahlua 'whatchamacallits?' A White Russian, that's it. They're really great! You know, I think they use half-and-half instead of milk. And, uh..." Cheri stalled, heart pounding suddenly at the thought of being left alone at the table with John. This would not look good if James heard about it, or, dear God, walked in on them.

"Uh, what?" Ginnie pressed humorously. "How about if I run into your admirer at the bar - anything I should tell him for you?"

"Now don't start that up again!"

"Don't have a cow. I'm only asking."

"And I'm telling you - don't encourage him, he's pushy enough as it is."

"See you in a jiff then."

Ginnie popped up out of her seat and was gone before Cheri

could think of any other way to delay her departure. Settling into her chair, she felt an awkward moment of silence descend between her and John, tempered slightly by the comforting buzz that was settling over her as the effects of the first drink kicked in. She could feel herself relaxing, the tensions of the workday and early evening gradually being exorcised from her mind and body. The music sounded great, the night was still young and now that she was out of the house with her friends, all her seemingly overwhelming problems were melting away like April snow under a spring rain.

"You know, Ginnie is so obsessed with that new baby of hers that she doesn't even trust her husband to watch it for an hour alone," Cheri confided to John, tossing that innocuous subject out on the table to try and dissipate some of the nervousness she was inexplicably feeling.

"Doesn't he do this for her every Friday night, though? I thought you guys were regulars here," John gamely pitched in. "You'd think he'd get the hang of it sooner or later, wouldn't you?"

"Yeah, we are regulars here and he does fine with the baby but Ginnie calls home about every other hour - they're so cute together! Which reminds me - where's your fiancee? After all I've heard about her, you show up alone and I don't even get to meet her?"

"Beverly flew home to see her parents for the weekend. And, to tell you God's honest truth, I wouldn't be half surprised if she didn't return when the weekend's over."

"Oh? Are things that bad?"

"Worse...but I don't want to bore you with my problems and look who's talking anyway."

"What do you mean?"

"I mean, you ask me about Beverly, as if I'm hiding her or something but where's your 'Mr. Wonderful?' James, right? I thought you two did everything together?"

"Yeah, we do...in fact, James and I had a big fight together right before I left the house," Cheri offered blithely. Feeling a pang of guilt, she added by way of explanation, "Well, to be fair, he's mad at me for coming here tonight without him."

"Can't say I blame him," John empathized. "An unescorted beautiful young woman like you is certainly going to attract a lot of attention from single guys."

"But I'm not unescorted right now, am I?" Cheri countered, immediately kicking herself mentally for implying that John was her escort.

"Look, why don't we forget about all these dull domestic problems and say, 'to hell with them!' How about a dance?" John asked.

And although she knew there was nothing wrong with dancing (was there?), Cheri's heart flip-flopped as she considered John's invitation. They were only good friends, right? Hadn't they just been discussing each other's respective mates? It wasn't like they were pretending Beverly and James didn't exist. They weren't doing anything inappropriate. Of course not. Hell, this was nothing but a bunch of co-workers out having a good time together. And she really felt like dancing. She loved to dance - except with James, who hopped around like a Mexican jumping bean to that spastic punk rock or new wave or whatever you wanted to call it, all of which Cheri passionately detested. But real dancing, to some up-tempo R&B or funky dance tunes, that was fun!

Not waiting for an answer, John got up and moved around the table to help Cheri out of her chair.

"Well, ok, I guess, sure..." Cheri surrendered.

Putting his left arm around her shoulder, John gently guided them past the chairs and tables toward the dance floor. Knowing that he meant nothing by it, having his hand on her still made Cheri feel vaguely uncomfortable. Unobtrusively slipping out from beneath his protective grip as soon as they cleared the tables, Cheri quickened her pace and jokingly commented, "If we don't hurry, by the time we get out there, the song'll be over."

Her backward glance caught John staring at her ass. Embarrassed at being caught red-handed, yet boyishly non-chagrined, he shrugged innocently and said, "Trust me, there'll be another song where that one came from."

Elbowing their way through various cracks in the wall of bodies jammed onto the dance floor, enveloped in the press of sweaty couples, they still managed to carve out a tiny space of their own and enthusiastically threw themselves into the music.

John wasn't the greatest dancer Cheri had ever encountered but he would do. His moves were somewhat outdated - he'd apparently not done a lot of club-hopping of late - yet he was graceful and in control of his body, one of the fringe benefits he'd obviously retained from his athletic past.

Cheri, although slightly disconcerted by the immediacy of John's physical presence and the cramped confines they were forced into together, was enjoying herself thoroughly. It felt great to shake out the last, lingering remnants of tension harbored deep down inside of her from the workweek and domestic front. Hell, it was Friday night! The pounding rhythm and jumping bass lines were all she needed to shed her inhibitions and let herself go. When the first song ended, they stayed for another, then another after that. Soon the two of them had the feel of each other's style and began to dance in more synchronized, coordinated steps. John occasionally reached out and took her hands to guide them through relatively more intricate moves or held her loosely in his arms, ballroom style, as they followed the lead of some of the more accomplished couples around them. It was during one of these movements that Cheri looked over John's shoulder and saw Helen dancing nearby with Ron. She was staring wonderingly at Cheri, a co-conspirator's grin lighting up her mischievous eyes as she nodded her head in approval then thrust her tits forward and shook them at Ron in a blatantly sexual come-on which she laughingly, (she was joking, right?) indicated Cheri ought to try out on John.

Frowning disparagingly, Cheri shook her head and turned away from Helen. She was too much - the nerve of that woman! Did she think Cheri was actually going to go out in the parking lot with John, like some little high school floozy and screw him in the backseat of his car or something?

Not that he wouldn't want to go - there was no mistaking what subject was of 'growing' interest to John. On more than one of their increasingly intimate dance steps she felt his excitement pressing up against her through his trousers. Like a skilled matador, she did her best to stay beyond reach of this bull's 'horn,' spinning and whirling out of harm's way, flashing some leg here, a little thigh there, drawing him in but always darting out of harm's way when he could no longer contain himself and tried to pull her in. Listening to his breathing grow labored, watching the glazed look of animal sexual heat creep into his eyes, slipping out of the clutches of his strong hands, pirouetting closely enough for him to draw in intoxicating whiffs of her perfume, Cheri had to admit that she was excited - exhilarated! - by her proximity to this panting, unthinking beast, thrilled by the danger of working without a cape, only one quick step ahead of disaster. If he actually caught her, would she be able - willing? - to break free of his grasp before he felt the answer he was looking for from her body? Did she dare find out the answer to that question herself?

As if in diabolical response to that query, the DJ sadistically shifted songs, this time putting on an unmistakably romantic 'slow dance' number. John's eyes lit up in amusement as the couples around them melted into various degrees of barely disguised foreplay. Holding his arms open to her, he invited Cheri into his embrace.

"Oh, go ahead - it's not like you're getting into bed together...yet," a familiar voice stage-whispered into her ear.

Turning her head in surprise, Cheri found Helen draped over Ron scant inches away. Scrutinizing Cheri closely, Helen encouragingly whispered, "Go ahead, give the poor guy a thrill. Look how hot and bothered you've got him already! Five'll get you ten he shoots his load by the end of this song."

Remembering John, Cheri turned to find him patiently standing there, arms open. Unconsciously taking a step away from him, Cheri abruptly made up her mind.

"No, I don't think so...I'm awfully sorry, but I've really got to go use the ladies room. John, you'll excuse me, won't you?"

John looked at her...admiringly? (oh, how to resist that look!) - shook his head in chagrin, then let her off the hook by joking, "Hey, if you gotta go, you gotta go."

As she turned to walk off the floor, Cheri again found herself meeting Helen's bemused, appraising gaze.

"Ah, yes, little Miss goody-two-shoes..." she gently chided.

"Yep, that's me," Cheri agreed, edging around the obstacle posed by Helen's swaying (tottering?) body and Ron.

"See you at the table," Helen called after Cheri in her most sugary tone, "and I don't mean under or on top of it!"

Cheri had to laugh at that one. Without turning around, she flipped Helen the bird over her right shoulder and left the dance floor.

In the harsh light of the women's bathroom, Cheri stared in the mirror for a long time, letting her heartbeat slowly return to normal, wondering who this wild-eyed woman was and what she really wanted. With a deep, heartfelt sigh, Cheri turned - suddenly weary - and made her way slowly through the crowd to rejoin her friends.

For the remainder of the evening Cheri hung out with the 'gang' at the table, laughing about work, downing drinks and genuinely having a good time. As if by unspoken agreement, she and John made no more visits to the dance floor. Finally, around midnight, he yawned and got up to leave.

"Why don't you walk me to the door?" he suggested to Cheri as he stood up and stretched mightily, vainly attempting to shake off the effects of the evening's alcohol.

"I'll walk with you as far as the coat racks," she offered gamely.

"Hey - you gotta watch her over there," Ginnie interrupted, slurring her words slightly. "Believe you me, I know. If she gets you by the coat racks, it's all over, Johnny baby - don't fall for that routine!"

"Somehow I think I'll be safe," John commented, "not that I want to be."

"Ok, enough of that," Cheri amicably broke in. "Let's go

hot-shot, I'll escort you as far as your coat."

The crowd had begun to thin out. The two of them made it around the bar and out to the hallway without incident. Finding his jacket and pulling it on, John commented, "Geez, I had a good time tonight - thanks for asking me out, I needed a break from work and... everything else too, I guess."

"Thank Helen, dearie, I didn't know you were going to be here."

"If you had, would you have shown up?"

"Sure, why not?"

"No reason at all - great! Then maybe sometime you'll let me take you out to dinner or something to thank you for being such a great friend over these last few months."

"John Lovingood, are you asking me out?"

"Call it what you like."

"I'll call it a very nice offer from a good friend who ought to be more concerned about finding his keys and his way home safely."

"That's a 'no' then, isn't it?"

"Yes."

John smiled, as if at some private joke, then shoved his hand in his pocket. Feeling around, he grimaced once or twice before triumphantly pulling out his keys.

"Ha - found em!"

"Great - you're on your way then. Be careful."

"Oh, I will - you too, ok?"

"Sure."

"Good night," he told her, turning one last time to look longingly into her eyes.

"Good night," Cheri whispered softly, allowing him the moment.

They looked at each other a few seconds longer - or was it minutes? - until John started to say something, thought better of it, turned and left.

Cheri remained staring at the door until another couple brushed against her making their exit. As if emerging from a deep sleep, she shook her head to clear it, then returned to the table.

An hour later, she pulled down the covers of her own bed and slipped in on top of the cold sheets. Despite the late hour, James wasn't home yet. A momentary surge of worry pulsed through Cheri's mind as she wondered where James was and whether or not she should be concerned because he wasn't home yet. After all, he'd been pretty angry when she'd last seen him.

'Oh well, he and Bobby must have found a band somewhere. They probably stayed to hear the last set. No reason to get concerned yet. He'll probably be home any minute now.'

But James didn't make it home that night.

Yukon Trail

Where the fuck am I now? Oh yeah, the Yukon Trail Bar, a real dive if there ever was one. I kinda feel like I'm waking up out of a dream...you ever get that way when you're partying and you've had a little too much to drink? What the hell am I doing here? Hmmm, that's right, me and Bobby were over at that crummy party some friends of his were throwing but it broke up early. Now I remember. Yeah, even though I dropped Bobby off at his house, I was still furious at Cheri for deserting me tonight so I decided to dawdle a bit before calling it an evening - fuck it, I'll show her! I ain't dragging my ass home all bummed out 'cause she don't want to go out with me, no sir. I'll have a few more beers first and - what the? Who knocked over that pool cue? Me?

Whoa, what's this, it's my shot? Who in the hell is this telling me to shoot? Oh, Christ, it's Winnie, Cheri's ex-sister-in-law. A mean-spirited, scrawny little bitch if there ever was one. I remember her from taking Melanie over to the ex 'in-laws' with Cheri on some extremely awkward holiday visits. I can't stand Winnie but she had the pool table when I got here. What a goddamn incestuous hick town this is. Every freaking person went to high school with every other freaking person in this burg and they all know each other. How's a person supposed to have any privacy in a fish bowl like this?

Whew, am I blasted, or what? Did that shot go in? I don't even know. I guess I drank more than I thought I did at the party...got to hang in there and reorient myself for the drive home. No problem! I'm a big boy and I can handle it. I've had to -

Now what on earth is that commotion over at the bar? Who the fuck is the asshole yelling at? ME? What? Why, you son of a bitch! I know him too - it's Winnie's boyfriend, Jed. He's one of those smug, wise-ass bastards whose teeth you'd like to knock right down their goddamn throat. Fuck you too, punk! You got something you want to say to me? That does it - yeah, you! You wanta get your goddamn face punched in?

I don't recognize my own voice in all the hubbub but I can see we've got the attention of everybody in this hole. But enough sightseeing - in your face, motherfucker! Yeah, you! That's exactly what I said. Whoa, here we go. Come up off the bar stool at me, will you? I've got you now, you ugly monkey. Boom! Down to the floor - how'd we get down here? Hmmm...look - the floor is made out of those little porcelain tiles like you see in bathrooms. Oh shit, who are these other guys jumping in on top of us? Of course, it figures, half of the people in this bar are his goddamn drinking buddies...damn, I should of thought of that - this could be trouble. They can't get at me, though, while I'm wrapped around their boy down here on the floor - and is he fucked up, or what? He can't even barely wrestle but that's ok 'cause this way it's easier to keep him between me and his friends. I guess I'm on my own here, and damn, I can't hear a goddamn thing anymore. Where has my hearing gone? It's like I'm swimming underwater or something. Ok, ok! We're breaking it up. Where in the hell did Jed and his buddies go? Everybody sort of disappeared and now I've got the waitress hollering at me. Jesus, what is she saying?

"Listen, buddy, let me give it to you straight - you better get the hell out of here while you still can and I mean NOW! These are some badass dudes and they are going to fuck you up. Do you understand me?"

She seems extremely serious and somewhat scared. I guess she can't handle these guys short of calling the cops and, after all, that's exactly the reputation the Yukon Trail bar has anyway, right? This joint is always in danger of getting shut down for all kinds of trouble. And I figure she doesn't really want to have to call the cops on her regular customers since I'm the stranger here.

"Ok, no problem. Thanks for the advice. I'm on my way," I reply.

And I am. No biggie. I don't see any of the guys I was fighting with as I casually saunter over to where my coat is hanging on the wall. Everybody I look at sort of averts their gaze except for a couple of 'tough' guys. Fuck you too! That's what I say. I don't doubt, though, that it's a good idea to get out of here while the getting is good - the bartender was right about that. This place is unmistakably hostile.

Man, it's brisk out here in the parking lot. I'd forgotten how cold it was tonight...must be about 10 degrees or so. Whew! Feels good, though, after that smoky bar. Lot's of stars out and the air is so frigid it seems like I could reach up and snap a piece off of it. Now where did I park my car?

Ah, there it is. And nobody followed me out here either - which is a good sign, right? Or is it? Those bastards... who the fuck do they think they are running me out of there? I wasn't doing a goddamn thing except playing a lousy game of pool.

That really pisses me off. I didn't have a goddamn thing to do with the start of that fight - Jed's the loudmouth who started saying some shit to me about God only knows what.

Now I'm getting mad. And those swine are probably in there laughing about how they kicked my ass out of 'their' bar. Those bastards. And they think I'm just going to leave because they're such 'badass' dudes? Fuck that!

The car door slams shut behind me and I'm out in the cold heading across the parking lot. It only takes a second to get to the entrance of the bar. I'm not sure exactly what I've got in mind but I kind of feel like Wyatt Earp, the old Western marshal, you know? Here I am heading into the saloon to clean out the riffraff.

As I return through the door and stroll jauntily over to the coatrack, I catch a number of double takes. Yeah, I'm back! And there's old Jed still looking very unhappy and pissed off sitting with Winnie at the end of the bar. I'll head right on down that way, I think.

The waitress sneaks a quick, skittish glance of alarm at Jed but he gives her a little sign which sorta looks like, 'It's ok - don't worry...I'm not going to start anything.' Or, at least, that's how I interpret it. She turns in relief and gives me a kind of half smile of welcome, nodding her head to acknowledge it's 'safe' for me to return. Ha! I smile pleasantly at her as I make my way past Jed and Winnie to the pool table. And my drink is still sitting there untouched...what luck! No one's even interrupted my pool game. I grab the cue, chalk it up and look out over the table. I can't believe how good I feel. This is the best I've felt since me and Cheri had that fight earlier tonight. I'm all revved up and ready to go!

What's this? Out of the corner of my eye I pick up a flurry of movement...Jed and Winnie are leaving? I have to think this over. Blank. Oh no, Jed, it ain't gonna be that easy. Dropping the pool cue, I hustle out the door right behind them. Where did they go? Ok, they're getting into that car over by the sign. Jed's on the passenger side - good, good, good! I catch up with them about two seconds later, yank open the door and slide in next to him, to his considerable, bleary-eyed surprise. I don't think he knows who I am until I punch him dead in the face.

"Now let's see how tough you are, motherfucker! Ain't no goddamn friends out here to jump on me. Here's another for you," I crow.

Feels good! Feels good! Whack! Whack! Yeah, fuck with me will you? Duck all you want but I've got your ass. Take that you dirty dog!

Whoa! What the...? Who's pulling me out of the car? Bang! Yow, that hurt. Down I go again. Oh shit. Guess I was wrong about his friends not being around. There's a couple of them here...ouch! Was that a boot I just took in the chin? I better -

I must have blacked out. I think it's a minute or two later for some reason. I'm sort of getting dragged around by both arms as far as I can tell and how did that happen? Blank. Blank. Blank. What's going on here? Somebody's whacking me across the top of my head. That's what's going on. I can feel the impact but it doesn't hurt at all. Whoa! And who's this zombie trying to line me up for a sucker punch? I suddenly realize that for some crazy reason I'm smiling. I'm still having a good time!

"Hey," I croak out magnanimously, "Careful now, you boys don't want to cause any permanent injuries, do you?"

Oh boy, that sure pisses them off! Let me drop to the ground again - it's harder to get hurt down here, although getting kicked like this ain't too much fun. Boom! Blank. Ciao!

***

At precisely 3:00 A.M. Wesley hears a knocking sound and instantly comes fully awake. The front door downstairs opens and somebody moves into the hallway. Wesley relaxes because that means it's probably one of his friends either drunk or stoned, looking for refuge. This isn't the first time that's happened. But, damn, 3:00! This better be good. Yet ever the humanitarian, he gets out of bed and starts pulling on his pants.

"Hon, where are you going?" Maureen whispers sleepily as she rolls over and wakes up.

"Somebody is downstairs - knocking at the door."

"What time is it?"

"Three."

"Who could it be at this hour?" she wonders aloud, a small note of alarm creeping into her voice.

"Oh, don't worry, it's just Paulie or Joey or somebody else messed up on something."

He leaves the room and pads silently to the top of the stairs to see who's on the way up. But nobody is coming up...that's odd.

"Psssst - who is it?"

No answer, or was that a groan?

"Wes..."

"Who is it?"

Another groan. Something isn't right. Wesley hustles down the stairs for a better look and finds someone leaning against the door.

"James?"

"Uuuhhh..."

It is James - and what's wrong with him? His entire face is swollen and puffy and there's blood all over everything!

"Holy Christ," Wesley calmly exclaims, having long since seen it all, "what happened to you?"

"Got beat uuuupp..." James mumbles, barely able to open his mouth. Does he look a sight. Wesley turns on the hall light for a proper inspection.

"How in the hell did you get here? You didn't drive, did you? Does Cheri know you're here?"

James stares at him vacantly, seemingly about to pass out.

"Hold on, hold on!" Wesley cajoles, propping James up.

"Wesley, what's going on?" Maureen, worry clearly expressed in her voice, starts downstairs wrapped in a housecoat to see what the problem is.

"It's James. Looks like he's been beaten up. I don't know how he got here - there's a cut on his chin that looks pretty bad...it's bleeding like hell. The front of his shirt is soaked with blood. His jaw looks awfully swollen too. Might be broken."

He turns his attention to James, who is slumping to the floor by this point.

"Here, sit down on the steps," Wesley suggests, guiding him to a more viable resting place.

"Got beat up," James mumbles one more time.

"I don't know, baby," Maureen comments, "he looks pretty bad - I think we better take him to the Emergency Room."

Wesley thinks about his warm bed and how cozy it is beneath the covers with Maureen. He looks at the front door and thinks about the bitter cold night outside. Then he looks at James, sighs deeply and with some degree of exasperation, concedes,

"All right...we're taking you to the hospital, kid. Goddamn children must play. Hey, wake up! Do you have any idea who did this to you?"

James stirs weakly, his voice barely audible, "Guys... couple of guys at the Yukon."

Then, rather curiously he adds, "My fault...my fault."

"Christ, the Yukon! That explains it —damn biker bar. What in the hell were you doing there?"

No further commentary appears forthcoming so Wesley lets it slide. Maureen, meanwhile, has gone upstairs to get dressed. Wesley opens the front door and steps outside for a minute. Brrrrrr!!! Goddamn, it's cold. How did James get here? There's no car anywhere...and why didn't he go to his own house? Wesley realizes his feet are going numb without shoes on so retreats inside where James is quietly mumbling to himself on the stairs. What a mess!

***

It is six o'clock in the morning, dawn's first light not yet in evidence. Cheri is lying in bed wide awake, fear nestled beside her instead of James, when she hears the sound of a car sputtering up the driveway. The sound of the exhaust gets louder as the vehicle comes around the corner of the barn. There is a moment of silence after the engine gets shut off. But what? Is that the sound of another car pulling in?

'If that son of a bitch has brought a party home, I'll...'

Throwing on her blue robe, Cheri jumps out of bed and tries to peer out her window. She sees Maureen, Wesley's girlfriend, helping James out of a black and white Subaru. Something's wrong with James. He can barely walk, it appears...he stands up shakily, obviously in some degree of pain. Wesley is parking the second vehicle - James' car.

Cheri rushes downstairs and has the front door open before they get a chance to knock. She finds Maureen and Wesley practically carrying an extremely disheveled James. A bandage covers his chin.

"Hi," Wesley greets her. "Your boy here got himself in a fight over at the Yukon. Somebody deposited him out at our place last night - although I don't know who yet. Anyway, he was in kinda bad shape so we took him to the emergency room. They put four stitches in his chin and x- rayed his jaw...it's probably not broken. Otherwise, he's only very bruised and battered. Here are his keys. I drove his car here from the bar."

"James...?" Cheri asks, her voice uncertain. "Are you all right?"

James looks up at her groggily as she makes a closer visual inspection. He manages a distorted smile, unabashed, still his normal self.

"Hi...kind of a long night...sorry I'm late. Hope you weren't too worried," he croaks.

Cheri hovers around them as Maureen and Wesley deposit James on the sofa.

"Can I get you two a cup of coffee or something?" she asks them.

"Yes, that would be nice," Maureen replies cheerfully. "I don't know about this one, Cheri, he gets himself into more trouble!"

The Party

Though the party started early and the hour is getting late, a hardcore remnant of the guests demonstrate no interest in departing. In fact, the remaining offenders seem to be settling around the kitchen table for a prolonged powwow, 'encouraged, no doubt, by their host,' Cheri fumes. The two footdraggers - both friends of James from his workplace - are obvious recent victims of Cupid's tender shafts and remain maddeningly oblivious to the pointed hints regarding 'how late the hour is getting' that Cheri directs their way whenever James is out of earshot. Isolated in their infatuation despite being enveloped by the raucous party, the young lovers spent most of the night staring soulfully into each other's eyes or giddily laughing over private jokes as they swigged from the bottle of 'vintage' French wine that Zack announced he'd obtained 'especially' for this evening's festivities. That turned out to mean especially for him and his swooning coquette, since Cheri had yet to see him offer any of his prized wine to the 'rabble,' as she'd heard him so blithely refer to the rest of the gathering during an unguarded moment.

Cheri noted early in the party that Zack appeared to be yet another in the unbroken line of eccentric friends James seemed drawn to, this one pontificating endlessly on all manner of pseudo-philosophical nonsense interspersed with - incredibly! - excruciatingly difficult geography quizzes he foisted upon unsuspecting victims much to their dismay. This behavior, of course, was driven by his desire to show off in front of his equally self-absorbed and smugly opinionated blonde-haired Bambi or Buffy or whatever her name was. Zack - jovial, big, ungainly - was largely content to preen in the spotlight his date cast upon him throughout the evening. Occasionally he made an effort at socializing which merely made people nervous as this rather large, imposing man (unselfconsciously wearing a black beret!) bluntly accosted them with outrageously pompous rhetoric, immediately followed up with persistent requests to 'go ahead, try and name JUST ONE of the islands located exactly half way between Alaska and Russia!'

Yep, he was yet another of the lot that James, inexplicably, seemed to be a magnet for, Jay and Wesley being two other perfect examples. Wesley was hypercritical and unapproachable, the backwoods sage who vastly preferred the company of trees to people (which might explain why he was not in attendance tonight, since he and James seemed rather estranged of late). Jay was brilliantly bookish and brooding, his bleak outlook poorly complemented by his morbid wit and utter lack of empathy for his fellow human beings.

And, come to think of it, there was yet another friend of James' that Cheri met for the first time tonight who unquestionably fit in this same category: Jim, gaunt and bearded, who regarded Cheri with what she interpreted as unconcealed rudeness as she tried her best to include him and his girlfriend in the general conversation. That conversation, not surprisingly, was a thoroughly engrossing discussion about sex, an endlessly entertaining topic among Cheri's friends. They constantly conducted sex 'quizzes' with their colleagues at work, the answers never proving half as amusing as the subject's reaction to being questioned so explicitly about their sex life.

Cheri was only partially kidding when she asked Jim what kind of foreplay he and his girlfriend, Sally, preferred but when Jim's eyes bugged out in embarrassment - considering the rough sledding she'd undergone so far in the face of his frosty silence - Cheri couldn't help but toss out 'cunnilingus' or 'fellatio' as examples of the type of detail she was looking for. Jim regarded her in tight-lipped disgust before abruptly snapping out, "We don't talk about that kind of thing."

Sally, interestingly, did appear willing to talk about 'that kind of thing' but one withering glance from her mate killed off that impulse before Cheri could glean anything revealing.

'Poor girl,' Cheri sympathized, 'stuck with this inhibited son of a bitch. And he's probably boring in bed too,' Cheri concluded, judging by his pained expression and dogged silence when Cheri followed up by asking, "Why - are you having performance problems?"

Sally tittered nervously as Jim glared at Cheri but eager as his date may have been to contribute to the conversation, Jim was having none of it.

Luckily, Cheri's band of friends contributed mightily toward making the party bearable. Helen, Ron, Ginnie and her husband, Benny, played records throughout much of the evening, alternating upscale, George Benson type R&B with funkier dance tracks. They also invented all sorts of new alcoholic concoctions in the blender while gossiping maliciously about the friends of James attending this soiree who'd had the misfortune of coming under their wicked scrutiny.

But all the other guests had long since gone home and the party was down to Cheri, James, Zack and 'Buffy.'

'What is wrong with these people?' Cheri wonders. 'Why can't they take a hint?'

Ok, so what if it looks like this is the first date either one of them has had in months. No matter, Cheri needs to get some rest. Zack and 'Buffy' can go find an all night diner if they want to continue mooning over each other.

Goddammit, though, James is pulling up a chair next to them and looking like he's far from ready to call it quits. His bloodshot eyes and bleary countenance speak volumes about the amount of booze he's put away this evening (not that Cheri has much room to talk on that score).

"Hey, so what's the highest altitude city of the northernmost mountain chain in the southern hemisphere?" Zack badgers James as Cheri slips into the kitchen looking for an opportunity to put an end to the festivities.

James clearly has no idea but determinedly squints his eyes and fakes thought.

"Damned if I know," he finally concedes, "but what's the longitude and latitude of Pago Pago?"

Zack's forehead wrinkles as he vainly searches for the answer, refusing to concede failure.

"Oh ho, so you don't know, do you?" James cackles triumphantly.

"Big deal, a technical detail! Like longitude and latitude matter to a dolt like you."

"Well, I can't imagine any self-respecting geographer not knowing how to figure out longitude and latitude," James reasonably points out.

"But there's the key," Zack exclaims triumphantly. "I'm NOT a self-respecting geographer - hell, I'm not self-respecting at all. That's one of my big problems. Longitude and latitude I can do without."

"Me too," Cheri intervenes, seizing the opportunity to hint once more, that it's time to call it an evening. "In fact, I could have done without it all night," she disdainfully dismisses the subject. "I can't imagine a much more boring topic," she tosses out peevishly.

"Oh, that's right, they don't cover geography in Stephen King novels, do they?" James comes flying to his friend's defense, startling Cheri with the suddenness of his assault and putting her very much on the spot. "You and your disco dolly friends are too cool for that sort of thing, aren't you?" he contemptuously adds by way of a parting shot.

Zack doesn't appear chagrined in the least by her rebuke as Cheri searches her mind for some clue as to why James is reacting so angrily. She reflects guiltily on the time she'd spent flirting earlier in the party with James' drinking buddy, Bobby, the sweeter, younger brother of a fledgling hoodlum Cheri went to high school with. Cheri had been well aware of the fact that James was jealously keeping an eye on her during the entire intentionally prolonged length of that conversation. Maybe Cheri's idle dalliance with Bobby had bothered James more than she'd intended?

But that was still one hell of a nasty, mean-spirited remark for him to throw out there on the floor, wasn't it? Maybe shed also made a few jokes about his friends tonight and that might have pissed him off as well. But here she'd been, dutifully hosting his entourage the entire evening, tolerating their stuck up, elitist attitudes as best as she could. Now he was going to thank her by implying that she was too stupid to understand geography because she read books that people actually enjoyed as opposed to the pretentious crap James liked to talk about reading but never seemed to finish?

"Well, if you're so goddamn smart, then why are you making minimum wage?" Cheri scathingly inquires, her ire unleashed, the cutting edge of her tone visibly startling the two remaining guests who sit romantically holding hands together beneath the table.

James absorbs her insult, starts to say something but then turns away and dismisses her with a contemptuous curl of his lip. That REALLY pisses her off!

"I mean, look at that pile of freaking bills sitting there behind you, Mister goddamn Minister of Finance," Cheri continues spitefully. "Why don't you bring over some friends who are economics majors so they can advise us on something more useful than geography? Then, maybe, we could begin paying off all our goddamn debts and not have to worry about scrounging up gas money every week."

She'd made it personal enough that he had to respond, if only to save face in front of his vapid little friends.

"Oh, yeah, right - like I'm going to work at that place forever?" James begins self-righteously. But realizing how lame that response sounds, he angrily compensates by increasing both the volume and nastiness of his rejoinder. "And, hey, if you don't like our relationship, why don't you get the hell out of it? I don't see any rich sons of a bitches standing around here in line waiting to take my place. Who are you kidding?"

That does it. Is the bastard implying that she - Cheri Melvey! - would have trouble finding another boyfriend? Cheri couldn't remember EVER having trouble finding a boyfriend.

"Who am I kidding? Ha! I can get on that phone right now and replace you in two minutes with another guy making a LOT more money, if that's all I wanted," Cheri witheringly informs him.

The second she says it, she regrets it. She's thrown down a gauntlet she can't pick up.

James hesitates, rattled, like a fighter who's taken a hard shot to the chin and is seeing stars. Cheri experiences a surge of hope - maybe he'll drop the subject! Uncharacteristically she finds herself wishing fervently to sidestep this reckless escalation before doing any further damage. Awaiting James' response she feels like an observer witnessing a glass getting bumped off a table, helplessly watching it tumble through the air, unable to do anything except wait for it to hit the floor and shatter.

"Is that right?" James belatedly challenges, following up his question with a wild verbal swing from below the belt. "Well, if you're such hot shit, why don't you get on the phone and prove it? C'mon, big shot, show us your stuff! Get on that fucking phone and call one of these rich bastards right now, ok?"

When Cheri fails to respond immediately, unprepared for this tactic, James steps up the intensity of his assault.

"What's the matter, can't remember any of their goddamn phone numbers? C'mon, tell me a name and I'll look it up for you!" he shouts in a fury.

Jumping out of his chair, he knocks it violently onto the kitchen floor. Oblivious to the scene he's causing, in a blind rage he snatches up their telephone book from a nearby shelf and shoves it to within inches of Cheri's face.

"C'mon - call!"

Staring into his furious eyes, realizing her complicity in this escalation of emotions, Cheri wants nothing more than to back down and let the moment pass. She's gone too far and is sorry. If he'll provide an opportunity to get them both off the hook, she'll take it. But she has a sinking feeling that it's far too late for either one of them to reverse course.

She mutely appeals to him, deeply afraid of what they're doing, knowing her own capacity to inflict pain, pleading mentally with him, relying on psychic transmission, 'James, stop, enough...please!'

But she can't get past his war mask - James is gone, replaced by an angry, drunken stranger she barely recognizes.

"Look, James," Cheri tries in a more conciliatory tone, "I don't have to -"

"The fuck you don't!" he shrilly interrupts her. "You say you've got guys lined up waiting to replace me? Well, then you go ahead and call one of them right now. C'mon, what's the matter, no guts? GO AHEAD AND DO IT!"

He slams the phone book down on the table with a thunderous crash and looms over her like some kind of crazed, avenging angel.

Cheri doesn't know if it's fatigue or anger or booze or what but when he throws the telephone book down in front of her, a blazing white light explodes behind her eyes, a fiery supernova burning bright. She registers a high keening sound like an alarm going off in her brain and then without further reflection, she's at the telephone dialing an old, barely recalled number. The two guests at the table, meanwhile, regard her like some sort of alien life form suddenly materialized in the kitchen prepared to ray gun them all into oblivion. Their eyes as big as saucers, their mouths hanging open in shock, the two visitors stare at Cheri in disbelief as she finishes dialing the number and turns to insolently face down James while lifting the phone to her ear.

James, though, decides not to stick around to hear whatever it is she has to say, to whoever it is that answers her call.

Bellowing, "FUCK YOU BITCH, I'M OUTTA HERE!" he bolts out the front door before anyone can react, slamming it so hard behind him that every object in the apartment trembles on its perch, teetering precariously prior to gingerly settling back into position. Outside, they can all hear the sound of a car engine gunned to life. Tires spin on gravel, the motor races, the sounds recede and then there is silence.

Except for the tinny voice insistently beckoning at Cheri's ear.

"Yes, hello? Hello? Who is this?"

It's the mother of an old boyfriend that, suddenly, Cheri can't believe she's dialed up.

"Oh, never mind, I'll call back later," Cheri abruptly declares, returning the phone into its receiver violently enough to crack the plastic casing.

Then, without a backward glance she storms upstairs leaving the two new lovers alone to think hard about what they'd just witnessed.

***

James, in the interim, has already gone from blind fury to bitter remorse and the hot stabbing ache of a broken heart. Where he's headed he has no clear idea as the car headlights illuminate darkened roadsides, crumbling stone fences, unlit habitations and the bare limbs of trees hanging overhead, their branches waving dolefully as he shoots past. Outside, the wind whips over the barren terrain, striking up a sorrowful chorus of lamentation, 'Why did you push her like that? Why couldn't you leave it alone? Why? WHY? WHY???'

Arriving at a lonely crossroad, he turns left and drives toward Poughquag and the Shamrock bar. He grimly acknowledges the fact that here is is, a refugee once again, returning to his original haunts in Dutchess County, hoping perhaps that if he starts there he'll be able to retrace his footsteps and understand how this thing between he and Cheri has unraveled.

His bruised and bewildered brain tries fruitlessly to make some sense of the rapid fire sequence of events that led to his speeding down this desolate highway alone in the middle of the night, his entire world overturned. He still can't believe it - he and Cheri through? Yes, through! They've really screwed up this time - cleverly outwitting even themselves, recklessly maneuvering each other into indefensible positions from which there are no means of escape. She'll never respect him again if he comes crawling home begging forgiveness. He has to leave her to exact suitable retribution. It's that simple. No more Cheri and James. No more apartment together. No more coming home after a long day at work to share supper. No more summer evenings sitting on the lawn watching Melanie play on the grassy hillside while he and Cheri laugh and talk and watch fireflies flicker to life along the tree line at the edge of the forest.

Pulling into the parking lot of the Shamrock, he's surprised to note that, for a Friday night, there aren't many cars in evidence. 'Must be later than I thought,' he considers belatedly, realizing suddenly that he has not the faintest clue as to what time it is, other than 'too late' for him and Cheri. Getting out of the car and stalking toward the entrance he recalls the times when he and Wesley frequented this place together. In those days there was always a happy-go-lucky crowd jammed inside, people crowded five deep around the bar, pool players racking up game after game, the jukebox blasting out tunes, drinks flowing freely. But tonight there are only two other people inside, both of whom regard James suspiciously as he steps through the door. He reaches the bar and sits down before realizing what else is wrong - they don't even have the jukebox turned on!

'Is nothing sacred?' he ponders bitterly. 'Isn't there anything left in this world that I can count on?' Almost instantly harsh reality grounds his flight of nostalgia.

'Yes, there is something else you can count on,' his wounded conscience reminds him. 'When you leave this place, your relationship with Cheri is finished, just like your first marriage. Maybe it's YOU that nobody can count on?'

Might that be the case? Were the situations similar? Had he repeated the same mistakes? He didn't think so. His first marriage came apart after he - however unintentionally - emotionally marooned his wife, selfishly pursuing a future that she justifiably concluded excluded her. This was different. He and Cheri were building a shared vision of a future together - right up until the point where he forced her to dial up an old boyfriend. It was all too complicated to think through so he decided upon a simpler solution.

"Hey, let me have a kamikaze, will you?" he asks the bartender, who is busily counting the money he's removing from the cash register.

"Sorry, man, last call was ten minutes ago."

"Ok, make that two kamikazes then," James requests defiantly.

The bartender turns around and stares impassively at James, his experienced ear discerning the solemn urgency of the request. Reacting to the unspoken gravity of the situation, a credit to his profession, he shrugs his shoulders helplessly, as if dealing with events beyond his control. Stepping away from the cash register, he turns, mixes the drinks and slides them across the counter to James.

"That'll be ten bucks and I'd like to get out of here in a few minutes, ok?"

"No problem," James responds, placing a twenty dollar bill on the counter. "Keep the change."

"Thanks," the bartender replies.

James sips deeply from the first of his two drinks. The citrusy tang of the decorative lime peel and the cloying sweetness of the syrupy base do a good job of masking the potent underlying kick of the Southern Comfort.

'Hmmm...a kamikaze,' James considers as he stares ruefully into his plastic cup. 'How appropriate!'

Two drinks and he'll put all he and Cheri have built together behind him. Two drinks and he'll have to walk away from the woman he loves.

***

Cheri lays in her room, staring at the ceiling, wishing to take back all the angry words she'd said, the actions she'd taken, but knowing she can't. She does know James will never forgive her for hurting him this badly in front of his friends. How could he? What kind of man would put up with what she'd done to him? But why had he been such a bastard to her in the first place? What choice had he left her as he bullied her into a corner and then refused to let her out? Wasn't he just as responsible for what happened?

But how to explain her brutally effective counterattack? Were deeper forces at work? Were her scalding words and explosive actions comparable to the shock waves released when opposing tectonic plates finally break free, the violent escape of energy reflecting the lengthy period of stress leading up to the fracture? Had some deep-seated tension in her and James' relationship finally erupted?

'Face it,' she tells herself, 'things haven't been so hot around here for a while.'

But when she considers, 'why?' a logjam of dubious reasons clutter her mind. Over the past weeks she'd felt increasingly hard-pressed and harried, like a canny fox that had joyfully participated in a long, thrilling chase, proudly displaying all the tricks in its vast repertoire, but which now, much to its own surprise, was in danger of finally being run to the ground, the hot breath of the hounds hard on its heels. Why did she feel this way? What was she running from? Was it the fear of having her hard-earned, fledgling identity as a fully independent person wiped out? Was it the fear of making herself emotionally vulnerable to another unpredictable man again? Hadn't she already learned how devastating a mistake that could be?

She also knew she'd not been truly happy since the carefree days of courtship and excitement last summer. Those were wonderful days when she and James enjoyed dreamy trysts beneath the moonlight, days when she felt so alive and invigorated that she had no need to sleep or rest, the two of them staying up late, flirting until dawn, listening to music together, drinking beer, making love joyfully, excessively, compulsively – reveling in the newness of each other, the excitement of the chase.

But now the chase was over. These days when Cheri came home from work she felt exhausted and demoralized. After getting dinner ready and preparing Melanie for bed, she watched sitcoms on T.V. while James read the paper, both of them retiring early, sex the last thing on Cheri's mind most nights. She crawled into bed worried about the rumored layoffs at the factory, fearful of losing her paycheck, her stomach knotting up at the thought of not being able to keep up with the bills, wondering disconsolately if James was ever going to be able to get a decent paying job or if this was a preview of the threadbare lifestyle they'd be destined for together.

James...her heart went out to him. Where was he right now? Had he finally decided enough was enough and given up? Of course he'd return, wouldn't he? But, God, what if he decided to leave her? Did she really want that? They'd had so much fun together, spent so much time and energy patiently getting to know each other. James and Melanie had just as carefully worked out a genuine bond between the two of them. Cheri recalled the wild glee in her daughter's eyes the first time James caught a snake and let her hold it while he carefully explained the difference between poisonous and nonpoisonous snakes to her. Cheri remembered watching the two of them carefully walk across the rooftop peak of their apartment complex, the breeze ruffling Melanie's hair as James held her hand firmly, a huge smile lighting up Melanie's face as she thrilled to the excitement of being so high up on the roof with James, who was inexplicably drawn to heights, to trees, to hilltops.

Cheri also recollected the flowers he'd picked for her, the love that shone so brightly in his eyes when he recognized Cheri behind the wheel of her car at the end of the workday as she wheeled around the corner of the barn to find him patiently sitting there out in front of his apartment with his stupid furniture and plants, waiting for her, wanting her, his mind concentrated on nothing else but his love for her.

They had true love...but alas, the age old question - is 'true love' enough? Would it get them through this terrible night? And if it didn't and she moved on to another guy, would she inevitably arrive at this same point in every courtship? Would changing partners save her from having to face life after infatuation? Was the tedious grunt work involved in maintaining a relationship a burden she couldn't bear?

And did she even have the option of keeping James anymore? A fierce knot of pain and remorse clawed at her insides. How could they possibly recover from the damage they'd inflicted on each other tonight?

***

James opens the door, enters the darkened apartment and flings himself face down on the couch. He isn't going upstairs to her... he can't. There's only one honorable course of action - he's leaving in the morning.

Lying there wracked with misery, he shuts off the emotion emanating from his heart, hiding it away like a gemstone in a strongbox so the damaging effects of this corrosive night won't further dim its once sparkling luster.

Cheri lays in bed quietly listening until she realizes he isn't coming up to her. She knows he won't. There's no further reason to delay. Taking a deep breath, her heart pounding so loudly she's sure he can hear it downstairs, she gets out of bed and pads naked down the hallway.

He hears her feet hit the floor upstairs and follows the sound of her footsteps. She comes down the stairs and into the kitchen. Lying silently on the couch, James braces himself for the worst.

"Don't worry, I'll be out of here in the morning," he woodenly states, launching a preemptive strike without raising his head from the pillow.

Cheri says nothing. He can't tell if she's still standing in the kitchen or has come all the way out into the living room. She's only a few feet away from him when she finally speaks, although he still can't see her with his face buried in the couch cushions.

"James...I –"

"Don't bother! I'll be gone in the morning."

He takes the time to reflect on the irony of the situation. Here he is doing his best to ensure things won't turn out the way he wants. Cheri is normally too proud to plead or beg and now he's cutting off what could be her last-ditch attempt to try and talk this thing out. But what is there to talk about? There's no way to get around what has happened. Talk can't erase that. Nothing she says can make the hurt and shame and humiliation go away. There's only one course of action he can take to regain her respect. He has to leave her. More irony.

Cheri, though, intuitive in the way that a woman can be, already knows they're far beyond the capability of words to save them, already knows there's nothing she can say to change what's happened, so she comes up with something else.

A sob bursting from her throat, she goes to the couch and in an act of supreme frustration, throws herself on top of James and bites him in the middle of his back.

Startled, then transfixed by the pain, James clenches his teeth and refuses to move or acknowledge Cheri's offensive action even as her incisors penetrate deeper and deeper into his flesh, all the anger and remorse and fear and longing between the two of them expressed through their silent complicity in this last, desperate attempt at reconciliation.

Before his skin finally breaks, Cheri releases her bite and gives herself up to helpless, inconsolable crying.

"James, I'm so sorry...I hate that guy - why did you make me do it?" she sobs.

Instantly all of James' guilt wells to the surface. What she says is true. He MADE her do it. And now she's putting aside her own ego to try and save them. Deep inside his chest, one of God's most miraculous creations - the human heart – demonstrates its incredible powers of recovery and renewal.

He fiercely loves this girl. He knows that. He can't bear hearing her crying...the suffering, the sadness, it's all too much to take. Rolling over, he pulls her into his arms and wraps them tightly about her, cradling her against his chest.

"I love you, baby," he whispers, tears running down his cheeks, voice choked with emotion, "please believe me, I love you!"

As if an infected, oozing pustule has been lanced, its poison released, their wound is washed clean by the regenerative power of their intermingled, salty tears.

"I love you too," she whispers.

Long after their tears stop flowing, they cling to each other in the dark. Then they go upstairs to bed together and sleep with the unspeakable relief of prisoners who've been given a last minute reprieve from the executioner's blade.

Bad Juju

Although it's terrifying to contemplate, I must grudgingly admit, fate outdid itself when it came to settling my account. Let me give credit where credit is due - oh, its subtle traps and snares!

The very next Friday, after mine and Cheri's terrible fight, Bobby and I head out together after work. He's an Italian kid who loves to party and run with 'his boys' and although 'his boys' are essentially a merciless pack of young cutthroats, Bobby, at times, displays a considerate, reflective side that elevates him above their mere hoodlum status. I met him at work and hooked up with him to play music together when I found out he was a drummer. Tonight we're scheduled to practice at my apartment (since Cheri's going out to Dick Smith's with her friends again) before catching a band later in the evening.

On our way out to my car, though, Bobby says, "Hey, why don't we stop across the street at Kelly's Lounge before we split? Eddie and Paulie are going over there for a drink or two and Eddie's got some dynamite sinsemilla. I'm sure he'll turn us on if we drop by."

No big deal. We've got all night and my 'baby' won't be home waiting up for me, will she? Hell no. It's a rainy, cold miserable evening anyhow, a drink or two oughta hit the spot.

I drive us over to Kelly's where we spot Eddie's car - a Dodge Challenger - park, and head inside. The bar is packed - it's Friday, work's over and the weekend's begun! Noise and commotion envelop us as we wander through the crowd looking for our friends. We finally spot our colleagues sitting over near the pool tables. And what's this? My old pal Angela is sitting there with Eddie and Paulie. Hmmm...I haven't exchanged a word with her in months. The two of us have completely ignored each other at the workshop since I tossed my lot in with Cheri. Through the grapevine I've heard that Angela broke up with the guy she was supposed to marry but hey, big deal, I don't have the slightest interest in her anymore.

This does pose somewhat of a difficult situation, though, doesn't it? I'd sure hate having to explain to Cheri why I'm sitting in a bar drinking with Angela. Bobby, Eddie and Paulie aren't responsible for my problems, however, so I nonchalantly pull up a chair and psychologically hunker down behind the fact that there's nothing even remotely improper about any of this. I can explain this to Cheri without making it sound like I'm sneaking around behind her back. And if Cheri does find out and it makes her a little bit jealous, is that so bad? Maybe then she'll think twice before running off and abandoning me every Friday night, right?

I don't say anything to Angela as Bobby and I sit down, laughing and making some wisecracks to the guys instead. But, inevitably, the moment comes when Eddie, Paulie and Bobby are all off playing pool and Angela and I are left sitting together at the table. This silence between us is idiotic.

To show there's no element of hostility on my behalf, I turn to her and say, "Well, this is kind of silly, isn't it? There's no reason I'm not talking to you."

"Likewise," she responds with an air of studied indifference.

"As far as I'm concerned," I continue, "there was nothing else that needed to be said between us when we stopped seeing each other. We never talked about that kind of stuff anyhow –" (a little dig there) - "because that was part of the rules, right?"

"Rules? What rules are you talking about?"

"You know, the rules you made up about how we were supposed to get along. I couldn't call you my girlfriend in public, we weren't supposed to act like we knew each other at work, I couldn't ask you about who else you were seeing - those rules. We couldn't burden each other with our personal problems, remember?"

"Well..." she answers slowly, "I'm a lot different now. And I'm sorry I acted the way I did during those days. It was a crazy time."

She looks straight at me with a secret smile on her face and adds in carefully measured tones, "I'd never be that way again."

Who cares? My mind returns to Cheri. I won't even get to see her tonight because we'll both get in so late. God, I'd love to be with her right now instead of sitting in this stupid bar! I hate that goddamn Helen and Ginnie for dragging Cheri away from me every Friday night.

"Excuse me, what were you saying?" I finally blurt out, realizing belatedly that Angela is still talking to me but I don't have the foggiest notion about what.

At that precise moment Bobby and Eddie return and I'm 'saved by the bell.' My quarter is up on the pool table so I head over there, ending mine and Angela's brief conversation.

I win the game in a breeze - the other guy still has five balls on the table when I sink the eight. Bobby's quarter is up next and he comes swaggering over like some sort of cheesy, two-bit mafioso in a gangster movie.

"Hey, James, ready to witness my version of the 'Massacre at Kelly's Corral?' But seriously now, after I wipe you out in this game - don't worry, I'll make it brief and painless - let's roll, ok? Eddie has to split soon but he said we can take a quick ride with him first to catch a buzz. I told you he's got that dynamite 'sense' with him, didn't I?"

"That's why we're here, right? I'm ready to leave anytime."

It's my break. I sink a low ball.

"Don't miss, you won't get another chance," Bobby taunts me.

"Maybe Eddie'll drive us up to the liquor store in Apple Valley plaza so we can get something for the road," I suggest, ignoring his comments.

"Yeah, that's cool - he'll do it or we'll kick his ass," Bobby offers helpfully.

Another low and - a miss! Bobby whistles dolefully and then runs six high balls off the table without interruption.

"You're right about needing to get on our way," I add. "We've got to hit my place before my landlord gets home or we won't be able to practice. He's pretty hardcore about that."

"That fairy...don't tell me you let him push you around? But don't worry - this game's over."

The little son of a gun pops another one in. All he's got left now is the eight.

"Hey, James, check it out. I'll put this one in with my eyes closed."

Damned if he doesn't, too.

"That was for a ten-spot, right?" he coaxes hopefully.

"In your dreams."

We head to the table to get our coats. Eddie, Paulie and Angela get up too and we all make our way out into the steady drizzle. Me and Bobby are razzing Eddie about him having to be home for dinner as we walk across the parking lot in the cold, wet dusk.

"Momma's boy, momma's boy!" Bobby catcalls.

"Yeah? You want to smoke some of this 'sense' or not?" Eddie laughs, knowing full well we do.

"None for me," Paulie interrupts. "Check you guys later - I've got to get to the firehouse."

Bobby jumps right on this opportunity to get in a zinger.

"Yeah, we're worried about that, Paulie, all you sweaty guys using that firehouse crap as an excuse for hanging around together every night. When was the last time they had a fire in Wappingers Falls? C'mon now, tell the truth - isn't that firehouse a cover for your gay commune?"

"Ahh, screw you, Bobby." Eddie retorts disdainfully.

"See what I mean? That's all you guys think about. You're as fruity as they come."

Eddie gets the door of his car unlocked - me and him jump in and grab the front seats, Bobby and Angela get in the back. I didn't realize they'd invited her to come along but I figure, 'oh, what the hell, we'll get high, Eddie'll drop me and Bobby off, we'll be on our way and that'll be the end of it.'

Bobby remembers our other errand too. "Eddie, why don't we shoot on up to Apple Valley so me and James can pick up some brandy - we're hitting the Capricorn tonight to check out a band and we want to be in a good mood when we get there."

"You guys are going to the 'Cap' tonight?" Eddie questions wistfully. "Man, I wish I could go with you."

"Well, you can't, you puss," Bobby busts his chops. "You've got to go home to mama and leave the partying to the real men."

"Speaking of partying," Eddie interjects, "here, try some of this."

He whips out a big doob, cranks up the stereo and we cruise on down the highway to the liquor store. The 'sense' is top quality - it tastes like rank dirt left in a damp cellar too long. We're all coughing our lungs out in moments.

"Holy shit," Bobby splutters. "You trying to kill us with this stuff or what?"

"I told you it was badass!" Eddie laughs. "It'll tear your goddamn head off if you smoke a whole joint."

"Yeah - look at James," Bobby offers helpfully. "He's turning green already. They ain't got no weed like that down in the swamps where he comes from."

We pull up in front of the liquor store and I run in to grab a bottle of brandy to ward off the winter chill. I crack it open upon returning to the car and we pass it around.

"Whew, what the shit kind of firewater is that?" Eddie groans after he takes his slug.

"Peach brandy," Bobby chortles. "Me and James drink that stuff down like soda pop. It's eighty proof! Five minutes from now you won't even know your own name."

"Five minutes from now I better be on my way home for dinner or I'll be kicking your butt," Eddie warns.

"Peach? I thought blackberry was your favorite, James?" Angela comments, remembering that blackberry was what the two of us used to drink together over on the rocks by the Hudson River and on our trips to New Paltz.

"I prefer apricot or peach now - not as much of a medicine

taste," I comment briefly.

"Oh, I see!" she adds, feigning surprise.

The group is in good spirits as we pull out of the shopping center parking lot, the car reeking of cannabis, the windows fogged up and everyone's face flush from drinking and smoking the killer weed. The windshield wipers keep a steady beat as we make the return trip to Kelly's Lounge.

Before we know it, we're climbing out of Eddie's car into the pouring rain.

"I'll see you guys later..." Angela comments as we near the entrance to the bar. "I guess I'm going to go inside."

She seems uncertain about the last part, looking at us hesitantly as if waiting for us to say something.

"Yeah, well, have a good night," I answer casually while continuing on toward my car.

"Later," Bobby seconds, likewise making tracks.

We reach our ride, hop in and I rev the engine a few times to get it warmed up before pulling over to the parking lot exit. I'm peering into the rain, gathering darkness and oncoming headlights waiting for an opening when a sudden sharp rapping on my window startles me.

"What the...?"

I roll down my window wondering if it's somebody me and Bobby inadvertently insulted inside earlier who's come out to settle a score, or the cops, or - but no, it's Angela standing in the driving rain.

"If you guys don't mind," she begins awkwardly, "I only went inside because I didn't want to be a bother. But I don't have anything else I have to do tonight and I don't feel like going home yet so would you guys mind if I went to the Capricorn with you to check out that band?"

I look at her, trying to gauge her intent. She returns my gaze. I glance at Bobby. He shrugs. Some quick mental gymnastics fly around my head - Cheri! What is Cheri going to say about this? She and I trust each other. Nothing is going on. Bobby is here as a witness. Cheri knows I dumped Angela for her. Not that she won't be a little annoyed if I let Angela come along, but Cheri will certainly believe me when I say nothing is going on, because it's the truth. And what the freak is wrong with Angela, has she no shame? Standing here in the rain practically begging us to take her along 'cause she's got nothing else to do? I can't believe she's been reduced to this.

"Well, you probably won't want to go with us because we're heading out to my place to practice for a while first so it'll just be a lot of racket and noise for a while," I stall.

"Practice? I don't mind. You guys forming a band?" Angela asks enthusiastically. "I can't wait to hear it."

Now what? The driving rain is running off her in rivers as she waits for my answer.

"Well, I guess so...all right," I answer hesitantly, not at all comfortable with the situation but certain I can handle it properly.

She hops in the backseat, settles in, lights a cigarette and laughs throatily, "What a car! Not like the old 'Cannon', is it?" she adds knowingly.

Ahhh, the poor old 'Cannon' - that was a truly great ride. Broke my heart when the transmission went.

"It's a little more beat up," I answer curtly, referring to my more than slightly used replacement Volkswagen Beetle.

"No - it's cute," Angela offers ingratiatingly. She's all smiles and flattery and I can't stand it. She can tag along but I'm paying only the most formal of conversational courtesy to her.

I don't know what in the hell she's up to but this is going strictly by the book. I've done my duty as a decent citizen by letting her come with us and that's as far as it goes.

"Yo - James," Bobby breaks in. "Did I hear you say, 'racket?' You're only talking about the greatest up-and-coming rock and roll band in the world."

"Sorry, Bobby, sometimes I forget."

"Yeah, well, just don't let it happen again, ok?"

"Ok, Bobby, that's a promise."

"Cool."

I put the car in gear and pull out on the highway.

***

Three hours later we don't have the faintest idea of where we're at. It seems like we've been driving for days in the pitch dark and a steady, relentless downpour. God, do I hate the winter up here! My gas supply is down to nothing and has been for the last fifteen minutes. Worse yet, I haven't seen an open gas station since we finished practicing and headed out into the boonies looking for this club Bobby was so sure he knew how to find.

"I think it's a little way further...the last time I was here I know we were on some deserted road that looked like this," he's telling me, his voice thick and slow from all the drinking we've been doing.

"Go a little further? We've been by here once already, haven't we?" I ask skeptically.

"Ha! You're right," Angela chimes in. "We passed by here earlier. I recognize this spot."

"We better get some gas soon," I warn. "It's way too cold

and nasty outside to be walking in this wilderness."

"Damn, where is this place? Is that the road? Hell, I don't know," Bobby interrupts. "Shit, I can't believe this. I've been there five or six times. Give me another hit off that brandy, will you?"

The road is completely deserted. I am really worried.

"Look - we've got to head back or we'll run out of gas," I emphasize. "I'm not kidding. We're going in circles - this is where we turned around last time."

I repeat the maneuver.

"Oh, well, we can find some other bar open along Route 9 and stop there for a drink," Angela suggests.

"Son of a bitch," Bobby breaks in, bitterly disappointed and feeling more than a little bit foolish for not being able to find the bar. "I wanted to see that band," he adds morosely. "We've been talking about it all week."

"Any other place with live music in Po-town?" I ask a few minutes later as we motor up Route 9 past the Fishkill mall.

"Not since 'The Good Times' closed last summer," Angela comments.

We catch a break. "Is that an open gas station over there, Bobby-boy?" I ask.

"Yes sir."

"At least we won't have to worry about running out of gas."

"I can't believe we couldn't find The Capricorn," Bobby groans one more time. "I can't frigging believe it."

***

We end up in Poughkeepsie at another local establishment, 'The Earl's Court,' located across the street from Vassar College.

At least there's some excitement and life here (albeit no live music), in large part due to the fact that it's within walking distance of the college. It's a little past midnight and this place is jammed with students and 'townies.' Bobby knows the bartender here and it pays off as we get served some ass-kicking, powerful drinks. There's such a crush of people in this joint that there's no hope of finding a place to sit. The stereo system is cranking at top volume and combined with the shouts and cries of the well-lubricated, standing room only crowd, this makes for a considerable din. Which is fine with me as I hang out by the bar sipping my drink. Where Angela is at this juncture I have no idea. She was still with us when we got here but I haven't seen her since. It has to be obvious to her by now that although she's been allowed to tag along, neither Bobby nor I intend to provide her with any sort of intimate companionship.

After about an hour at 'The Earl's Court' Bobby decides it's time to walk around the block to yet another hangout for the late night party crowd. Angela materializes out of nowhere as we make our way to the door and informs us that she's run into some old friends and will get a ride from them back to her car. Thanking us for letting her hang out all evening she disappears into the crowd again.

As Bobby and I walk out the door some asshole follows us swearing up a storm aimed in Bobby's direction. It's not clear to me whether he's pissed off about something that happened tonight or if this is some old, unsettled grudge we're dealing with here but since I'm not in the line of fire I can simply stand by at the ready and wait for events to unfold. Out of nowhere the guy suddenly throws a drunken punch at Bobby but it misses by a mile and before things get out of hand a bunch of people jump between them and haul the irate fellow back into the bar. Good thing too - a patrol car noses around the corner and cruises slowly down the block in our direction as Bobby laughs it off and we continue on our way.

It's cold out here too! We're about frozen by the time we cover the distance. In the spirit of warming up we get into a wrestling match outside the new place. Something to do with the hockey series between the N.Y. Rangers and Philadelphia Flyers, I don't know exactly. We end up lurching around the pavement, banging off buildings, having a grand old time, drawing a drunken, cheering crowd before we arrive at a stalemate and head inside for another round of drinks.

Turns out Bobby knows the bartender here too, so we end up drinking more powerful firewater - there are advantages to partying with the local crowd! This place is a zoo, too. Where do all these people come from at this time of the morning? I even run into Billy, Cheri's 'ex', which isn't a problem because we get along fine. In fact, I kind of like the guy. We exchange pleasantries, I introduce him to Bobby and we go off on our separate ways. The night rolls on in a hazy, pleasurable blur until, before I know it, some bozo is hollering, "last call!"

What, two o'clock in the morning already? Where does the time go?

Bobby and I join the crowd (considerably thinner by this point, I have to admit) emptying out into the freezing cold again. We've got enough energy left for one more titanic wrestling match that ends up with the two of us crashing through some hedges across the street before we call it quits.

Hopping in my car, we roar away into the night, both of us too tired to talk. I drop Bobby off at his Dad's house and arrive home myself shortly before three a.m.

And you know what? Cheri is home. My spirits soar - all is well! I'm grinning crazily as I try to slip into bed without waking her up. I pass out before my head even hits the pillow.

***

But in the morning, all is not well. Cheri is in the kitchen when I wake up groggily to a new day. More than slightly hungover, I go downstairs looking for some aspirin.

"Oh, so you finally decided to wake up this morning, did you?" Cheri questions me sharply. "And you've got a nice headache too, huh?" she observes, watching me search through the medicine cabinet.

I judiciously refrain from answering, preferring not to provide Cheri with any additional ammunition, neither confirming nor denying her hypothesis.

"Well, I'm not surprised, considering all the noise you made coming upstairs and getting into bed last night," she continues undeterred. "I don't care what time you're out to but can't you at least have a little damn consideration when you come home that late? And I suppose you were driving too, in that condition? One of these nights you're going to get a DWI. I swear to God, I don't know why you get behind the wheel when you've been drinking like that."

All thoughts of reconciliation and a nice Saturday immediately go out the window. I'm stung by her criticism and retreat into a defensive posture.

"Yeah, well, if I had a girlfriend who'd spend a little time with me I wouldn't be out driving around partying on Friday nights, would I?"

"Jesus Christ almighty, is that the only thing you know how

to say? Aren't you ever going to get tired of trying to make me feel guilty about that? It isn't my goddamn fault you have to go out and get drunk with your buddies, so don't you try and blame me for it."

She's on a roll, keeping me on the defensive, not giving me any room to maneuver. I decide to launch a counteroffensive of my own, hoping to shake her confidence a little.

"Speaking of drinking buddies, guess who ended up driving around with us last night?" I question smugly, certain I've got just the thing to put a little crack in her armor.

"I have no idea."

"Angela."

Cheri stops dead in her tracks and fixes a stricken stare on me. Tears instantly well up in her eyes and she covers her mouth with her hands.

"Oh, my God," she moans softly. "Oh, my God."

Like a little kid who's played a prank that suddenly veers horribly out of control, I scramble to undo the damage.

"Nothing happened! Ask Bobby, he was with me the whole time. She was at Kelly's lounge with Eddie and Paulie and asked if she could go to The Capricorn with us to see a band. How could we say no?"

Cheri is crying softly, grief-stricken, not listening to a word I've said.

"Cheri, I swear, nothing went on!"

"James, I wish I could believe you," she manages to whisper, her voice barely audible, hurt and pain frozen on her face. She stares at me as if I'm a complete stranger standing in her kitchen and I feel my stomach drop out a hole in the bottom of my gut. I'm terrified by the damage I've done.

"You see what happens because of this goddamn bullshit of

going out separately on Friday nights?" I holler shrilly. "Are you happy now? This never would have occurred if you were with me. I can't fucking stand this - nothing went on between me and Angela!"

But I can't take the words back. Tears still trickling from the corners of her eyes - God, please make her stop doing that, it's breaking my heart! - she shakes her head slowly from side to side, cuddling herself with her own arms, rocking herself mutely. This is killing me. It's killing her.

"Cheri, I..."

"Oh, God, I can't take this!" she cries out, sobbing openly as she runs for the stairs. I start to follow but she turns, eyes blazing, and screams, "Don't you come up here! Leave me alone - I thought I could trust you."

I'm left standing in the kitchen, a helpless bystander at my own train wreck, aghast at the destruction I've caused. Twenty or so minutes later, she comes downstairs again, eyes red from crying, strangely subdued. She says she accepts my statement that nothing happened. But she refuses to look me in the eye. We spend the rest of that Saturday in silent, lonely misery unable to console each other. The crevice between us has widened into a chasm. I can barely see the other side anymore.

Coup de Grace

Endicott Sylvain organizes the 'live' entertainment for the annual Christmas party at the sheltered workshop for retarded citizens where I work. These are uproarious affairs that generate a genuine holiday spirit. The workshop provides employment opportunities for mentally handicapped individuals with conditions ranging from Down syndrome to traumatic brain injuries. These 'clients' get paid by the piece to perform menial tasks such as inserting books into display boxes or stapling right and left hand gloves together prior to packaging. Staff members such as myself instruct the clients on how to properly perform the jobs to meet the quality standards of the companies subcontracting this labor to our workshop.

A 69 year old retiree, Endicott works part time picking up a little extra cash to fund his hobbies, one of which happens to be guitar playing. He has a beautiful Gibson semi-hollow body six-string and a full assortment of effects pedals to go with it. While he is by no means a virtuoso on the frets and his tuning is purely hit or miss due to a partial loss of hearing in one ear, he's an enthusiastic and dedicated amateur musician.

A wiry, intense guy with a wonderful, expansive sense of humor and an unabashed love for the art of bullshitting,

Endicott thrives on cutting up with the younger guys and gals on our staff at work. Never in a bad mood, he comports himself with the ease and assurance of a man entirely satisfied with his station in life. He's a 'senior citizen' in the most revered sense of the phrase, a good man who's lived a long, productive life, raised a fine, upstanding family and who still can't resist taking various 'stray' youngsters (such as myself) under his wing.

A year ago, I was a goner the instant Endicott learned I was a fellow musician. I'd not been working with him a week when the first of his 'annual' workshop Christmas shows came into being. Somehow he'd opened his mouth and got himself stuck with a commitment to play carols and gospel favorites in front of the staff and clients. Desperate for accomplices as the day of the performance approached, he'd somehow discovered that the new kid on the staff (me) played guitar. On the day of that first Christmas show he bedeviled me all morning until I agreed to go home at lunchtime and get my guitar to join him as part of the afternoon's musical entertainment. We practiced all of thirty seconds and let me tell you, it takes more than thirty seconds to blend influences as diverse as Count Basie (his) and the Sex Pistols (mine).

But God watches over those with good intentions. I remember laughing hysterically and having a helluva good time throughout our performance. We were a rocking, rollicking success and the event was elevated to the status of an 'annual' affair.

This year Endicott's bass-playing son and two saxophonist friends are joining us. I also scored the stunning triumph of getting my buddy, Bobby, to play drums. This will be Bobby's first public performance and he isn't sure about debuting in front of a few hundred writhing and hollering clients. I was nervous this morning when he showed up (he's a fellow staff member at the workshop) without his drum kit but after convincing him that his name was 'mud' if he didn't play, he relented, protesting all the while, "I don't know, James - for chrissakes, Christmas carols don't have beats, do they?"

"Don't worry," I kept reassuring him, "it'll be just like when we practice at the house except you'll have hundreds of fans going wild! Just follow whatever beat Endicott sets and I guarantee you'll have a great time."

Bobby regarded me dubiously but finally conceded, "maybe I'll just bring the snare and a high hat."

We pick up his drums at lunch time. Cheri, in fact, takes us over to get his stuff. She's running some errands and needs me to cash my check since she's going out with her crew again after work (yes, Friday night the week before Christmas - rest assured, I'm not too happy about that either).

By the time Bobby and I return with his drum kit the workshop is a madhouse, clients running all over the place dressed up in their Sunday best following the luncheon buffet set up by the Board of Directors - roast beef, ham sandwiches, salads, cakes, the works. I'm telling you, this Christmas performance is a big thing in our little neck of the woods.

Another tradition the staff indulges in on this particular day is getting shit-faced, stumbling drunk. Bottles are hidden in every nook and cranny of the building for discreet 'sipping' in the morning and flat out guzzling in the afternoon. Prior to the musical performance a number of us knocked off a bottle of white wine as well as a jug of vodka and orange juice hidden in the tool shop.

But not to worry - the show goes great! We blast out favorites ranging from 'Rudolf the Red-Nosed Reindeer' to 'God Rest Ye Merry Gentlemen,' all at an ever more frenetic, ever more rambunctious pace, the clients screaming and moaning and shaking in a world of their own as the band gleefully pours fuel on the fire. In between Christmas carols, we take the crowd through Endicott's favorite gospel and popular tunes and finally, having exhausted Endicott's set list, Bobby and I throw in some Ramones and Clash numbers. The other participating musicians fit right in as we freelance our way through one of the most enjoyable, entertaining Christmas parties ever. As we return the reins to Endicott for his closing remarks, everyone in the audience is drenched in sweat from their fevered dancing and gyrations.

Bobby and I migrate to the tool room, basking in the congratulations of our fellow staff members and rejoining them in the - by now - serious drinking that's going on. There's more vodka and other hard stuff and the day begins to blur and slip in and out of focus, faces becoming redder, people offering effusive holiday toasts as the booze flows and tongues loosen. Our organization has completely broken down by midafternoon. Buses finally come and pick up the clients. It's time to call it a year. The workshop closes down for the week between Christmas and New Year's Day and everyone on the staff heads off on their separate ways to celebrate the holidays.

Unfortunately for me, as the day goes on, my gloom increases steadily. Yes, the party was a blast, but so what? Cheri isn't going to be home when I get there and my stomach knots up whenever that thought crosses my mind. Oh sure, she has her reason - the people where she works are having their very last Christmas party together. It's been announced that their semiconductor manufacturing plant is closing permanently come the new year and everyone is getting laid off. I can understand her wanting to be with those folks on this poignant occasion. But to me, it's merely another Friday night without Cheri. Another night of wondering what is happening to us.

By three o'clock in the afternoon the clients are all gone and it's like Grand Central Station in the tool room. All my drinking buddies are there, along with the agency director, the executive director, the secretarial staff, other group supervisors and... Angela.

Angela. God, I could strangle her! I can't help but blame her for the fissure that has widened dangerously in my relationship with Cheri. The night Angela went out with me and Bobby shook Cheri badly. I saw the loss of trust in her suddenly distant eyes and felt the icy wind of separation blowing between us. The signs of serious trouble were there before, yes, I admit it. But that night - innocent though my role in it may have been! - that night I hurt Cheri. Despite my fervent, impassioned explanations and excuses, I damaged Cheri's trust in me.

I look at Angela now - why, why, WHY did she ask to come with us on that fateful evening? What was I supposed to do? How could so small, so innocuous an act, such a few brief words, 'Yes, all right, you can join us,' lead to such disaster? How could my world disintegrate so quickly? Why doesn't Cheri believe me when I say nothing happened? I've never lied to her. I've never been interested in another women since I've been with her. I love her. But she won't be home when I get there tonight to tell her that. She's never home anymore.

The end is near. One innocent mistake. Our ship glanced off an iceberg - a gentle bump - what possible harm could it cause? Yet below the waterline, the sea floods in through our fractured hull, a list slowly develops. Up on the deck, it's a beautiful starry night but beneath the surface, our vessel is irreparably damaged. It's only a matter of time until the ocean inexorably sucks us down beneath the waves.

Who'd have imagined it working out this way? We tried so hard. We really did. We loved each other. And to what grim end?

They're breaking open another bottle of wine. Someone calls out, "Merry Christmas, Merry Christmas to all!"

The events that follow are unclear. I remember staying at the workshop until well after four o'clock in the afternoon, drinking steadily with my buddies all the while. When the party finally breaks up, the group decides to move the festivities across the street to 'Kelly's Lounge.' Eddie's giving me a ride home (Cheri dropped me off at work because all my musical equipment didn't fit in my car) so I don't have much of a choice when he decides to stop by the lounge with the others. I have only a spotty recollection of being at Kelly's, perhaps some merciful subconscious filter blocking out memories of my most recent disaster there when Angela asked Bobby and I to let her hang out with us. Eddie finally drives me home, that much I recall.

The apartment is dark and deserted (what else is new?) when I unlock the door and go inside. There's no sign of my buddy, Jay, anywhere. He's supposed to join me for dinner tonight at my place. I called his place earlier from Kelly's Lounge, leaving a message with his roommate informing Jay that I was running a little behind schedule. I call Jay's apartment again but no one answers. Either he didn't get my message or else he's on his way. No matter, I'm hungry, so I decide to go ahead and prepare the meal. In the refrigerator I find steak marinating along with a bowl of sliced peppers and onions. Cheri had offered to help me by preparing dinner ahead of time, knowing Jay was coming by. Wasn't that gesture worth something?

How pathetic that these tiny shards of hope are all that I have to cling to. How utterly sad. Two lost souls slowly drifting further and further apart...to what end? I picture Cheri's beautiful face. I vividly recall the spring day I moved in next door and how we fell in love out there beneath the pine trees.

But our love is dying. I wake up every day afraid of the new problems it will bring Cheri and me. What new stress lines? What new hurt or slight? I keep telling myself, 'it's nothing personal - she swears it's not our relationship that's flawed.'

Sure...and the Titanic just needed a few more lifeboats.

***

I wake up. It's late. What's that smell? Coughing, I sit up, groggy, bleary-eyed but conscious that something is wrong. Why can't I see? And what IS that horrible odor? Suddenly it dawns on me - the apartment is full of smoke. What? The pepper steak! Oh, my God, I fell asleep again with food cooking on the oven.

Rushing out into the kitchen, I discover it's not too late - there's no fire licking at the walls. Only two blackened, heat-warped pans with thick plumes of acrid smoke billowing up to the ceiling, nothing left of the meal but ashes.

Looking at my watch I see that it's 11:30 p.m. I've been asleep on the couch for four hours. What ever happened to Jay?

But back to the present, man, what a stink! The smoke is so thick I can't even see across the room. Shutting both burners off and putting the scorched pots in the sink, I run cold water in them while opening the front door to air out the apartment. It's a futile gesture though, something to do with the finish on the pots. The biting, plastic smell stings the nose and clings to everything. The meal is a total loss. Twelve dollars worth of steak reduced to cinders. Cheri's attempt to help me out with dinner - buying the ingredients, chopping up the vegetables, marinating the steak - all for naught. What a disaster.

I hear a car coming up the driveway (I'm used to listening for that sound these days) and I know it's her. She is going to flip out when she walks into this mess. And she's even early, like she said she'd be. She tried. A little, at least. I hear the car door open and then slam shut. The click-clack of her heels echoes on the concrete walkway.

Cheri comes through the door and immediately recoils in confusion. Her eyes squint as she fans the smoky air trying to determine why the door is open and smoke is pouring out into the night. She sees me standing in the middle of the kitchen, red-eyed, and instantly she figures it out. She storms into the kitchen, temper absolutely at the breaking point.

"Uh-huh, uh-huh, uh-huh! Where's Jay?"

Oh yes, I know the tactics so well. Curt, biting tone, tightening of the jaw, vicious glare. When she's really mad she takes her time, setting up the kill perfectly, leaving no fact uncovered, no screw-up hidden.

"You passed out, didn't you? All that food ruined? Great, just freaking great!"

She slams a few things around in the kitchen, pocketbook here, coat there, working herself into a fury as she looks in the sink assessing the damage.

"Two pans ruined? Unbelievable."

I know I should keep my mouth shut - this is going to push

her over the edge, but I can't help myself.

"The pots aren't ruined," I assert defiantly, pissed off myself, ready to fight.

She loses control of her voice slightly, lashing out in an uncontrollably loud, harsh manner, "Not ruined? They're supposed to come with the paint burned off of them and the sides caved in? Not to mention, you could have burned the place down!"

"Big goddamn deal! Who gives a shit? Not you, that's for damn sure - 'cause you'd be here if you cared. Maybe if my so-called girlfriend wasn't out running around all over town with God knows who, I'd never get in this condition in the first place, you know what I mean? So fuck you too! And by the way, just who WERE you out with at this hour? 'Don't worry, I'll be home early tonight, dear!' Bullshit!"

"I can't believe this," she states, shaking her head in genuine wonder. "You almost burn the house down and try to blame me? You nasty, stupid shit! I can't stand it anymore. I want you out of here tomorrow, ok? I mean it."

Without a backward glance she whirls around and heads up the stairs. After a moment I sit down at the table, my mind spinning. I can't believe this is happening. Tomorrow is Christmas Eve.

***

There is nothing left to accomplish downstairs so I follow her up to the bedroom, conflicting impulses darting crazily through my brain, disbelief foremost among them. Did she really tell me to move out? I come through the door into the bedroom assuming a forced attitude of calm. I did, after all, almost burn down the apartment, which was, when all is said and done, inexcusable. I swear I'll remain patient and clear-headed until we get this resolved.

Cheri doesn't so much as glance up from the book she's reading as I slip in beside her.

"Out?" I ask impatiently. "Is that what you want?"

She keeps reading.

"Listen, if you don't want me here, then I don't want to be here," I plow on. "Why waste our goddamn time? You want me out of here, just say so."

Cheri lets the book drop down on the covers.

"James. Get the fuck out of here. All right? Are you happy now?"

Ka-boom! That one caught me completely by surprise. Suddenly I'm hopelessly tired and depressed, beyond further expression of emotion one way or another. Who in their right mind would want to stay in a relationship that has degenerated to this point? And to think, God gave both of us a second chance...what a shameful waste. Lots of people aren't lucky enough to meet someone they can fall in love with once, never mind twice. And here we are pissing it away. That's what tears me up inside. Why?

We lay there in silence for a considerable time. Cheri finally reaches up and turns out the reading light. I no longer possess the mental energy necessary for concentration so I let my mind drift aimlessly over the events of the evening, unable to comprehend the enormity of what's been said.

Cheri moves, settling into another position and I can tell she's still awake. I know it'll be a while before I can sleep - the anxiety has my mind racing uncontrollably. Inexplicably, I'm having a flood of tender, protective thoughts about her. I can't help but admire her fierceness, her raging, unrelenting struggle. If only I knew what she was struggling against. But even then I don't think it would help us because I'm afraid it's 'life' she's fighting against and the choices it forces us all to make and live with.

Entirely unexpectedly, I feel her hand softly touch my leg. She snuggles up against me under the covers. She's still trying – maybe it's not over yet!

I put my arm around her and pull her closer.

"Goodnight, baby," I whisper, longing for nothing so much as the merciful release of sleep.

"Goodnight," she whispers, inching still closer.

We fall asleep huddled together like two orphans seeking solace on a cold winter's night.

Fini

Melanie and I spend the better part of the next morning tromping through the snow-covered woods near our apartment in search of the 'perfect' Christmas tree. We closely examine each spruce and pine and fir we come across, wanting a tree tall enough to command respect in our high-ceilinged front room but not so tall that it won't fit. And yes, the selection and decoration of the Christmas tree should have been done weeks ago but such is the tattered state of mine and Cheri's domestic affairs that neither of us made the time to attend to the task earlier, so here Melanie and I are on the day before Christmas trying to complete this most basic of yuletide preparations.

Our progress is made all the more difficult by the fact that a recent heavy snowfall has bent many smaller trees nearly to the ground, leaving me uncertain as to whether they will recover their upright state once thawed out. Melanie does not understood all the subtleties of the selection process and is puzzled as I reject tree after tree for apparently spurious reasons. Good trouper that she is, though, she gamely clomps through the snow behind me, cavorting about and amusing herself in the picturesque winter wonderland. It's a beautiful afternoon, the sky as blue as it can be, the sun shining down on a picture-postcard perfect 'White Christmas' holiday scene. I would enjoy it too if my heart wasn't so heavy with foreboding.

Cheri is at the mall finishing some last minute shopping while Melanie and I handle this outdoor work. Today neither Cheri nor I mentioned the scene we went through last night, avoiding that subject throughout the morning, drifting along in our own private, disconnected worlds, neither of us capable of any more fighting.

By the time Melanie and I accomplish our mission, settling on the 10-foot-tall crown of a much larger tree, the late afternoon light has faded and the shadows are lengthening in the forest. When we get to the apartment Cheri isn't home yet. It takes me a while to help Melly out of her boots and snowsuit and into her pajamas but finally we get around to breaking out our decorations. Cheri arrives home in time to help us trim the tree with tinsel and ornaments and brightly colored electric lights. It's almost enough of a cozy holiday scene to make us forget the night before.

But not quite. The decorating over, the three of us are standing around in the kitchen preparing dinner. I feel a sharp stab of guilt as Cheri pulls out the battered frying pan she gamely salvaged (scrubbing and scouring for what seemed like hours) from my cooking disaster last night.

We're making our favorite dinner for 'special' occasions. Melanie is helping me peel shrimp one moment, helping her mom melt butter for scallops the next. There is little in the way of conversation.

The telephone rings and Cheri catches it immediately.

"Hello? Oh, hi, Ron! Merry Christmas to you, too. What? Oh...where is she now? At her mother's, I assume. Haven't you heard from her since she went down? No, not that kind of 'down,' you idiot!"

Laughing and smiling, Cheri retreats behind the downstairs bathroom door, fully absorbed in the conversation, phone cord trailing behind her. I start getting madder and madder. How can she be so downcast and quiet with her family but so upbeat and enthusiastic chatting with some damn virtual stranger? The poor guy is alone on Christmas Eve, so I guess I shouldn't be a total Scrooge about him wanting to talk to someone but dinner is almost done, Cheri isn't paying any attention to us and listening to her giggling with Ron isn't helping my mood any.

Twenty minutes later they're still gabbing away. Dinner is long since ready. I put the dishes and glasses out on the table creating as much noise and commotion as I possibly can. Getting the hint, finally emerging from the bathroom, still laughing, Cheri exchanges a warm Christmas wish with Ron before hanging up and coming to the table.

"That Ron, he's impossible," she offers gamely. "I've told him I'm not going to discuss the subject of him and Helen any longer. He's got nobody to blame except himself for these problems - she told him she was married on their second date."

"Yeah, but it's what they did on the first one that counts, isn't it?" I retort.

Sensing from my clipped tone that the subject isn't a good one, knowing my feelings about Helen and Ron and her hanging out with them, Cheri switches topics.

"How's the shrimp, baby?" she asks Melanie, who's happily gnawing on a butter-sauce garnished crustacean.

"Good, mommy, good."

"How's yours?" she asks me.

"Fine," I tersely reply, still angry about her prolonged phone call with Ron.

We lapse into silence, no topic safe enough to broach without risking controversy or argument, the atmosphere so oppressive and claustrophobic that conversation, which used to be a joy for Cheri and I, is essentially impossible. At times like this I understand perfectly well why she enjoys hanging out with Helen and Ron and their entourage. With them she can talk freely, laugh and joke without the suffocating weight of a dying relationship hanging around her shoulders. She doesn't have to bicker about where she's been or what she's doing. She can go out, have a few drinks, a few laughs and let the rest of the world get along without her.

The phone rings and Cheri quickly jumps up from the table to grab it. It's her mother. Cheri picks one more scallop up off her plate and deposits the dish in the sink before closeting herself behind the bathroom door with the telephone once again.

Melanie takes the opportunity to run off and amuse herself in front of the television. I finish eating our 'special' holiday meal alone then silently gather up the dishes and place them in the sink, anger and bile burning a hole in my stomach as I bite back words that I know will only inflame the situation. As I'm washing the dishes, Cheri remains in animated conversation behind the bathroom door.

What was that? Something Cheri says to her mother catches my ear - "I don't think it's going to work out. No, I'm going to tell him after this weekend."

I can't believe I heard that! Tell me what? That it's over between us? Paralysis sets in and all my efforts are directed towards sucking in a big gulp of air so that breathing can resume. The lights on the Christmas tree seem to flicker and pulse momentarily as the room spins around me.

That's it. I heard her say the words. Cheri has given up. A long, tearing stab of pain works its way from my throat and chest down to my gut.

I find myself suddenly bellowing, "You're going to tell me WHAT after this weekend? That it's over? That you've given up? Goddammit, then tell me now!"

Cheri peers out from behind the bathroom door, startled.

"Go ahead and tell me now!" I rage. "Don't wait until after the weekend - have the guts to tell me now."

Comprehension, then anger, flickers across Cheri's face. Pressing the earpiece of the phone against her side, Cheri explodes, "Oh, so now you listen to my phone conversations too? Why don't you mind your own goddamn business?"

She slams the bathroom door in my face. I stalk angrily into the living room and sit down, stunned, on the couch. Melanie remains wrapped up in her T.V. show, studiously ignoring the goings on around her. Poor nut, she's such a good kid! Why should she have to suffer because of mine and Cheri's inability to function as responsible adults? All I can hope is that Melanie doesn't understand what's about to happen to her world as we go through the charade of celebrating Christmas Eve like a real family.

This is all too much for me to comprehend. I've had time to prepare myself for this moment but still can't believe it's happening. I find myself staring at the blinking tree lights again. For God's sake, it's Christmas Eve!

The bathroom door opens and Cheri charges out to slam the phone down on the receiver. Without a word to me she makes a big show of Christmas cheer for Melanie's sake and then carts her off to bed.

I sit on the couch seething, staring blankly at a newspaper, trying to distract myself.

'No more hollering,' I vow. No more recriminations.

Cheri comes downstairs and takes a seat on the big chair near the couch. I remain buried in the newspaper. Five minutes of silence go by before she finally speaks.

"So what are you going to do? Read the paper all night?" she finally breaks in.

"Yeah, that's right. I'm going to read the paper. What's it to you?"

I'm amused at how calm I sound. No emotion. I like that.

"We have to talk about...things," Cheri states neutrally.

"What's there to talk about? I'm calling my brother to come pick me up in the morning. I'll be out of here by noon."

"You're calling your brother...?"

She actually sounds shook by my statement. Odd response, isn't it? Especially in light of what she said to her mother.

"Oh, come on Cheri! You're on the damn telephone telling your mother it's all over between us, that you'll wait until after the weekend to tell me and what the hell am I supposed to think about that? You don't have to hold goddamn secret conferences to get me out of here - I'm gone. Wish I could say it's been fun, but I can't remember that far back."

I return to the pages of my newspaper, preparing myself for whatever new verbal salvo she's prepared to fire. Strangely enough, though, we sit in silence for a minute or two before she quietly continues.

"James, I don't know what you heard but you didn't hear me say anything to my mother about me and you being through."

She sounds sincere enough, in fact, she seems close to tears. Is she telling the truth? I haven't even considered the possibility that she could have been talking about some unrelated matter that I've misinterpreted.

"So you're saying I heard wrong? You have no desire to break up with me? Who were you talking about then?"

"I don't remember what we were talking about when you interrupted me but it wasn't that."

We sit quietly digesting each other's comments. I idly turn a page of the newspaper as Cheri sits quietly pondering our fate.

"What am I supposed to tell Melanie?" she asks in a quavering voice. "That I broke up with her father first and now I'm taking you away from her too? She loves you so much...oh, God, how will I tell her?"

"You should have thought about that a long time ago," I answer coldly, aware only of the fact that Cheri is passing up the opportunity to reassure me about the two of us staying together. She is choosing, instead, to worry about her own tactical problem of explaining my apparently imminent departure to Melanie. I can only assume by her questions that Cheri accepts the fact that we're through.

"What are you going to tell her?" she asks me. "That it was all my fault? That you hate me? Will you hate me?"

I have to laugh - more out of surprise than anything else.

"Hate you? Of course I'll hate you! All the time we've spent together - wasted? All the effort we've put into this relationship down the drain? And you can't even tell me why it's over?"

I'm getting angry again thinking about it and although I know I'm raising my voice, I can't help it.

"Hate you? You're goddamn right - I'll hate you the rest of my life for taking away what could have been the best thing I ever had," I rant on.

"Then don't leave me. I don't think you should do this."

I can scarcely believe my ears. Now she's telling me not to go? Even though these are the words I've been dying to hear, I don't feel any better. Cheri seems tired, confused, defeated. I'm not convinced that she means what she's saying.

"Stay for what?" I continue. "You don't seem to get any comfort or pleasure out of me being here. All you do is avoid me. I'm a wreck from what we've been through the last few months. I can't eat, I can't sleep and I spend every minute of every day worrying about what's going to happen to us next."

I pause to look up at her. She's staring into space, a faraway look in her eyes, as if she's lost in a dream and can't get back. I love her so much! I want to rush over and take her in my arms but I can't. The sadness of the situation is overwhelming. This is the rarest of moments, she's actually letting me say what's been on my mind without interruption or resistance. I know that this is my last chance to get through to her.

"I can't live this way, Cheri. You're taking advantage of me. You're killing my heart. I feel like it's a piece of meat that's been torn out of my chest and thrown on the floor for you to walk all over. If I stay, does anything change? You've been telling me for months now to have patience and to give you time. Well, I've given you plenty of time and nothing's changed. You'd still rather run around with your bullshit friends than be with me, right? Great! You can have them. I hope they're a great source of comfort to you in the future."

Cheri remains silent as I return to the paper. A moment later she gets up, goes upstairs, then comes back with two piles of games and toys for Melanie that need to be wrapped. She plops them down on the living room floor along with the scissors, wrapping paper and tape. Tears are glistening on her cheeks.

"Can I give you your Christmas presents now?" she asks me

tonelessly. "You might as well take them."

Something inside of me snaps.

"No - hell no! I don't want them. Don't you dare give me any goddamn Christmas presents - give them to the next sucker."

She accepts my anger passively and sits in silence for a moment before continuing, puzzled.

"What am I supposed to do with them?"

"Throw them in the goddamn garbage! Ok? Just like everything else in this relationship - throw it all in the goddamn garbage."

She puts her head down, arms limp at her sides and almost starts to cry. But she doesn't. Making a visible effort to pull herself together, she takes a deep breath and goes on.

"Will you please stay long enough to go with me and Melly over to my parents' house tomorrow so she can open her gifts there? Please? Then I'll bring you here and your brother can pick you up, ok?"

So there it is in her own words. Despite all her protests that I misunderstood her comments, here she is planning for the fact that I'll be gone tomorrow.

"All right - for Melanie's sake. That's the only reason I'll consider it."

I still can't believe this is happening. I love Cheri. I know she loves me. But we're breaking up tomorrow.

Cheri is wearily wrapping the last of her presents, going about the task mechanically, soundlessly.

I get up and go to the closet where my presents to Melly are hidden. Taking them into the living room I begin cutting wrapping paper.

"James?"

"What."

"I don't think you should go. I don't think it's over. I wish you'd think about it more."

"I've done nothing except think about it for months. I'm sick and tired of thinking about it."

That's unfair and cruel...and true.

Cheri takes a deep breath and holds it. I know what an effort it must be for her to swallow her pride and ask me to stay. I'm being stubborn and God knows I don't want to go but what's the point of staying if nothing is going to change?

Within fifteen minutes the wrapping is all finished. It's very late. Cheri gathers up all her gifts and dejectedly puts them under the tree.

"I hate Christmas," she says, getting up to turn off the Christmas tree lights. "It's not Christmas here."

She looks at me. "Are you coming to bed with me? Or do you want to stay down here on the couch - I'll understand if you want to, but I wish you'd come up to bed with me."

I follow her up the stairs.

***

We make tender, passionate love to each other, luxuriating in the one thing that always comes easily, without effort, to us. It's everything it can be as we hold each other tight and make the world go away.

When it's over (for the last time?) and we're lying entangled in each other's arms, exhausted, the sense of unreality pervading the evening is gone. We've reached each other once again, however brief the moment may yet prove to be. In the snug shelter of the bed, in the warmth and darkness under the covers, the world seems far away, our problems erased. This is how it used to be. To throw it all away seems unthinkable.

"Oh, God, I don't know what I want anymore," Cheri finally whispers. "I know I'm not happy right now but I don't know why. I don't think it's us...I'm sure it's not. I just want to get through the rest of the holidays without any more problems."

I lay there in the dark absorbing her statement - that's what I want too, isn't it? We could go to sleep right now and pretend this whole evening hasn't happened. But it has. The events of the last thirty minutes don't change that central fact, as much as I wish they could.

Rolling over, I sit up and turn on the light so I can see her better. In this relaxed state, her tender innocence and beauty are heartrending. She's only a baby herself! She looks at me curiously, eyes blinking from the unexpected illumination. Worry quickly furrows her brow. I've already ruined the hard-earned moment of repose we worked so hard to find. I hate myself for doing this, but I have to.

"Cheri, nothing would be easier right now than for me to say, 'fine, everything's ok,' but it's not. We haven't done a single thing to fix whatever it is that's tearing us apart. Let's either repair this relationship or end it. I can't go on the way we've been going the last few months. I don't want that kind of relationship. I'm sorry. If nothing is going to change, we're not going to make it."

As we lay there looking at each other, we can feel the protective cocoon we've just finished weaving start unraveling. We stare at each other in silence. We aren't touching anymore.

"I can't promise I'll change," Cheri finally states quietly, "and I don't know if I want to."

I nod, bowing my head down in resignation.

"James, it'd be so easy for me to say things are going to be different but I can't promise that. I don't know why I'm acting the way I am. I don't know what I want. I'm in a horrible, horrible frame of mind and it's getting worse and worse and I don't know what to do. I've been in bad moods before but never this bad, this long. I need more time to come out of it. Sometimes I wish I were alone so I could figure out what it is I really think by myself. I can't get over the fact that I've never, ever really been on my own in life."

I'm very tired. It's a combination of physical and mental exhaustion. She's never been alone. Maybe she needs time to be alone. Great. For her, maybe. But I don't need time alone now. I've been alone and don't want to be alone anymore.

"So what happens to us while you're off by yourself 'thinking' about what it is you really want?" I ask. "Am I supposed to disappear? What about Melanie? She's not going anywhere. It's too late to say, 'I want to be alone.' Too many people are involved."

"I don't know if that's what I need or not."

"So we'll just break up while you're trying to decide and I'm not supposed to take that personally?"

She looks at me with pleading eyes.

"I don't think that's what I want," she continues. "But if this is hurting you too much, I know I can't ask you to put up with it indefinitely either. Leave me if it hurts too much. Right now I like doing the things I'm doing. I like going out and seeing my friends on Friday nights. I'm not going to stop doing that."

I fall back on my pillow and stare blankly at the ceiling. So here we are, right where we started. Nothing's changed. NOTHING. I look over at the clock. The hour hand is past twelve. Good Lord, it's Christmas day!

And here we lay 'on a cold winter's night that was so deep' as the Christmas carol 'Noel' plainly states. All avenues of hope are exhausted. It's the end of the line.

"Ok, Cheri," I start off, not even sure she's awake anymore, my voice breaking once or twice as I swallow hard and take the deep breaths necessary for continuing. "It seems to me that we've only got two options left. We break up or –"

She doesn't respond, not even by moving a muscle.

"Are you awake?" I ask finally.

A long pause follows, then, a reluctant, "Yes."

"I've got next week off since the workshop is closed. After that I can take a leave of absence, along with some vacation time. I'll go visit my family. You can be alone. I'll wait a while – however long I can stand it. You take whatever time you need to figure things out, ok?"

I can't go on or even comprehend what I'm saying as tears well up in my eyes. Did I just say I was leaving?

"I can't ask you to do that," she responds mechanically.

"I'll call my brother to come get me when we wake up in the morning. My Volkswagen will never survive that trip. I don't want to go but if you think it'll help, I'll do it. The only thing I want to know is, should I pack up all my stuff and take it with me or not? If you have the slightest suspicion that this is really the end, please, tell me. Let me take all my stuff with me so I don't ever have to come back here and see you again. I don't think I could stand that if our relationship is really over."

"I don't know James...can we decide in the morning?" she asks.

"Sure..." I reluctantly agree.

I don't know when it comes, but finally – FINALLY! – sleep takes us both in its merciful embrace.

Christmas

In the morning, it's over quickly. Melanie rips into her presents with greedy, gleeful, exultant joy. Cheri kisses my cheek and gives me my presents like nothing out of the ordinary has occurred between the two of us. I accept my gifts with a subdued 'thank you' and point out where Cheri's card and presents lay under the tree. After opening our gifts, we drink coffee together and watch Melanie cavort about in the discarded wrapping paper. Then, before we know it, it's time to go to Cheri's parent's house for more gift giving and 'celebrating.'

The car ride over is without incident since neither of us speak, letting Melanie rattle on without interruption. I vacantly stare out the windshield, from time to time glancing at Cheri's drawn features, thinking that she's never looked so beautiful. At moments like this I can almost pretend nothing is happening – hey, here we are driving along in the car together, right? Just another tour of the countryside. Maybe she's forgotten that we're breaking up today. I'm almost convinced that this is business as usual until we pull into her parents' driveway and Cheri speaks for the first time in the entire trip as Melanie races off to her grandparents' doorway.

"Let's not say anything to my parents, ok?" Cheri requests,

exiting the car. "After Billy comes over to pick up Melanie we can talk on our way back to our apartment, all right?"

She heads for the house without waiting for my answer. Inside we go. Presents, more wrapping paper, a pathetic attempt to be cheerful and 'Christmas-y' in spirit for the sake of everyone else. There's a huge dinner to work through. Cheri and I eat next to nothing, which is duly noted and commented upon. Out comes dessert. I force down an indigestible lump before excusing myself from the table.

Cheri's ex-husband, Billy, shows up to collect Melanie, who's ecstatic about the prospects of receiving yet a third round of Christmas gifts. Minutes after Billy and Melanie exit, Cheri and I make our apologies to her parents and depart. We drive a mile or two before I dare open up the final topic.

"So what do you want to do?" I blurt out, my gaze fixed on the slippery, slushy pavement in front of us, heart pounding, gut churning.

"I don't know..." Cheri responds slowly. "I just know that I can't go on like this. I need time to think by myself."

I feel as if a curtain has suddenly fallen between us. White hot emotions course through my veins. I hate her, love her, want to be away from her but am terrified of leaving her, all in the same instant.

We drive the rest of the way to the apartment in silence. Walking in the front door I stare at the rooms in wonder, like I'm touring an old, abandoned soundstage from one of our favorite T.V. shows that's been canceled, the cast not returning for another season.

'This is the apartment Cheri and I used to live in,' I reflect ruefully, sweeping a loving eye around the rooms.

Taking off my coat, I go to the telephone.

"Who are you calling?" Cheri asks, visibly startled by my decisive action.

"My brother. He has to get started on the road or he won't get here until midnight. And I've got to tell my parents we won't be coming down for Christmas. They're expecting all three of us, remember?"

"Wait. I don't want to hear this," she replies. "Your parents are going to hate me now too. Please, don't call until after I start the water in the bathroom. I'm going to take a shower while you're talking to them."

My mother answers the phone on the first ring.

"Hello, James, 'Merry Christmas' to you and Cheri and Melanie!" she enthuses. "What time are you leaving to come down here?"

She sounds so sweet and cheerful and happy. It's Christmas!

"We're not leaving, at least not all of us. I'm sorry, we -" I begin, then stop, unable to complete the sentence, choking up, swallowing back a sudden wave of overwhelming sadness and grief.

"James, are you ok? What's wrong?" my mother questions.

"Cheri and I are separating today and I need Eric to come pick me up, if he can."

"Oh, James, I'm so sorry. Are you all right? How are Cheri and Melanie? Are they going to be ok?"

It's like my Mom to be as worried about Cheri and Melanie as she is about her own son.

"Everyone's fine," I brazenly lie. "Can I talk to Eric?"

"He's not here right now, dear. I think he's at one of his friend's houses. I'll have him call you the second he comes in the door, ok?"

"Thanks, Mom. I don't feel much like talking, so if you don't mind, I'm going to hang up."

"I understand, dear. We love you and can't wait to see you."

The compassion in her voice almost makes me come unglued. The things that are happening to Cheri and I are so harsh and bitter that it takes equally harsh emotional control merely to cope, my teetering brain unable to allow itself any undermining feelings that will make the pain intolerable. The love I hear in my mother's voice mercilessly exposes the pitiful charade Cheri and I are substituting in its place.

Hanging up the telephone, I sit down on one of the creaky kitchen chairs Cheri has been wanting to replace.

'Not my problem anymore, is it?' I mindlessly reflect.

Cheri emerges from the bathroom, water dripping off her hair, bathrobe casually wrapped around her. It's unfastened, revealing her incredibly beautiful, classically proportioned body, the timeless female nude the great historic painters tried so hard to capture on canvas.

I get up and start to remove my collection of books from the shelf next to the entrance hall. I've only pulled down the first handful when Cheri speaks up.

"What are you doing?"

"I've got to start packing, right?" I reply. "If this is the end, I don't want to have to return here."

"You'll have to return if you give them two weeks' notice at work that you're leaving, right? I mean, even if we decide..."

She leaves that last thought unstated, then continues.

"So there's no need to take everything with you now, right? Why don't we just see how...'this' goes?"

I put the books back on the shelf.

"All right. I'll only take what I need to survive for a few weeks," I agree.

The phone rings, surprising us both. Cheri answers it.

"Hello? Oh, hi Eric. Yes, he is...'Merry Christmas' to you too. One second."

I take the phone, "Hi brother, how are you?"

"Pretty good, but it doesn't sound like things are going that way for you, I'm sorry to hear. I can pick you up right now, no problem at all. I'm well rested and I like driving."

"Thanks, Eric. I really appreciate it. See you in a few hours," I conclude.

"No problem," he confirms.

Putting down the phone, I let out a big sigh. The wheels are in motion.

The phone rings again. I pick it up. It's Eric.

"Forgot to wish you a 'Merry Christmas' brother," he informs me.

"Thanks, Eric, 'Merry Christmas' to you too," I reciprocate.

"Is he coming?" Cheri inquires cautiously as I put down the receiver.

"Yep."

***

When Eric arrives a few hours later, I go outside to meet him. We pack my meager possessions in his van in one quick pass. Eric gets in the driver's seat. I walk back inside the doorway of the apartment to where Cheri is waiting inside.

"I'll be calling you a lot on the phone," Cheri tells me. "Don't worry, I know I will be."

"Well, maybe we should wait a couple of days so we can both get a chance to settle down and see what we're feeling away from each other," I suggest.

"Ok. It'll take a while to get used to not having you around all the time," she agrees.

We both reflect on the full implication of her comment.

"Take as much time as you need," I state emotionlessly. "But, please, Cheri, once you make your decision, don't let this drag on. Let me know right away if it's over."

"I don't think it's over, James, I really don't. I just think I need some time to be by myself."

"Ok."

Embracing each other, we kiss. It's a warm, sweet, affectionate goodbye. Stepping back, we face each other without pretense.

"I love you, Cheri," I tell her calmly.

"I love you too," she replies. "Be careful!"

"I will. You too."

I turn and leave our life together.

After Eric and I drive down the road a mile or two, I ask my brother to pull off on the shoulder and stop the car. Getting out of the vehicle, I walk to the edge of the highway and fall to my knees in the snow. While my brother watches helplessly, I cry until my aching heart breaks completely in two.

VI

Exile

Late December 1980

Tuna Out

It's a bleak and cheerless winter day, never brightening sufficiently to merit a substantive 'as the light of day faded away...' capstone eulogy. Gray rock ribs protrude dull and wet through surrounding hillsides like the exposed slats of a disintegrating deer carcass. Long streamers of mist hover in low patches. Bowed saplings stagger beneath a two foot burden of freshly fallen snow. Rock-strewn, stone-hewn, the heavily forested landscape flashes by outside the van windows, the scene liberally interspersed with hair-raising, treacherous curves and unforgiving roller-coaster grades.

James registers none of that; instead, a 'mindscape.' He's downstairs in the 'old' apartment he just vacated. It's dark and cold, only the tiny, hooded nightlight over the stove providing dim, shadowy illumination. His eyes search the length and breadth of the room - where is she? Adjusting to the gloom he sees the ancient radiators suspended halfway up the plastered walls, the cold tile floors oozing winter dampness and there, in the living room, the Christmas tree he and Melanie had painstakingly hauled home scant days before.

Listening intently he peers at the narrow staircase leading upstairs. It's black as night up there. Had he heard the sound of movement? Suddenly he's terrified at the idea of climbing those stairs - what if the attic doors had been left unlocked? Who knew what could have escaped from those two huge, cavernous, walk-in storage attics filled with the abandoned clutter of past denizens, accessed via 'trap' doors at the rear of each bedroom? A skeleton key provided entry to those ill-lit, haunted house chambers, full of musty, broken furniture, jumbled boxes, dangerous flooring, unexplored recesses and clutching cobwebs. He'd never let the entrance doors swing shut behind him, propping them open beyond all possibility of error. Yet he'd also never crept into those attics without a grim sense of disquiet and foreboding - and then during daylight hours only, never forgetting Beelzebub's attic entry in 'The Exorcist.' When he exited the attics – blessed relief! - he always made certain that the doors were securely locked behind him. Sometimes late at night, lying in bed reading, he could hear noises emanating from those unlit, tomb-like reaches. 'Squirrels - it has to be squirrels,' he always told himself. But he never went in to check because he was afraid of not finding squirrels.

He thought of those attics now, as he stood at the base of the stairs in his dark contemplative mindscape. Something could have gotten out, could be waiting for him up there, lurking in that claustrophobic pitch! Nervously edging away from the steps, heart in throat, he retreats into the living room.

It's only then that he spots her. She's been downstairs the entire time, evading his search...an elusive, beautiful shadowy figure wearing the royal blue robe he's admired her in so many times. He can't see her face - only a quick glimpse of white and then a dark swirl of hair as she turns away. He watches her impassively, heart frozen, unable to call out. She knows he's there, of that he's certain. He steps toward her in the dark - it looks like she might come to him. But, no, without a backward glance she flits up the stairs like an apparition and vanishes as the picture collapses.

Night comes rushing toward him in waves of inky black. In the far distance he hears the gates slam shut - barred solidly from within by some massive dead bolt the tribe muscles into place. Inside those walls the clan gathers, roasting meat over roaring fires, breaking open kegs of wine and ale. Boisterous, rough voices ring out in merriment and camaraderie, some chanting incantations designed to ward off evil spirits. That is all denied him now. It's not his tribe anymore - they are not his people. He's trapped outside the fortress walls at nightfall. The gates will not open again this evening.

He can sense the forces of darkness stirring as the sky deepens into an oppressive, ominous gloom. He discerns low, guttural moans on the wind; squeals, howls, and what is that? A disturbing shuffle, the unmistakable sound of heavy, muffled footsteps approaching from a long-forgotten, haunted corridor of his consciousness. Panic! What's out here in the night with him? Some malignant, demonic intelligence has picked up his blood scent, he can feel its malign attention turning toward the outcast crouching by the gate.

Through good fortune and good luck people sometimes get to 'forget' fear - or at least successfully bury it. But it's always there, down deep, waiting to well up and spill over, paralyzing and numbing the victim, only as far away as that lump growing steadily larger under an armpit, or the blood in one's stool, or worse yet, in a loved one's. Real fear falls with a sledgehammer blow, it's an overriding reality that crashes uninvited into the here and now. The inconsolable anguish of lost love lets it in as well. James' heart aches and writhes sickeningly - he and

Cheri tried so hard! Yet here he is, cast out into the wilderness, overcome by loneliness and despair - most corrosive and unendurable of human afflictions.

More wet and desolate highway lies ahead. 'How am I going to handle the night?' he worries, keeping his anxiety to himself.

'Alone,' comes the cruel reply, 'Alone!'

Glancing about fearfully he looks closely at his brother who is calmly seated behind the steering wheel. Scrutinizing him intently, James suddenly wonders, 'Who is this? My brother, angel of mercy delivered by the Lord? Or Charon, oarsmen for the damned, ferrying lost souls across the River Styx? Am I even now being delivered to my doom? Is this the last mortal between me and the howling darkness of the pit?'

Dread and panic well up inside his chest, breaking through his fragile equilibrium. What is he going to do? Hopelessness threatens to drag him under and it isn't even nighttime yet.

> 'Out - tune it out! tune it out! tune it out!
> Out - tune it out! tune it out! tune it out!
> tuneitout tuneitout tuneitout tuneitout
> tuneitout tuneitout tuneitout tuneitout
> Out! tuneitout, tuneitout, tuneitout!'

Where this ridiculous ditty comes from, he has no inkling. After a few moments of mentally reciting it, however, his only thought is, 'It works, thank God, it works!'

Interesting variations immediately occur to him - 'speed up the frequency', 'vary the intensity' and even 'free associate' (for example, 'tuneitout' disassembles into 'tuna out' and he pictures a stern-faced librarian pointing angrily at the door as a school of crestfallen tuna rise from their seats and quickly file out of a public reading room).

> 'Out - tuna out! tuna out! tuna out!
> Out - tuna out! tuna out! tuna out!'

It's music to his ears - occupies space, keeps the bad stuff out, although, of course, poses its own problems. After all, you can't keep this up forever, can you? No, then you'd be crazy, right? If you stay away too long, what if you can't get back? And it's also a continuous loop, a continual reminder of the problem, inevitably leading to the question, 'tune WHAT out?' And then, there 'it' is again, knocking at the door.

But, make no mistake – mindlessly reciting the ditty is better than nothing, an improvement! It requires concentration. That's precisely the benefit and refuge. Sometimes you have to hunker down and grit things out, however you best can. Sure, there's a certain hysterical element to it - that's understood - yet it's got to be put in perspective. It's a matter of hanging on and waiting and praying for a change in the winds of fortune and fate. A measure of relief.

'Where are we now?' James wonders. Night sky - dead of night - billion pinpricks of light. Moon casting a silver glow, clouds breaking up and racing in tatters across the horizon.

'There's nothing between me and the cold black of deep space, is there?' James ponders.

Cars whip by zipping down the asphalt ribbon of the turnpike.

'Our turnpike! Cheri used to drive down this turnpike with me,' James recalls. 'I remember the first time we went to the Jersey shore together...so long ago. I got a ticket in Manhattan for driving the wrong way down a one way street. It was summertime. I was the new guy in her life and we were in love. Why couldn't things stay like that - Cheri, Melanie and I driving down to the shore on weekends, visiting my family, swimming at the beach, splashing in the water? Man, Cheri looked great in her bathing suit! But where is she now? Why isn't she here beside me?'

> 'Out - tune it out! tune it out! tune it out!
> Out - tune it out! tune it out! tune it out!
> tuneitout tuneitout tuneitout tuneitout
> Out! tuneitout tuneitout tuneitout!'

'Whew, that was close,' James reflects. 'It's hard to keep the ditty going all the time. I've got to stick with it and concentrate:

> Out - tune it out! Tune it WAY out!
> Out - tune it out! Tune it WAY out!'

Chinatown

I've slipped into a disconnected subconscious state, surfacing only infrequently. In this place, wild fantasies of reuniting with Cheri flare up, burn furiously and then collapse under the weight of their own ill-conceived structures. An acrid pall blankets all, blurring focus, tearing eyes, clouding prescience. I perceive a black vault of inestimable depth and dimension surrounding me. A storm is howling, waves of nausea and crippling anxiety surge angrily over my seawall, flooding power stations, triggering massive mental blackouts and wreaking devastating outages in my cortical grid. Sparks electrify the darkness, a few neural junction boxes buzz and snarl angrily like overturned hornet's nests as their wiring scorches and melts. What remains of the proud mechanism?

And while my brain may be breaking, it's my heart that's in its death throes, a punctured, quivering brute laboring valiantly yet perhaps, nonetheless, irreparably damaged? In much the same way as the Arabs leave crippled camels behind to perish in the desert, perhaps it's time for me to leave my ruined heart in this wasteland. Everything reminds me of her. I picture her face: her skin smooth and flawless; her lips soft and sweet; her beautiful brown eyes full of promise and passion. But thinking of her only brings me inconsolable anguish and misery. Why? Is it fear of being alone again or simply proportional mourning at the loss of a magical love? It's actually a very scary place down here. Sometimes I wonder if I can make it back 'out' - dear God, please don't abandon me now!

Philadelphia - Chinatown? Yes, that's right. Eric and I stopped to get something to eat. Crowded restaurant, bright lights, shiny red and gold bunting, a whiff of incense, exotic wall tapestries decorated with elaborate scenery and indecipherable oriental calligraphy. Nearby tables are piled high with steaming plates of freshly sliced vegetables, heaping bowls of fried rice, egg rolls, hot soup, cups of tea - the overpowering aroma of cooking and spices all pervasive. Happy, smiling people - lovers, families, friends - occupy every booth.

If only I could eat. Uncontrollable cramps and convulsions erupt at the mere thought of swallowing. Light bulbs explode before my eyes, my limbs feel detached and it seems like my central nervous system signals aren't reaching their peripheral stations. There is an incredibly loud clatter of clashing silverware, banging plates, voices hollering - the din is splitting my skull wide open! I'm sure blood is going to come spurting out of some hole in my head if this awful clamor doesn't stop. Who are these people? Why are we all here? Wide-eyed, I regard them with astonishment. Oh no, I can't stand this, I'm going back down inside...

Better Things

Collegetown, Pennsylvania - port of refuge, safe harbor. Late night docking under a gallows moon. The town throbs with life - a university crowd never sleeps. At our lodging, we're met with open arms. My kid sister, Corrie, and her boyfriend, Jack, greet us in the entrance hall of an off-campus communal 'castle' they share with my brother (when he's not home visiting our parents like he was when I called looking for him this morning) and numerous other housemates.

"Hi, James, Merry Christmas. Great to see you - how have you been? How was the drive?" asks Corrie cheerfully.

"James, bub! Merry Christmas. What's up? How're - " (quick recovery) "...things?" adds Jack.

"Merry Christmas to you too. Things are fine, just fine, thanks," I lie, as is becoming commonplace with me regarding the big topic of my breakup with Cheri.

"Great. Well, uh, glad to hear it - c'mon in and meet the gang," Jack encourages.

Inside, party cheer. The stereo is rocking to Philadelphia's finest FM station. Other rent-paying denizens wander through the common rooms exchanging nods of acknowledgment. The household atmosphere is wonderfully upbeat. I love parties!

My stomach lurches and growls resentfully, memory cringes, but I'll hold my ground and try to enjoy this.

"Bub, look what I've got here."

Welcome distraction, Jack, relentlessly cheerful and thoughtful, has his fist clenched around a large untapped bottle of blackberry brandy - he remembers my favorite beverage!

"What do you say, Bub? I got this especially to celebrate your visit. C'MON EVERYBODY!" he hollers. "Let's have some shots of brandy. Glasses! We need glasses - ah, the hell with the glasses."

He cracks the seal, twists the cap off and takes a big slug of the brandy to get things started. Eyes bulging, spluttering and grimacing, he passes me the heavy bottle.

Why not? Take a gulp - DEEP gulp...whew-ee. Yow! What a concoction - sickeningly sweet, almost cough syrupy. Head spins, lights brighten and flicker unsteadily. I reel as the fiery liquid burns its way down my esophagus.

"Aarrghh...tastes fantastic," I splutter. "Just what the doctor ordered."

"Great. I thought you might still have a taste for that nasty stuff, even after what we went through last New Year's Eve," Jack comments gleefully.

He's referring to an evening of drinking at Times Square with me, him, Corrie, Eric and...Cheri...that didn't turn out too well. Eric eventually puked in the backseat of 'our' then brand new car after I insisted on driving everyone through the town where Corrie, Eric and I were all born in nearby North Jersey. Cheri was none too happy with me that night.

"Well, if you recall, getting it down isn't the bad part, it's keeping it down that's tricky," I emphasize.

"Oh, yes, I do recall. And, boy, did Cheri - oops!"

"Hey, it's ok, really..."

"Ahh, what the hell, bub? I'm blitzed already, what can I say?" Jack apologizes.

He gamely forges ahead, "It's great to see you. I hope everything works out ok."

"Me too, 'bub', me too," I confess.

The crowd gathers around in earnest and the bottle flies from hand to hand, people hitting off it like there's no tomorrow. The smell of reefer fills the air and the noise from spirited conversations rivals the stereo's blare. More and more people arrive, somehow finding room to jam into the packed house.

My sister materializes out of nowhere, grabs my arm and leads me to the house stereo setup.

"There's a song I'd like you to hear - it's off 'The Kinks' comeback album," she tells me.

Leaning over the turntable, she lifts the needle arm and places it carefully on a spinning platter. Moments later, the song she's selected blares out:

> "Here's hoping all the days ahead,
> won't be as bitter as the ones behind you.
> Be an optimist instead, and somehow,
> happiness will find you.
> Forget what happened yesterday,
> I know that better things are on the way."
>
> - The Kinks, "Better Things"

I'm touched, but not in the way she intended. Memory, you cursed wretch! Hadn't I left you behind with that last swig, that last hit, that last shout?

Innocently my sister follows up, her inquiry leaving me shell-shocked with its matter-of-fact presumption, "So what are you going to do now that you two have split up?"

Say it ain't so! Paranoia - does she know something I don't know? Has she spoken to Cheri on the phone? A bolt of horror rockets through my system, something cold and clammy grips my gut, such chilling finality in her question.

"...it's probably for the better, anyway, the way you two seemed to fight all the time," she continues brightly, offering sympathy, trying to help.

Stung. Hot blush of shame. I want to cry out, 'That's only circumstantial evidence!' I want to tell her, 'We had true love, couldn't you see that too? Who here among us can understand the ways of God and man? Who can foresee where the twists of fate will deposit us?'

But I don't say anything, a crushing load of bleak resignation settling upon me instead. My sister is too young, too full of youthful clarity and confidence to understand the unpredictable, untimely and occasionally harsh dictates of fate. She's happy and newly in love - what can I say to her? She can't begin to grasp the particular dynamics, the unique, intertwined paths that brought Cheri and I to OUR moment, our destination, our collision in space and time.

And no one else knows how much I miss her right now, how much I ache to be with her. What a bitter pill to swallow, coming face to face with the realization that the world - if my sister's comments are any indication - has already written the two of us off. Those who know us best have closed the book, expecting Cheri and I to move on to bigger and better things. Human communication seems so pitifully inadequate at times like these.

'It's that God fellow,' I want to tell my sister. 'He's the one that's orchestrating this! Don't ask me why it's all happening.'

But I can't explain that one either, it's too maudlin, too self-pitying, too complicated. The jungle drum resumes its frenzied pounding inside my skull. Mutely I absorb the body slam my beloved sister has unwittingly delivered me.

I can't imagine feeling any worse than I do at this particular moment but then a streak of black humor manifests itself and I recall the old saying, 'Things are always darkest before they go pitch black.'

And lo, what's this? Here's a welcome distraction. Jack is back, God bless his cheery soul. He's got the bottle of firewater in hand. Sure, I'll have some. Why not? Darts? Hell, yeah, I'll throw darts. And, please, pass that bottle again, would you? Give me a hit off that. C'mon, let's guzzle that swill!

Look out, clear the way, we're throwing some darts here. RUN FOR YOUR LIVES you ornery little devils. Heh-heh-heh, almost got you there, didn't I? Sorry. Zing! Son of a gun. I can't believe I missed by that much. Watch out folks! Who's got the bug juice? Turn up the stereo! Now we're having some fun. Where's Cheri, she must be around here somewhere?

Nope - don't go down that path. Hey, pass me the bottle, quick! Ceiling whirls, faces appear and disappear, a warm glow spreads. I'm blasted, ripped, where can I find a flat spot to lay down and rest? Ah yes, brilliant strategy, how about the floor here? Yes, this'll be fine. I'll lie here and listen to tunes on the stereo. The sounds of music and happy voices swirl around me. Maybe I'll close my eyes for just one moment...

The Noose

In the morning, things are worse - noose tightening, circle shrinking. The cold, weak light of December offers no solace. A dull, hollow ache emanates from my cranium and my gut is a churning cauldron of bubbling acid. New day, same life - without her.

To the van we go, drive - don't think! ('Where is she now? What is she doing this morning without me?')

My mental fabric is fraying, something has to give - a sense of overwhelming fatigue has me increasingly unable to combat the nitro-fueled, clutch-popping, pavement-scorching blasts of despair from my increasingly erratic mind. There is only one theme left to be played out - 'Is it REALLY over?' Faith is the slender reed I'm hanging onto, my breathing tube as I slip into the deep water. The months of struggle leading to this point have left me too exhausted to keep my head above the surface much longer. Yet, though I may postpone my drowning, I'm afraid there might be a clot forming somewhere inside my skull, clogging up one of those innocuous little arteries in the gray matter, causing it to swell and distend to obscene dimensions before it finally pops in a wet splatter of bright red droplets. A stroke like that can be fatal - although sometimes, I understand, a vegetable remains sucking at the ventilator tubes.

Oh God, it's much too grim to contemplate! Drive on, brother, drive on. I'm convinced that motion helps. I've concocted the patently ridiculous notion that if we keep on moving, bad news won't be able to catch up with me.

Homeland

And finally, ancestral homeland, last stand, flat as a billiard table, hidden amid the 'Pine Barrens,' a huge undeveloped evergreen stronghold complete with a folklore and culture of its own. Here, the stomping grounds of the 'Pineys' and the infamous 'Jersey Devil,' these woods representing the north-most extension of the vast conifer belt dominating the southeastern United States. The pines - eastern white, loblolly, scotch and pitch - thrive in the area's sandy soil, competing fiercely for space with the ubiquitous native scrub oaks. This sprawling forest is also shot through and through with prodigious quantities of mouth-watering blueberries, thickets of red-berried, spike-leafed holly bushes, tangles of gnarly, flowering wild laurel and stands of reclusive white cedar. The latter species is found only deep within the fastness of the woods, clumped secretively about dank, oozing bogs or hidden, meandering springs where the light of day never penetrates fully to the thorny underbrush of the moldering forest floor. In spring the foliage sways with a shimmering ripple of dizzying green. In summer, dazzling blotches of sunlight flood the open spaces between adjoining groves and the monotonous droning hum of cicadas chirping on a hot afternoon induces a dreamy, sleepwalking stupor.

Unfortunately for the legions of unemployed who reside here, this enchanted wood is not commercial grade and the entire region remains a chronically depressed economic zone. The few jobs available are mainly provided by an aging glass industry that once capitalized on the extensive, high quality silica sand deposits and water resources of 'South Jersey.' Telltale 'gravel holes' pockmark the landscape, mute testimony to the boom days when blast furnaces glowed an angry red around the clock and workers sweated and strained melting the sand into glass, frequently experiencing temperatures in excess of 120 degrees Fahrenheit in the shadows of the ovens. Entire smokestack towns grew up around these mills and factories, providing employment for every able-bodied, hard-working, heat-resistant 'man jack' and their children too, once they grew up. But the plants have long since been shut down, with one or two notable exceptions (and even they announce layoffs daily), leaving the area with one of the highest unemployment rates in the northeastern United States.

The towns that thrived around those factories are interesting historical anachronisms, essentially rural outposts that boomed during the prosperous years of the late industrial revolution; the feed store still a prominent fixture on 'main' street, the architectural style distinctly small town, the business district characterized by ornate, antiquated storefronts straight out of an Edward Hopper painting. These establishments overlook a steadily dwindling trickle of pedestrian traffic and the occasional American Legion or Little League sponsored fireman's parade. Today's main street is mostly symbolized by boarded-up 'five-and-ten cent' stores that never anticipated the era of shopping malls and by an ever increasing number of largely empty parking lots that mysteriously appear overnight in locations where successful businesses once flourished. The local high school football team remains the biggest show in town with regional sports rivalries taking on exaggerated importance due to the fact that nothing else of interest happens locally. Outside the towns, a rudimentary truck-farming industry survives (this is after all, the 'garden' state), but large scale agriculture has also abandoned the region and most of the produce is sold at roadside stands manned by mom and pop and the kids.

Where the land ends, the water begins. To the west lies a vast stretch of mosquito-infested swamps, pungent marshes, sunken forests, tidal flats and estuaries. This scenery gradually gives way to the open waters of the Delaware Bay, a heavily trafficked waterway routinely plied by ocean-going vessels conducting business upriver at the Dupont plants in Delaware and the ports of Philadelphia and Wilmington. This 'bayside' is also a vibrant wildlife sanctuary, its protected waters providing shelter, sustenance and spawning grounds for schools of sport, game and commercial fish populations. Its meandering muddy channels, oozing black muck, impenetrable chest-high reeds and cattails (accessible only by small, flat-bottomed skiffs), provide an unspoiled haven for all manner of resident and migratory fowl and, believe it or not, bald eagles. The area represents a last stronghold for this majestic bird in the eastern U.S., a breeding pair roosting at 'Turkey Point' with a few other young or solitary eagles scattered about these isolated reaches.

Generations of fishermen, crabbers, clammers and oystermen made their living from these bountiful waters, with another set of isolated communities (Shellpile, Bivalve, Port Norris, Dorchester, Port Elizabeth, Fortesque) owing their existence to the annual harvesting of what had once undoubtedly seemed like an inexhaustible supply of shellfish. But pollutants and over-fishing spelled the demise of that industry too, although today an occasional oyster boat or trawler can still be seen tied up at a dock along the region's extensive inland network of lazy creeks and rivers. The vast bulk of today's sea-going craft in the bay, though, are pleasure boats: sport-fishing charters, sailboats and the occasional yacht. Legacies of the shell-fishing past can still be found, however, by driving along the back-country roads. There abandoned canneries, rusting warehouses, rotted wharves and poverty-stricken shanty towns lie, literally buried beneath huge piles of long-since shucked oyster shells that continue to generate a fearsome stench, reeking to high heaven in summer when the sun burns brightly on the decaying mounds.

In the winter months these marshlands are eerie in their remoteness, the wind whistling in off the bay, rattling through the cattails, whipping up angry whitecaps on the frigid waters. A dreary, foreboding atmosphere seems to hint that the end of the world may be nearer at hand than we ever suspected.

To the east, though, lies a different world entirely; a place of clean, sparkling beaches and cold, blue swells where the north Atlantic surges gently against the continental shelf and washes sedately ashore. This, the 'real' Jersey shore: Atlantic City, Wildwood, Cape May, Ventnor, Margate, Sea Isle City and Ocean City. Here summer is worshiped. At first it's a fleeting dream in the back of the mind, slipping in unobtrusively whenever March relents and offers up enough unexpected sunshine to draw the weary denizens out of their stale quarters. During the exuberant days of April, a traveler to the shore will find signs of stepped-up activity everywhere. Storm windows are replaced with screens, new coats of paint are slapped on bungalows and musty canvas awnings are stored away for another season. In the weeks leading up to the time-honored Memorial Day official summer 'kickoff' weekend, armies of newly liberated college and high school students descend on the beach towns, manning the summer jobs that underlie the feast or famine cycle of the local economies. These temporary workers count change in the arcades, ring up souvenirs in the gift shops, slice pizza, wait on tables and hawk games on the amusement piers. In their free time they soak up sun on the beach during the day, then change into party clothes and spend their hard-earned cash making friends, lovers and memories along the boardwalk at night. Getting tans, crashing parties, listening to music blaring out of beachside bars, they do all the things that will make this summer memorable years later whenever a snatch of a song from this special season drifts out of an open car window, recalling a time when they were young and free and life was full of exhilaration and unexplored possibilities 'at the Jersey shore.'

Escape

The radio is bringing me music from the future - twenty-first century, perhaps? It's here, I'm gone, wired into tomorrow, piggybacking wild planet waves, nerve net inextricably engaged, cosmic consciousness blasting through me. Here it comes again - yah! Intensely physical, orgasmic, spasmodic, all electric - it cranks directly through my portals, surging uncontrollably, firing synapses in trip-wire, explosive progression.

It calls to mind another experience - I was climbing a six foot high cyclone fence next to my apartment garage one rainy Saturday morning in San Antonio, tossing trash in the neighboring motel's industrial strength dumpster. Clambering over the barrier, perched precariously, I reached up to my garage roof's overhanging metal rain gutter for balance and ZAPPPPPP!!!! Repairmen working on the garage roof the day before had inadvertently brought the main power feed into contact with the drainpipe. The current for the entire garage apartment promptly detoured through me. I vividly recall the astonishing moment of my electrocution - elemental, titanic power seizing total control, becoming part of me, instantaneously snapping me fiendishly, ferociously erect, every hair on my body literally standing on end. My eyes bugged out toward heaven, pure electricity invaded my body as I involuntarily screamed like a woman experiencing orgasm! Then, gravity came to my rescue, toppling me off the fence, sending me crashing to the ground. I landed in a pile of greasy, discarded automobile parts, lying there in the rain and mud, nothing but a burn on the tip of my finger and a vivid memory to show for the experience.

This moment is similar. A subtler visit, it comes in intense physical rushes and waves, accompanied by otherworldly, futuristic music - full of light and space, lyric and melody, color, power, inspiration, seduction.

Jeff

"Hey, boy, you still alive, there? Ready for a little more 'go-fast'?"

The voice materializes like an unexpected apparition, catching up to me as I drift without anchor in the far reaches of altered consciousness. Is this part of that otherworldly symphony I was listening to?

Confusion reigns ('Where am I? Who's talking to me? Open your eyes!') until focus returns. Directly above me I see exposed beams, aging slats and suspended roof struts climbing to the peak of a sharply inverted V. Decorative fish nets hang from exposed nails driven into the ceiling, contributing to a bohemian 'Summer of Love' ambiance. An eerie, soft purple glow illuminates the room, emanating from a fluorescent black light located strategically in the corner. As I slowly scan the scene, groggily cataloging my vaguely familiar surroundings, two large stereo speakers loom into view, each perched on an unoccupied chair in a futile effort to maximize space. I remember that due to the sharp pitch of the roof, standing erect is only possible under the center beam and even then it's a most hazardous undertaking, fraught with skull-cracking peril. Dials flicker busily on a stereo receiver ('The one picking up signals and music from the future?' I wonder) that sits nearby on a formica-topped table amid a clutter of paraphernalia.

Jeff sits at the table. Using his forearm, he clears a broad swath, grinning mischievously (the same grin he use to flash as a 12-year-old after pilfering a selection from his dad's 'Playboy' magazine collection for us to examine). He opens his hand to reveal a large, dirty white 'rock' the size of a peanut.

"Just got some more 'go-fast'!" he cackles merrily behind his bushy, mountain-man beard, bent eagerly over his wares, reminding me of a kindly old country doctor making a house call. His ways may be unorthodox (not to mention illegal) but he's a happy fellow, which ain't all bad, considering that so many people never take the opportunity to be happy. And Lord, does he have a boundless enthusiasm for his beloved 'crank.'

And then there's Jeff's 'patients.' He lives way down along the southernmost reaches of the Maurice River, deep in the heart of heavily forested swamp country in a tiny outpost of civilization. The oddest thing about his town, though, is that, near as I can tell, the only thing people do down here is 'speed' around the clock. I swear, I've never seen anything like it. Night and day, a never-ending stream of burnt-out, wasted hulks files through Jeff's door in search of more 'go-fast.' That's why he's abandoned the bottom two stories of his house. To escape the relentless press of humanity knocking on his door and peering through his windows, he's retreated up here to his attic stronghold.

Jeff is a virtual prisoner in his own home. He keeps his car hidden in the woods a mile or so away so no one can tell when he's in. Sneaking down an abandoned railroad track, he slips unobtrusively into the woods behind his house so he can see who's waiting for him on his front porch. When the coast is clear, he sprints to his back door, slips in, darts upstairs and then bolts the attic door behind him. Once that door is locked, he won't open it for anyone.

"So, whaddya say, ready for a little more?" he inquires eagerly, his voice bringing me back to the present.

I don't have to think about it too long.

"Well, what the hell, if you've got enough..." I manage to croak out in response.

"Sure do, SURE enough do!"

"Great, I'm ready then."

"Hot damn, I was hoping you'd say that."

See, the thing is, we're childhood buddies and we share an intimacy that can only be acquired from that experience. We spent our adolescent years together tromping around in the woods, building tree shacks, camping, fishing, riding bicycles and motorcycles and then discovering music. In fact, the black light up here in Jeff's attic is the one he drove his parents crazy with when he lived next door to me, creating his own Day-Glo kingdom in their cellar as he listened intently to everything from early Gary Puckett to Black Sabbath. We went to junior and senior high school together.

Jobs, girlfriends and distance finally came between us and I've been away a good number of years but whenever I'm in the neighborhood, Jeff and I get together to play some music (he's a helluva pianist) and party. Once my brother dropped me off at my parents' house after my separation from Cheri - effectively concluding his rescue mission - I instinctively gravitated toward Jeff's hideaway deep in the heart of the forest.

The deed is quickly done - and here comes the good part. A moment of constrained excitement. Now I feel it! Heart starts jumping, chest expands, breath catches, pulse throbs like a jackhammer, pure heat starts melting down my insides and it feels SOOOOO damn good. 'Better than sex,' the good doctor advertised, shaking his head in disbelief as if unable to imagine such a proposition. And yes, it's an illusion, and no, you can't hide from the world forever but for a few minutes I feel like Superman with his finger stuck in a wall socket. No despair - King! Ruler! Tyrant! A purely physical sensation of outrageous pleasure races up and down my spinal cord, a warm glow extends to the very end of my fingertips. Raging, unbounded energy is unleashed and torrents of feverish conversation erupt from our untethered tongues. Flashes of insight burst forth with startling clarity, ideas flush and scatter in every direction like flocks of startled quail. Multiple channels of thought are simultaneously - but unsuccessfully - pursued because you never can quite catch up with all of them. Try as you might, they're going too fast. Our minds zoom along at an astonishing clip, racing through seemingly endless streams of impressions and perceptions, spitting out observations and insights in fearsome displays of verbal pyrotechnics.

And suddenly, unexpectedly, it's over. A crushing fatigue wells up out of nowhere and brings everything to an abrupt halt. It's time to find a soft spot, curl up in a fetal ball and listen to songs from the twenty-first century.

Asylum

The first couple of nights here have been kind of 'wonder full' in a sort of cliff-hanging, snatched from disaster kind of way. As might be noted, Jeff is a total wild man living a life like Kurtz in Joseph Conrad's novel, 'Heart of Darkness.' The only difference is that Jeff's wife and child still live with him and no violence is being done to anyone. Other than that, anything goes. His prodigious appetite for 'go-fast' completely dominates all his waking hours, of which he has many, considering the fact that he 'speeds' around the clock. He occasionally drops out of sight to crash for a few hours but soon enough he's up and on the prowl again, a never ending, perpetual motion machine, truly a wonder to behold as he dashes off on his bull-headed rampaging frenzies, self-absorbed and dedicated to his quest for more speed, more sex, more music, more fun! The man is on a single-minded quest to burst through the limits of human endurance, apparently for no reason other than the sheer pleasure of snatching the lightning bolt out of Zeus' grasp. It strikes me as rather heroic although I doubt his long-suffering, incredibly patient and loving wife, Belinda, would agree with me on that point. It's certainly not the type of lifestyle that can go on forever but nonetheless, Jeff is taking his shot at it, surrounding himself with chaos and disarray. He's everywhere at once, alive, incandescent, burning with his desire to experience it all, have it all, consuming life in his own banzai, flame-throwing fashion.

His 'castle' is an accurate reflection of his state of mind - a million incomplete reconstruction projects under way, each launched with great enthusiasm then abandoned whenever a new, more interesting project presents itself. Every wall on the first floor of his house is stripped down to bare beams and wiring. Exposed between each wooden brace is a strip of insulation with a shiny, silver aluminum foil surface that reflects light in shimmering fragments, creating a visual effect similar to living in an unfinished lunar outpost or abandoned space station.

In this topsy-turvy world I've found refuge. Oh sure, there are some productive activities we do from time to time. Since it's the dead of winter and the house runs entirely off of heat generated from burning firewood, one of the big events of any given day is rounding up whoever happens to be downstairs when the wood supply runs out. We all then pile into a couple of cars to blast off to some isolated stretch of forest where our impromptu work party scurries into the trees and hastily grabs up whatever logs and kindling are available. It's like watching a raiding party hit an unprotected village as wild-eyed, partied-out zombies lurch clumsily through the woods ripping down saplings and low-hanging branches, uprooting dead or dying trees, cursing and grumbling in the cold and the snow as they shiver in their skimpy coats and sneakers. Jeff even brings a saw and ax so we can do some real damage. But soon enough we've got all the wood the cars can hold, then we race back to the house, and, voila, let there be heat! The partying starts up again.

That's the modus operandi around here - 'Let the Good Times Roll!' It's been a blessing for me. There's nothing I can do to change my current situation other than wait patiently for events to run their course so if in the meantime I have some fun and blow off steam, what's the harm? I talk to Jeff whenever I get a chance and otherwise it's music, guitars, speed and more speed.

And it's helping. A stranglehold has been released from my throat. My despair is having its butt temporarily kicked by crank. Sometimes, I even have fun! When human beings are faced with overwhelming difficulties and it all seems like too much to cope with, nothing beats the sheer, unrestrained pleasure of escapism, does it? In these circumstances it's almost a duty to just say, 'screw it - I've had all I can stand and I can't stand no more,' and then go off and play hooky, call in sick or go to the beach. Adopting such an escapist attitude may well be the difference between coping effectively or getting an automatic weapon and opening fire on the unsuspecting. As the saying goes, 'the tree that bends before the storm doesn't break.' Coronaries and strokes take their toll on the stoics, the martyrs, the ever-suffering and the inflexible. Hey, this earth is a crazy kind of place and it takes all kinds of strategies to cope. You gotta go with what works for you as long as you aren't making someone else suffer.

I know I haven't found a long-term resolution to anything. All my problems are waiting for me 'back there' in the real world. But I've managed to get through the last few days, haven't I? I'm still out here punching away. And though it may not do forever, it'll do for now.

Deep Freeze

Late at night, I'm trying to sleep, shivering and shaking instead, prisoner in the grip of bone-crushing cold. A prolonged deep freeze has its arctic grip on this unending evening. Huddled miserably beneath a threadbare, borrowed sleeping bag, face and limbs numb, only my fevered mind is still burning. I'm certain the end is near. Downstairs the wood stove has run out, no raiding party has replenished our meager fuel supply and the last flame has long since flickered into extinction.

Oh wretched fate! Fitful slumber, fleeting periods of unconsciousness - all behind me now as I lay wide awake in total darkness, unwilling to make a move to save myself. I stare blindly at the attic ceiling, vividly picturing the elemental, absolute cold of intergalactic space pressing down against my aerie, its slipstream originating deep in the vast reaches of the universe, nothing between it and me except cedar shingles and my pitiful rags.

BBBBRRRRRRRRRRRAAAAAAAAAAPPPPPP!!!!!!

A hellacious blast of sound shakes the very foundation of the house. What the...? A quick glance at my watch reveals that it's 3:30 a.m. What's happening? Jumping to my feet I clamber awkwardly down the attic steps, scoot through the vacant bedroom, rush down the stairs and -

BBBBBBBRRRRRRAAAAAAAAAAAPPPPPP!!!!!!!

A whirlwind of flying wood chips and churning sawdust greets me. The dining room lights are ablaze - commotion reigns supreme. There's a body in there somewhere - it's Jeff gone berserk with a chainsaw!

BBBBBRRRRRAAPP!!! BRRRRAAAAAAPP!!!

The reek of gasoline, grease and scorched wood is overpowering, clouds of dust and exhaust make breathing well nigh impossible. The floor is a half inch deep in shavings and shredded tree bark, an absolutely incredible mess.

Jeff drops the chainsaw to the floor with a clatter, sprints out the front door of the house without a word, then quickly returns dragging in a huge branch, a tree limb he stashed away somewhere for an occasion such as this. He picks up the chainsaw again and -

BRRRRAAAAAAAAA!!! BRRRRAAAAAAAA!!!

Another stunning blast of noise - cover your ears! I hold the bough while Jeff carves it up with a few savage, rendering slashes of the whirring blade. The log quickly succumbs to his assault, yielding three or four sizable chunks of fuel, joining the half-dozen or so others Jeff has already cut up. A pall of smoke settles on the scene as we view the battlefield carnage - but no time for that, quick, let's start a fire! C'mon - cram that stove full of wood - get that baby cooking - we need warmth. A few squirts of lighter fluid, some newspaper kindling and the flames shoot high. Sweet, blessed silence surrounds us as we huddle near the woodstove, shoving more kindling on the fledgling fire. Jeff gazes in reverential awe at the wreckage around us, the fruit of his decisive action, never mind the mess. He's proud of what he's accomplished - his family and friends are safe. There's wood to burn!

Cannonball Express

Ok, so here we are - last stop on the Cannonball Express. Don't get me wrong. Nothing melodramatic (or even climactic) is going to occur. I'm just thoroughly bored with the 'gofast' (therapeutic though it may be) and in this day and age - probably every other, too - you have to know when enough is enough, right?

Now what? Obviously, my 'big' problem remains unsolved. Why hasn't Cheri called me? I don't know...and my heart flip-flops spasmodically whenever I consider the question. Despair still threatens to overwhelm me as each day goes by without word from the north. In fact, I'll admit it, the other day I broke down and cried like a baby.

But what options do I have? My solid Roman Catholic upbringing leaves self-destruction entirely out of the question and with two loving parents pointing the way, I tend to be the eternal optimist about human relationships anyway. I truly believe in my heart of hearts that God has not abandoned me, that Cheri and I are being 'tested' and one day soon the telephone is going to ring and it's going to be Cheri saying, 'Come home, baby...'

This whole story is a histrionic case study of how, ultimately, no adequate replacement for stolid, boring, middle-class virtues - devotion to family, desire for love and the need to be a responsible provider - has yet been developed. Why is it that mature, well-adjusted, fully contributing members of the human race seem characterized by their ability to rise above their own desires to be concerned about 'others?' In a deeply personal sense, isn't that what loving someone else teaches us to do? Loving a spouse, loving children...don't we have to put aside our own desires to do that properly? Isn't 'loving' thinking about someone else before considering our own greedy, grabbing impulses? Maybe that's why we so highly treasure the concept of 'love.' It lets us demonstrate the good things we human beings are capable of. It's the exact opposite of selfishness.

Since the very first recorded scribblings (and long before that, if prehistoric cave drawings are any indication), mankind has grappled with the awkward and awesome fact of existence. All these years later have we progressed much past those initial basic fumblings when it comes to answering the question, 'Why are we here and what are we supposed to be doing?'

We tend to think we can figure everything out ourselves but it's humbling to realize how little we really know even about things we think we're very familiar with. Take vision. We 'think' we look out into the world and see things, right? 'Look, over there - what a beautiful sunrise,' etc. But when the scientific evidence is examined, the fact is, we don't look 'out' at all! Electromagnetic waves of varying frequency are either absorbed by, or bounce off objects around us. Then they enter holes in our faces called 'eyes' where they trigger biochemical reactions in our retinas. Our nervous system transports this bioelectrical information to a piece of flesh buried somewhere deep inside our skulls. We then construct an internal representation of these signals, allowing us to 'see' what's going on around our completely encased brain. Now, if our senses can fool us that convincingly, how can anyone confidently declare that there is nothing to life but what we 'see?'

So there it is, my personal credo all laid out neatly in front of me now that the shit's really hit the fan. I've come to the conclusion that the universe we inhabit is a pretty mysterious and tricky place. I'm sticking with my intuition and my intuition tells me 'God ' is out there somewhere waiting to see what I'm going to do next.

I feel pretty confident about how this whole thing is going to turn out. The time for whining and crying and pissing and moaning has come to an end. It's time to have faith.

The Dream

The hour of the gloaming is hard upon us and the blizzard has yet to abate. Backs bent, eyes averted, we trudge silently through the fallen snow in my otherwise deserted, desolate dreamscape. Heavy wet snowflakes tumble down soundlessly from the darkening maw of heaven, burying us beneath an all embracing, ever deepening mantle of frozen arctic white. Visibility is limited to a matter of feet and I am only dimly aware of the formless shapes I am following as I labor on, breathing heavily, shivering, desperate to ward off the cold, snow crunching underfoot. It is getting darker and the wind continues to rise. How long will this continue? Who am I following?

We crest a large ridge. Suddenly the sun breaks through and a dazzling silver shaft of light plunges to the earth below, a sturdy bridge linking heaven and earth. We are on the rim of a large bowl, a saucer of snow. Below us, in the bottom of the depression, there is a pool of shimmering water. But the strangest thing is, the sky and the ground around it are jammed with an endless press of beautiful white birds of every size and shape - egrets, cranes, herons, pelicans, storks. It's like we've stumbled into a breeding ground or rookery.

The scene resets and the birds are gone. The snow stops

falling and bright daylight illuminates the setting. I notice that the pool of water is full of ice chips and the sun is reflecting brilliantly off the glittering, sparkling facets.

Cheri and Melanie stand near the edge of the pond. Cheri's body is long, lean and beautiful. Mother and daughter effortlessly slip into the water and begin to swim and splash about, laughing and calling out gleefully. Cheri gazes fondly at her child, eyes full of maternal love, the child innocent, delighted, impossible to keep up with as she joyfully cavorts about. The scene is one of overwhelming serenity and grace. The whole earth is silent as I happily watch from the distance. God is here.

Eventually the girls have had their fun. Emerging from the water dripping wet, laughing, happy, they look up to me with smiles of affection and love. My heart bursts with pride and joy as they come to me.

And then...

It ends, simply enough, with a phone call.

"Hi, it's me," I open the conversation. "How are you?"

So much depends on her answer. Fear and its companion product, adrenaline, suddenly shoot through me. My legs go wobbly and I feel my heart palpitating.

'Steady, man, this is it,' I fatalistically steel myself. 'Stay calm, don't allow her the pleasure of detecting any emotion in your voice if she's decided to drop the boom.'

"Well, I'm...fine," she responds, as if somewhat surprised by the answer herself. "Or at least I think I am. And I guess I should know, huh?"

Have I ever mentioned what a pleasure it is merely talking to Cheri on the telephone? And you don't have to only take my word for it. Her sexy, sultry voice is so engaging, so melodious, that at her last place of employment she discovered that whenever she called their overseas European sales affiliate, that district manager pulled the male members of his team into his office and intentionally prolonged the call simply to allow them the pleasure of listening to Cheri talk on the speaker phone.

Mine and Cheri's conversation flags momentarily, however, as we fumble with the burden of expectation being piled high upon every word, every nuance, every pause. What's coming next? How will we get to 'the' subject? My mind leaps ahead like that of an over eager school boy trying to anticipate the teacher's next question. Sure, Cheri said she's doing 'fine' but what does that really mean? It could be that clear cut - she is doing fine - or it could mean she is fine because she's finally come to a decision she could live with...even if that decision means not living with me.

"I'm glad to hear that - me too," I offer.

"Oh, and why is that?" she playfully banters, reflexively challenging me, as always a step ahead, keeping me off balance.

"Because it's so good to hear your voice again," I volley back.

"I feel the same way hearing yours," Cheri acknowledges pleasantly, without guile.

"What have you been up to? How's Melanie?" I ask, trying not to rush the moment of truth, willing to lose myself temporarily in the pleasure of listening to the sound of Cheri's voice, immersing myself in conversation with this bewitching woman.

"She misses you," Cheri confesses, refusing to elaborate, as if not wanting me to think that external forces could be brought to bear upon her decision making process.

I can feel the suspense building. Moment by moment, we both know we're creeping ever closer to 'that' topic.

"How about you?" I lightly toss out, unable to pass up another opportunity to ask a question designed to reveal the direction of Cheri's thinking.

"I miss you too," she straightforwardly declares, not providing any further detail, unwilling to be rushed, in firm control, keeper of the rules.

"Do you know anything more about what you're feeling?" I

gently nudge. My pulse accelerates, this could be it! Once Cheri reveals her hand it will be either joyful reunion or...a future too awful to contemplate.

At the same time, I feel a great weight being lifted from my shoulders. The subject is out on the table. Determining what happens next is out of my hands.

"Yeah, I guess I do," Cheri confesses. "At least I think I know."

Maddeningly close!

"Know what?"

"Know...I don't want it to end."

Torture, sheer torture.

"Don't want what to end?"

Her pause prolongs my agony, my heart writhes like a stricken beast.

"I don't want...you and I to end."

It takes a moment for me to absorb her words. They're like the first drops of a sweet, summer rain soaking into the desert of my heart. I feel life and hope growing inside of me for the first time in weeks – months! God, merciful God, is giving me my life back.

"I can't tell you how happy I am to hear you say that," I manage to respond. "Can I come home?"

"Yeah," Cheri sheepishly responds. "I think it's probably about time we reclaim you."

***

On a bright, sunny winter's day, I find myself in a car with Cheri speeding toward my beloved Hudson valley. Every time I look at her my heart swells with joy. For Christmas her parents gave her an elegant new winter coat, charcoal gray, very stylishly cut, that for some reason reminds me of Cossacks, Moscow and Russian winters. I can't keep my eyes off her, she looks great! She's cut her hair shorter in the interim and her eyes sparkle alertly beneath her bangs as she drives us up the Jersey turnpike, over the George Washington bridge and onto the bucolic Taconic State parkway.

Everywhere, recognizable scenery speeds past outside my window. I revel in each twisting bend of the highway, relish the sight of every familiar forest, meadow, stream and rocky hillside. I gaze awestruck at the magnificent valleys and mountains - this is the place Cheri is from, this is where I found her, this is the place we're going home to!

That's how Cheri and I reconciled and started rebuilding our life step by step, day by day. There's no master plan, we've come to no new agreement, we have no particular knowledge of how we're going to accomplish what we're setting out to do. We just know we're going to do it together.

VII

Epilogue

1981

The Settlement

Late one afternoon while exploring the tree line beyond our landlord's property, I discover a path leading up onto the hillside overlooking our little valley. I'm intrigued, having tried unsuccessfully to conquer this slope in the past, rebuffed by its steepness and the prickly tangle of thorns and brambles clinging to its rocky face. But on this particular day I get lucky. Stumbling across what appears to be nothing more than a deer run, I soon realize this rut is inexorably working its way up my heretofore impregnable mountain. Assiduously following the winding track, I scramble uphill alongside a crumbling stone wall and cut sharply across a heavily eroded, slippery grade before finally being deposited on a barren knob near the summit.

Turning to examine the view from my hard won, lofty vantage point, I'm stunned to see our entire little 'settlement' of Moore's Mill laid out virtually at my feet. I'm looking straight down on our apartment, the landlord's refurbished barn and the other dwellings at the end of our driveway. I can see the pond and waterfall, everything nestled snugly at the foot of the hills surrounding the area. Although I can't spot the main road through the canopy of leafy trees, I can hear the occasional car making its way down Route 82.

As I overlook this idyllic scene, the day is fast moving toward my favorite hour, that pause before twilight, the moment when the very turning of the earth seems to slow down, all sounds exaggerated and magnified as the day's momentum is broken, its initiative surrendering to evening. It's the hour when children are called in for supper and families gather around the dinner table.

The shadows are lengthening perceptibly. I listen to a multitude of insects and creeper frogs tuning up for this evening's performance, their chirping already filling the air. The occasional peep of a bird, the bark of a neighbor's dog and the beckoning call of a voice in the distance are audible as well. It's hard to describe the feeling of contentment I'm experiencing watching the yellow line of daylight recede beyond the darkening hills.

Porch lights wink on along our driveway. Evening begins its descent and the hum of airplanes, cars, animals and people dies away. There's a hush and an expectant pause in the air, as if something new and significant is about to happen. And yet, to think, it's the same old thing happening over and over again - families, lovers, children, friends, husbands, wives coming together at the end of another day.

Up here there's nothing to keep me company but a rustling in the trees as a breeze ruffles the hilltop foliage and brings relief from the day's heat to the inhabitants of my little valley. The woman I love is down there waiting for me - she's probably setting the table or washing off Melanie's face before supper, wondering what on earth I'm up to.

I laugh to myself as I think about it. Yep, no doubt, Cheri'll take a piece out of my hide for being late to dinner and Lord, don't I love her for it? No matter that tomorrow brings its thousand devils or solitary struggles, as night falls I look out over God's grand creation and know unequivocally, 'It's life, it's GOOD and it's mine.'

THE END

Made in the USA
Columbia, SC
27 June 2024